ALIEN STORM

"Hey, look, it's been great," the biker stammered. "But me and my crew didn't sign up to fight a war..."

Bright held up his hand, palm forward, fingers splayed. "Then you should go."

There was a dull thud as the biker exploded in a puff of red mist. Eco wrinkled his nose at the burning smell that had filled the air. Without its rider, the bike toppled over onto its side. A scrap of the biker's leather jacket floated through the air and landed on the rear wheel. The other two bikers jumped off their machines and stumbled backwards, away from the major and Eco.

"Does anyone else want to disappear?" Bright asked mildly.

About the Author

A.G. TAYLOR was born in New Zealand and grew up in East Anglia. He studied English Literature at Sheffield University and teaching at Cambridge. For the last ten years he has worked as a teacher in England, South Korea, Poland and Australia. He currently lives in Melbourne with his partner, her whippet, his Italian greyhound and numerous computer games consoles.

ALIEN STORM

A.G.TAYLOR

USBORNE

For my parents

First published in the UK in 2010 by Usborne Publishing Ltd., Usborne House, 83-85 Saffron Hill, London EC1N 8RT, England. www.usborne.com

A CIP catalogue record for this book is available from the British Library.

JFMAMJJA OND/10 02556/1 ISBN 9781409520184
Printed in Reading, Berkshire, UK.

1

The nightmare had visited Sarah Williams every night for a week.

In her dream she was trapped in a burning plane, desperately trying to fight her way through people towards the exit – except the exit was a swirling mass of desert sand that jumped out to engulf her. It was when the red dust filled her mouth and nose, suffocating her, that she awoke, sitting bolt upright in bed and staring into the darkness. The dreams she shared with Robert, her brother, were growing in intensity. Breathing deeply, Sarah brought herself back to reality. She knew she would have little sleep for the rest of the night.

Sarah eased herself from under the duvet, slipped on a dressing gown and walked barefoot across the cool tiles of the bedroom. She brushed her long, dark hair back with her hands and fixed it with a tie from her pocket as she headed for the door. Sarah Williams was fifteen years old, but she had more to worry about than taking GCSEs or making friends – during the last six months she had become the leader of a group of kids on the run. If someone had told her a year before where she would be, Sarah would have laughed in their face.

How quickly things change.

In the corridor outside, Sarah paused at the doorway of the boys' room. Nestor, Octavio and Wei were sleeping soundly, but Robert was not there. Looking round, she saw the outline of his head silhouetted against the balcony window in the lounge.

Although the late summer day had been unusually hot, a cool change had come to Melbourne that evening and now the night air had a real chill to it. As Sarah stepped out onto the balcony, the sound of a baby crying in the tower block opposite carried across the deserted car park. Robert looked round briefly and then back to the glittering view of the night city. He was a blond-haired, blue-eyed kid of ten. When he smiled, his eyes sparkled with humour, but that night his expression was serious.

Sorry, I guess I woke you, Robert told her, although he said nothing aloud. Communicating with their minds had become second nature to them over the previous few months.

You were dreaming about the plane crash, Sarah replied. She put her arm around his shoulder and gave him a squeeze to show it was okay. He smiled, but then his expression darkened again.

What's it like? he asked. *Living someone else's nightmares, I mean.*

For a moment, Sarah didn't answer. Six months before, when they were just coming to terms with the death of their mother, the plane carrying them to Australia had crashed in the outback. Like thousands of others, their lives had been changed for ever by the meteorite that hit the desert that day – creating an electromagnetic pulse that knocked their plane out of the sky.

But the meteorite also carried with it a visitor from outer space: the fall virus.

Sarah and Robert had been among the lucky ones – rather than falling into the coma that adults exposed to the alien virus suffered, they had been gifted with extraordinary powers as a side-effect. Now, along with four other kids, they were on the run from anyone who might exploit them because of their talents. Sarah's enhanced psychic ability meant that she shared the dreams and nightmares of her brother, the person closest to her.

It's not so bad, she reassured him. *At least I know you're not going through it alone.*

I sense you there, Robert said with a nod. Then he looked away, out over the city again. *You'd never leave us, would you?*

Sarah frowned. *Leave you? Why would you think—*

"Because you don't need us," Robert interrupted, speaking aloud for the first time, voice thin and strained. In the city-light Sarah saw tears forming in his eyes. "With your powers you could go anywhere or be anyone. All we're doing is holding you back."

He fell silent. For a while neither of them said anything at all, but Sarah didn't move her arm from around his shoulder. The power she'd been gifted by the fall virus was the ability to read and even control the minds of others, so the thoughts and motivations of those around her were often an open book. In the months since the change, she'd almost forgotten what it was like to be unsure of people around her – to not know their plans or ambitions. She gently pulled her brother round and looked into his eyes.

"I'll never leave you," she replied softly. "That's a promise."

Robert finally cracked a smile. Sarah patted his arm. *Now, it's time you got some sleep.*

Robert nodded. *Thanks, sis. You always make me feel better.*

She was about to say something in reply, but Robert disappeared in that instant – his own special ability. Teleporting from one place to another around the apartment was second nature to him, but it could be disconcerting to her and others. She made a mental note to remind him about it again as she stepped back into the lounge.

On her way through the apartment, Sarah looked into the boys' room. Robert was already back in his bed. She closed the door quietly and returned to her room.

What's going on? Louise, her nine-year-old room-mate, asked sleepily as Sarah climbed into her bed. *Are we okay?*

Sarah pulled the covers over herself and said softly, "Go back to sleep. We're all fine."

Louise smiled and turned over. Sarah sensed the

younger girl's thoughts overtaken by sleep once more, but as she had expected, it was a long time before she slept herself.

We're okay, *we're fine,* she thought as she stared at the ceiling, but it was impossible to escape the dark feeling that had come over her during the past few weeks.

Something bad was coming.

And if they didn't all get out of Australia soon, none of them would be safe…

2

Dr. Rachel Andersen removed her glasses and rubbed her tired eyes. She hadn't slept much that night, but she hadn't slept much at all since being made head of HIDRA Asia–Pacific, the international task-force in charge of containing the fall virus in the region. Rachel's background was as a scientist, but that morning she had to deal with the military operations of HIDRA – something that always left her feeling drained. She stifled a yawn as a communications screen opened on her computer desktop. In the window, Commander Craig appeared.

He was the young officer who was in charge of HIDRA's military operations in Australia. He kept his fair hair slightly longer than the ordinary soldiers – a privilege of rank – and was dressed in the black and gold uniform of the HIDRA elite.

"Dr. Andersen?" he snapped with typical military bluntness. "Are you there, sir?"

Rachel turned on her camera. "Yes, Commander. Sitrep, please."

Sitrep – military terminology for "situations report". She was getting used to throwing a few bits of army jargon into conversations – it seemed to make the soldiers more comfortable with her. As a scientist, it was taking a long time to win their respect, but she was getting there. And at least she had persuaded them to stop calling her "Colonel Andersen". She had been given the honorary rank after taking over HIDRA Asia–Pacific to sort out the mess left by Colonel Moss.

"Very good, sir," Commander Craig said on the other end of the video link-up. Behind him, Rachel could see the desert and blue sky flying past the windows of his vehicle. "We're ten minutes from the enemy base. We've got four hovercopters moving in from the east. I'm in the lead copter. There's also a ground convoy of thirty soldiers being deployed from the south."

Rachel nodded approvingly. She picked up the satellite photograph of the *enemy base* – a collection of caravans and trucks parked in the middle of the Australian outback, three hundred kilometres north of Adelaide. This was the hiding place of Major Bright, the right-hand man of Colonel Moss, the former director of HIDRA's military operations. Bright was the only member of the old HIDRA military command that hadn't been arrested for his actions following the meteorite strike. Together, Moss and Bright had imprisoned the children who had developed powers from the fall virus. Bright had been responsible for torturing those children to expose their powers and he had been the first and only person to be given the serum developed from their blood. As a result, he had developed an amazing mix of powers that made him very dangerous.

And now he was hiding out in the desert with his own little army of followers – mostly thieves and outlaws.

"I hope you understand what you're going up against, Commander Craig," Rachel warned, looking back at the camera. "Major Bright's powers combine the strengths of all the virus-altered children."

"If he still has those powers," Craig added. "He's probably run out of serum by now."

Rachel considered it, but shook her head. "Colonel

Moss created enough vials of serum for almost a dozen doses. We never found those vials, even after he was arrested. We can only assume that Major Bright has them."

"And if he has the serum," Commander Craig said, "he has his powers."

"You should be ready for a fight."

Craig grinned at the camera. "Don't worry, sir. HIDRA Special Forces are always ready for a fight."

Major Bright sensed them coming as an image in his mind's eye – four hovercopters moving almost silently through the skies above the Central Australian desert. It was part of the psychic early-warning system he'd inherited from Colonel Moss's experiment with the fall virus. He was supposed to be the leader of a new generation of superhuman soldiers, but now there was only him – stuck in the outback amidst outlaws almost as wanted as himself. The forces of HIDRA were coming to capture and imprison him, just like they had Colonel Moss.

Swinging his legs off the bed, he reached into the water bowl on the nearby table and splashed the lukewarm liquid on his face. Looking in the cracked shaving mirror on the table, he ran his hands over his closely-cropped hair and stroked a finger down the old battle scar that ran the length of his cheek. He frowned at his reflection. After six months of hiding out in the desert he'd put on a little weight in the face, but his body was still hard and muscular – barely a gram of excess fat. Bright flexed his bicep and nodded approvingly. He was ready to go to war.

At the doorway of his caravan, Eco stood to attention in readiness for any command. Eco – the eighteen-year-old kid who'd become his ostensible second-in-command at the camp during the past few months. When Bright had an order to give to the collection of almost a hundred crims and misfits who lived around him, it was Eco who delivered it.

"Is there anything wrong, sir?" the teenager asked, his thin face almost invisible in the darkness – the window shades had to be kept down during the day against the searing heat of the desert.

Bright dried his hands on a towel and looked round. "Wake the camp. We're going to be attacked. Tell them we've got about ten minutes."

Even in the darkness, Bright could see the kid's mouth fall open stupidly. Months of rage and frustration bubbled away under the major's calm exterior, but he suppressed it. Bright was used to commanding highly-trained men (the very type of men who were being sent to capture him), but here he was reduced to living with common criminals and ordering around a teenage misfit looking for a father figure. Eco continued to gawk as if he'd just spoken in Latin.

"Well?" Bright snapped, just as he would at one of his underlings when he had been in control at HIDRA. "Wake the camp! Get to it, soldier!"

"Yessir!" Eco yelped, giving some kind of half-salute as he stumbled into the blinding light of day.

Major Bright shook his head as the gangly kid exited the caravan, and then went to the cupboard near the bed. He removed a single item on a hanger and tore off the protective plastic. Even in the dimness of the caravan the brass on his old uniform sparkled – the rips and tears from his last battle with Sarah Williams and the other children had been repaired so it was almost as good as new.

Soon he would be a commander of men once more, not boys or criminals.

Laying the uniform down on the bed, Major Bright took a plastic case from the cupboard and flipped it open. Inside sat a syringe-gun and glass vials, each containing a sample of the virus serum that gave him his powers. Every few weeks he felt his enhanced strength draining, and that was when he had to inject more of the serum. He counted the vials – *only two left*.

Bright placed one of the precious vials in the gun and held it against his left arm. With a pull on the trigger, the serum shot into his bloodstream like molten iron. He gritted his teeth to stop from crying out in pain and gripped the side of the bed as his entire body was racked by muscular spasms.

One more vial, Major Bright thought as the pain subsided. *I need more serum.*

Luckily, he knew just where to find it: the original children from Colonel Moss's experiment – *Project Superhuman*. He sensed them in the east with his attuned psychic sense: Sarah and Robert Williams, the Colombian twins and the two younger ones. Their blood was the key to their powers. When Bright had their blood, he could make serum on demand. When he had that, he would be truly indestructible.

With a smile, he began to dress for battle.

Meanwhile, Eco ran around the camp, unkempt blond hair flying around his face as he went.

"Wake up!" he yelled, banging on the door of a

caravan. "We're under attack! Get to your defensive positions!"

Before he reached the next vehicle, someone caught his arm, almost pulling him off his feet. Eco looked up into the eyes of a bearded biker with tattoos on his face.

"What are you shouting about, Shrimp?"

Eco gritted his teeth. *Shrimp*. He hated that nickname, but people didn't use it when he was around Major Bright.

"HIDRA is coming," he said, pulling his arm free. "Time to show your loyalty to the major."

The biker gave him a look like he thought he was crazy. He turned and signalled to two of his mates, who were dressed in jeans and leather and sporting full beards despite the crushing heat. They walked in the direction of their bikes.

"Hey, where are you going?" Eco demanded, running after them. All around the camp people were emerging from vans and caravans, blinking in the sunlight.

The biker looked round as he swung a leg over his Harley and fired the engine. "It's been cool hanging out here, but I ain't taking on no army for that freak."

Eco was aware of half the camp watching their conversation. He stepped in front of the bike. "You're not going anywhere."

The biker looked round at his friends and they roared with laughter. The man leaned over the handlebars of the motorbike until their noses were almost touching.

"You know, kid," he said, "for a snot-nosed teenager, I kinda like you. So don't make me ride this hog over your head."

Eco looked around the camp. "We can defend this place! The major will protect us!"

A murmur went up from the people watching the scene. The biker sighed and revved his engine for quiet. "Major Bright ain't got nothing but a bunch of party tricks up his sleeve. Anyone stupid enough to stick around for those HIDRA boys to roll in here—"

His voice trailed off as the door to the caravan opposite slammed open as if it had been kicked. Major Bright stepped out into the light. Everyone in the camp looked round at the towering figure – now dressed in his black and gold uniform. For a moment he didn't move, regarding them all with his cold, blue eyes. Nobody breathed. Finally, Bright started down the caravan steps and walked slowly across towards Eco and the biker.

"Is there a problem?" he asked as he reached Eco's side.

The kid looked round, relief written all over his face. "This guy wants to leave."

The major looked at the man on the bike and raised an eyebrow questioningly.

"Hey, look, it's been great," the biker stammered. He seemed to have shrunk half a metre in height since Bright walked out of the caravan. "But me and my crew didn't sign up to fight a war..."

Bright held up his hand, palm forward, fingers splayed. "Then you should go."

There was a dull thud as the biker exploded in a puff of red-tinted mist. Eco wrinkled his nose at the burning smell that had filled the air. Without its rider, the Harley toppled over onto its side. A scrap of the biker's leather jacket floated through the air and landed on the rear wheel. The other two bikers jumped off their machines and stumbled backwards, away from the major and Eco.

"Does anyone else want to disappear?" Bright asked mildly, casting his eyes around the silent audience. "No one? Sure? Then get to your positions. NOW!"

The crowd broke and ran for their assigned places around the perimeter of the camp. For the last month, when they weren't out on scavenging missions to the nearest towns, Bright had been drilling them in how to defend the camp from infiltration. Eco felt his heart race as he saw men and women grabbing makeshift weapons and scurrying behind barricades. He looked up at the major.

"Don't worry, sir. We'll see them off or die trying."

The major traced a finger down the scar on his right cheek.

"Sure. You will."

3

Ten kilometres from the camp, Commander Craig tapped an area on the windscreen of his hovercopter and a Heads-Up Display, or HUD, opened showing a magnified view of the desert ahead. The camp in the distance was little more than a collection of rusting cars, trucks and caravans. To the edge of the screen a window showed a dark-haired woman in her late thirties – his boss, Dr. Rachel Andersen. She was overseeing the desert assault from the safety of her office, hundreds of kilometres away at the HIDRA base in Melbourne.

"Okay, Commander," she said. "Tell me what I'm seeing."

"The aerial assault is inbound on the camp, sir," Craig informed her. He tapped a section of the HUD to the west, where a dust-cloud was rising. On Rachel's screen back at the base the vision would be highlighted. "That's the ground convoy. We've got six troop transports heading into the camp."

Rachel Andersen said again, "I hope your men understand what they're going up against, Commander."

"A group of outlaws and scum hiding out in the desert? Forgive me, sir, but this should be short and sweet."

Rachel gave him a hard look. "I'm talking about Bright. I want him restrained and in a cell by the end of the morning. No mistakes."

"Yessir," the commander replied briskly as he reached for his comm. "Ground force, hold position one klick from the camp. Air support move in."

The three other hovercopters surged towards the camp while Commander Craig kept his in a holding pattern.

"We can watch everything from here, sir," he told Rachel as the magnified HUD showed the copters circle the perimeter of the camp. "They're conducting an initial scan. This should tell us exactly how many hostiles we're dealing with and where the weak points are."

In the window, Rachel nodded as data appeared on the screen: close-up pictures of the camp and thermal scans of the vehicles. People inside the camp showed up in red.

Commander Craig studied the thermal overview. "Looks like we've got about sixty warm bodies in there, sir. There's a scattered group of about twenty moving to the south on foot. Probably deserters from the camp making a run for it. We'll pick them up later. Our intel suggests we've got at least thirty wanted criminals amongst this mob."

"I want zero casualties," she reminded him. "You have permission to proceed."

"We have a go," Craig said into the comm. "Air support, take out the unoccupied vehicles. Let's clear a path for the ground assault."

The first missile hit as Eco was running across the central area of the camp. An ageing camper-van to his left exploded, rising into the air and coming down with an almighty crash that rocked the entire camp. Eco's legs fell from under him and he hit the sand, rolling onto his back and blinking in confusion. The sound of the explosion was quickly replaced by a ringing in his ears. He looked around and watched people running left and right, their mouths working as if they were screaming, but all he heard was the ringing.

I'm deaf, he thought as something like a massive, black bird appeared overhead – a helicopter hovering directly over the centre of the camp. Eco watched in fascination as it made a leisurely turn, taking in its surroundings, completely unconcerned with the chaos it had created below. The machine stopped its rotation and fired a second missile, lighting up a bus that formed the back door of the camp. Eco pulled himself to his feet and walked backwards, noticing for the first time that the helicopter had no spinning blades. He wondered how it stayed in the air, as two identical machines appeared above the camp.

"Hey!" Eco yelled as a man ran from his hiding place near the east wall. "Do something! Shoot at them!"

The man tossed his shotgun at Eco's feet. "You shoot at them!" he said and fell on his knees, hands on his head. "I'm surrendering!"

Eco was about to call him a coward when he noticed that at least thirty other people had abandoned their positions and were walking into the open area. They followed the man's lead and threw their weapons down, kneeling before the three machines hovering above them. Shaking his head to clear the ringing, Eco bent down and picked up the shotgun. It was heavier than expected and felt alien in his hands.

"Kid, don't be a fool!" a woman on her knees beside him hissed. "Look!"

Eco held the gun limply and followed her gaze. Through the hole torn in the bus by the second missile he saw a line of black shapes approaching across the heat haze of the desert. Humvees – Eco had seen them in a film about Iraq. A few seconds later the first tank-like vehicle blazed into the camp, smashing aside the remnants of the bus and drawing up fast before the kneeling occupants of the camp. Doors on both sides of the machine swung open and six armoured soldiers ran out as the other Humvees pulled up.

Eco's legs went weak and the gun slipped from his fingers. The woman tugged at his T-shirt.

"Get down!" she said. "You're gonna get shot!"

Eco didn't move. He was fixated on the soldiers forming a line around the kneeling camp-dwellers. One of them raised a loudhailer to his mouth.

"Everyone else, come out with your hands up!" he ordered. "You won't be hurt if you give up now."

Immediately, twenty or so others emerged from the

vehicles around the camp and assumed the position in front of the soldiers. The soldier with the loudhailer looked at the captain next to him and grinned.

"Mission accomplished, sir?" he said.

His superior looked around the camp. "Where's Bright?"

The door to the major's caravan swung open once more. The soldiers tensed as Bright stepped out and crossed into the middle of the camp. Twenty dart-rifles swung round to point at him.

"Knees, now!" the captain ordered. "We're taking you in, Bright!"

Major Bright looked at him. "Or what?"

All around, people dropped from their knees to their stomachs, faces in the sand. Someone started sobbing with fear. Major Bright looked around the cowering mass with contempt. Only Eco and the soldiers remained standing.

"Fire!" the captain screamed.

Twenty rifles went off at once, the tranquillizer darts slamming into the major's arms, chest and legs. He staggered back, almost losing his footing, but managed to keep his balance. The soldiers stopped firing. They looked at the still-standing target with amazement, lowering their weapons.

Major Bright winced and roughly brushed the darts away that were embedded all over his body, as if he were removing dust from his uniform. He looked back at the soldiers with an annoyed expression and said one word: "*Ouch.*"

The soldier with the loudhailer looked at his captain. "He's taken enough juice to sedate a zoo, sir."

The captain took a step back. "Yeah. Perhaps we need to—"

A howling sound filled the air, drowning out the last of the captain's words. On impulse, Eco ran to the major's side as he raised his hands. The ground beneath them vibrated. Bright looked round at him, his eyes blazing red now.

"My turn," he said.

All around, a tornado was beginning to form, creating a wall of sand that ripped around the soldiers and the inhabitants of the camps. The wind grew in intensity, but Eco and Major Bright were safe in the eye of the storm. Bright raised his hands higher and the tornado raged faster. Eco watched soldiers being lifted off the ground and into the expanding twister.

*   *   *

Commander Craig watched the rotating pillar of sand engulf the camp, expanding as it turned. Within seconds the edge of the sandstorm was only a few hundred metres from where their copter was hovering. Ahead of them, the wall of the twister grew closer by the second.

In the link-up window, Rachel Andersen's eyes widened as she saw the camp swallowed up. "Commander, get out of there!"

Commander Craig yelled into the comm, "All units! Full retreat!"

His voice trailed off as a black object was spat out of the tornado and arced through the air towards them. As it flew closer it was possible to make out what it was – one of the Humvees.

Commander Craig's mouth fell open. "That's our—"

The two-tonne vehicle slammed into the side of the hovercopter, sending it into an uncontrollable spin. The windscreen shattered from the impact, showering the occupants with glass. The copter hit the sand a second later.

The storm had passed – and so had the camp...and the copters...and the soldiers...

Eco stood in the centre of a giant crater where the

camp had once been. As the dust in the air settled he made out the shape of half-buried vehicles. It was as if someone had taken the entire desert and shaken it. Beside him Major Bright stood stock still, eyes closed, arms still held up, in some kind of trance.

A few metres away, one of the survivors of the camp emerged from the sand, took one look at Major Bright and ran off into the desert.

"Hey!" Eco yelled after him. "Where are you going? There's nothing out there!"

Major Bright opened his eyes and shook his head. "Leave them, Eco. Fools."

Eco looked round at the strange tone in the major's voice – almost dreamy, as if he were half asleep.

"Uh, Major," he said, "are you okay?"

"We must travel east," Major Bright went on, as if speaking to himself. "That is where the children are. Melbourne."

"Children?" Eco repeated, still not getting it.

"The children with the powers," Bright continued. "Sarah Williams and her brother. Nestor and Octavio. Louise and Wei. I need more serum. I need their blood."

Eco looked round at the sound of vehicles and saw the silhouettes of more Humvees approaching. The twister hadn't wiped out all of the HIDRA forces.

"I think we have a problem, sir," Eco said. "We should run."

An uncustomary laugh escaped Major Bright's lips. He grabbed Eco's wrist in his massive hand and clasped it tightly. Eco gave a cry of pain – the major really didn't know his own strength.

"Why run?" Bright hissed. "When you can teleport?"

Eco let out a cry as white light began to expand around them. He fancied he felt his skin and clothes burning. Through the brightness he saw the HIDRA vehicles driving towards them at full speed. If they didn't dodge they were sure to be run over, but the major held him firm.

"Noooooooooooo!" Eco closed his eyes and screamed as he waited for the impact...

It didn't come.

To his surprise, Eco felt a cool breeze and several spots of rain against his cheek. Slowly, he opened his eyes.

The rolling red dunes of the desert were gone, replaced by lush green trees on either side of a deserted road. The air was thick with moisture and the sweet, cloying smell of eucalyptus trees. Blinking, Eco took in his new surroundings as the major released his wrist.

"Where are we?" he murmured, shivering at the

sudden change of temperature. It was clear they were far from the desert now.

Without warning, Major Bright staggered forward, and Eco reached out to support him. Bright pushed him away, but it was clear he was struggling to stay on his feet.

"What's wrong?" Eco asked.

"The distance of the teleport has weakened me," he said. "We need to find a vehicle. Now."

As if on cue, a four-wheel drive appeared over the crest of the road, heading towards them. As they were standing right in the middle of the highway, Eco moved to the grass verge, but the major didn't budge. The Range Rover swerved to avoid him. Major Bright reached out with his left hand and caught its side. With a metallic tearing and a screech of tyre rubber, the vehicle spun around in the road and came to a halt. Seconds later, the door flew open and the stunned driver stumbled out.

"Run if you want to live!" Major Bright spat as the driver opened his mouth to say something. Without any further prompting, the driver turned tail and ran into the trees by the side of the road. Bright said to Eco, "You drive."

"Where?" Eco asked, still taken aback by what had just happened.

Major Bright jerked a thumb at a sign by the side of the road: *Melbourne 150km.*

Without another word, Major Bright walked to the Range Rover and slumped behind the passenger seat, face lined with exhaustion. As Eco got behind the wheel of the unfamiliar vehicle and gunned the accelerator, a cruel smile passed across the major's lips.

"Sarah Williams," he murmured, "I'm coming for you and your friends."

4

The ringing bell on the pawnbroker's shop door brought the owner hurrying from his portable TV in the back room. The old man was hunchbacked from years of bad posture at the desk-work that was his speciality. Thick glasses supplemented his ruined eyesight. He walked up to the serving grille and peered through.

The man on the other side was a giant, easily two metres tall, with a shaved head and a leather jacket that bulged in the arms and chest. The big man looked around the racks of pawned items behind the counter –

electronics, musical instruments, jewellery. All items of value that people had given up in return for money.

"You're a day early," the pawnbroker said.

The giant stepped up to the counter. "You've had three weeks. Don't tell me the items aren't ready."

The pawnbroker held up his hands. "Of course they're ready. Do you have my payment?"

The big man dropped something in the money exchange slot. The pawnbroker's eyes widened as he looked down and saw a diamond sitting there. Reaching out with his wizened hand, he picked it up between his thumb and forefinger and held it up to his spectacles.

"Amazing quality," he said, before reaching to press the button that would turn off the security cameras. He then shot the locks and opened the section of counter before him. "Come."

The giant bowed his head as he stepped through. The pawnbroker ushered him towards the back room. A news report was playing on the ageing TV set: something about teenage gangs with psychic powers roaming the city.

"Imagine," the firm-jawed reporter said, "a group of teen thieves with the power to make people on the street simply hand over cash, jewellery, credit cards. Science fiction? It's happening in every Australian city, all thanks to the after-effects of the fall virus."

"Delinquents," the old man said as he turned off the TV. "I hardly dare set foot outside my door these days." He indicated one of the tattered armchairs. His cat gave a screech and ran for the kitchen as the big man approached. "Don't mind Tabitha. She hates everyone."

As the giant took a seat, the pawnbroker grabbed his eyeglass from the table and gave the diamond a closer examination.

"Only Daniel Williams could find product this good," he said with a sigh.

The big man leaned forward and cracked his knuckles impatiently. "The passports?"

The pawnbroker produced a padded envelope from the side of his chair and passed it over. The giant checked the contents: six European Union passports. He picked one out and checked the information page. It showed Sarah Williams's picture, but the name underneath read *Michelle Bishop*.

"It's a perfect forgery," the pawnbroker said. "New identities for all six children. Now, the rest of my payment?"

The giant replaced the passport in the envelope and looked at the pawnbroker. The fear in the old man's face was apparent. The giant reached inside his pocket and produced a bag containing two more diamonds. As the old man reached for it, the giant held onto the bag and leaned forward.

"When I walk out this shop," the giant said slowly, "you won't remember me."

"Of course." The pawnbroker met the giant's gaze and found himself transfixed by the penetrating stare of the man. It was as if the room around him was melting far into the distance, until there was only the two of them. A soothing voice began to sound in his head: *forget, forget, forget.*

The pawnbroker blinked twice and rubbed a hand over his face, feeling as if he'd just awoken from an unexpected nap.

"Goodbye," the giant said and rose from the chair.

Still dazed, the pawnbroker didn't respond as the big man disappeared through the front of the shop. With the chime of the doorbell, the old man looked round in surprise. He frowned as he tried to remember who had just been there and why.

A few doors down from the pawnbroker's shop, Robert Williams watched the main entrance open. It was not the giant who exited, however, but his sister. Emerging

from his hiding place, he ran to catch up and they fell
into step. Sarah indicated a side street and they took it,
walking a few metres into the shadows before they
stopped.

"How did it go?" Robert asked.

She grinned and held up the envelope containing
the new passports. "Got them," she said, rubbing her
forehead with her hand.

"Headache?" Robert asked with concern.

Sarah nodded. "I had to work the old man's mind a
bit. It's always a strain."

The ability to change her appearance in the eyes of
others was just one of the amazing gifts she had
developed as a side-effect of her exposure to the fall
virus. Another was a deeper mind-manipulation skill that
had allowed her to wipe the pawnbroker's memory. She
was getting better at it, but it always left her exhausted.

Robert took her hand. "What now?"

"Now we get the plane tickets," Sarah replied. In her
guise as the giant man, she'd already reserved six open-
ended round-the-world tickets. The money for both the
tickets and the forgeries had come from the diamonds
left to them by their father, Daniel, who had been in the
process of smuggling them into Australia when the
meteorite struck. Sarah was more than a little relieved

that the last of the diamonds had been disposed of. There was no doubt about it, they had been illegally obtained by Daniel and whoever it was he worked for – in the years their father had been absent from their lives, he had become involved in some very dodgy business. But now Sarah was determined that some good would come from them: a new life not just for her and Robert, but also for their friends. All that remained to be done was to submit their new passport details at the travel agent and pick up the tickets.

"Then we're really getting out of here," Robert said, as if he could hardly believe it. "Are you sure we're doing the right thing? HIDRA are still looking for the fall virus cure. They need blood samples from kids like us, don't they?"

Sarah placed a hand on his shoulder. "We'll find a way to get them to HIDRA, but it's time we started a new life where nobody knows who we are. As long as we're Sarah and Robert Williams, there will always be people looking for us. Now let's go."

As usual, Sarah and Robert found the lift out of order when they arrived at the apartment block in the north of Melbourne an hour later. The tower block was one of three built next to one another thirty years before to provide cheap housing in one of the poorest areas of the city. Now the towers were practically falling apart – half-empty slums that should have been torn down years before. Not a nice place to live, but perfect for people who didn't want to draw attention to themselves.

Sarah reminded herself of this as they trudged up the fifteen flights of stairs to the apartment they rented on the top floor. Disguised as the giant, she'd leased the "penthouse" two months before from one of the crooked landlords who operated the towers. Paying six months' rent up front had ensured no questions were asked.

"I could get us up here in the blink of an eye," Robert grumbled as they walked round a black rubbish bag that had been left out on the landing on the fourteenth floor.

"Don't even think about teleporting," Sarah said, shifting her grip on the loaded shopping bags she carried.

"I know, I know," Robert muttered. "Keep a low profile."

They reached the fifteenth floor and walked down the corridor to the third door on their left. The walls here were a faded yellow that hadn't been repainted since the tower was thrown up in the seventies. There was a constant smell of damp carpet, even on the hottest days.

Robert rapped four times on the door and then used his key to open it.

On the other side, Wei – a round-faced Chinese kid dressed in jeans and a *Transformers* T-shirt – was waiting for them.

"You didn't do the proper knock," the ten-year-old protested, brushing a lock of jet black hair out of his eyes. "It's supposed to be three quick and three slow."

Robert threw one of his shopping bags into Wei's arms and brushed past. "What are you going to do, vaporize us?"

"Maybe."

Sarah kicked the door closed behind her and looked at Wei. "No vaporizations."

Wei smiled sweetly. "Just kidding, Sarah!"

Just kidding. With the ability to spontaneously create fire with the power of his mind, Sarah knew that Wei was more than able to set the entire apartment ablaze on a whim.

Putting that disturbing thought aside, Sarah passed through the lounge in the direction of the kitchen. A blonde-haired girl a little younger than Wei sat in front of the TV playing an Xbox game. Louise didn't look round as they entered, so intent was she on manoeuvring a car through an exploding building. The only unusual thing about the scene was that she wasn't using the controller – opting instead to play the game using telekinetic power alone. This allowed for incredibly fast reaction times – she always got the high score. Louise blinked and a rival car exploded to make way for hers.

On the sofa, Nestor looked up from a book. "Let me help," he said, moving his tall frame off the couch. The same age as Sarah, he was a dark-skinned Colombian kid with friendly eyes that put people at ease the minute they met him. When things had been tough over the previous six months, Sarah had often been glad that she had Nestor to back her up.

She gave him the bag of vegetables and looked round the apartment for his twin brother. "Where's Octavio?"

Nestor gave a sigh as they walked into the kitchen and began emptying the bags. "Out on the balcony. Sulking again."

"Louise?" she asked and Nestor nodded.

Although, at fifteen, Octavio was six years older than Louise, a natural rivalry had grown up between them during the few months they had been together as a group. This was probably the result of the almost identical ability they shared – telekinesis allowed them to move or control objects from a distance with the power of their mind alone. What really rankled Octavio was that a kid almost half his age could equal him in most areas.

"I'll talk to him," Sarah said. "Put this stuff away, will you?"

She left the kitchen and walked back through the lounge. Wei was now sitting next to Louise, cross-legged on the floor, content to watch her play for hours on end. The two of them were inseparable. Sarah walked past them and slid open the door onto the narrow balcony outside.

Octavio sat slumped in a plastic folding chair at the other end of the balcony. He didn't look round as she closed the door behind her and leaned against the railing. Although they were twins, Octavio's temperament was the complete opposite to Nestor's optimistic openness. His dark hair fell all around his face, completely obscuring his expression, and Sarah knew he would be staring blankly at his feet – mind full of dark, unspoken thoughts that she didn't try to read. Octavio could tell when she was inside his head and it drove him into a temper. Also, she knew it wasn't fair to use her telepathic power on her friends – who wants to be around someone who can read your mind all the time?

"Are you okay?" she said finally, taking a breath of

fresh air. At least the balcony was free of the musty smell that infected the entire apartment.

Octavio grunted, bobbing his head fractionally. *He needs a haircut,* she thought. *We all do.* Then she laughed out loud at her maternal concern.

Octavio's head jerked round at the sound. "What?" he asked indignantly.

"Nothing," she replied. "Just that I'm turning into my mum."

Octavio sneered. "Some mother. You've brought us to live in a slum."

Sarah bit her tongue and looked out at the other two towers on the estate. Most of Melbourne's suburbs were made up of single-storey buildings, so the towers stood out like sore fingers. In the nearest one, just a couple of hundred metres away, she could hear music playing in the apartments and the sound of a couple arguing.

"We have our new identities," she said finally. "We have money. We can get a plane out of here anytime we want."

"And go where? To live in slums in Europe? How about South America? I hear the *favelas* in Brazil are just great. Or perhaps you'd like to use some of that diamond money to get us somewhere that doesn't smell like a sewer."

"You know we have to keep out of sight while we're here," she said. "The fall virus and kids like us are still all over the news. In Europe things can be different. We'll find somewhere far away—"

"I don't want somewhere far away!" Octavio interrupted, voice full of bitterness. "Nestor and I used to be treated like kings at HIDRA! Now look at how we're living!"

Sarah suppressed the urge to remind him of how he'd sided with Colonel Moss – a man who had wanted to turn all of them into slaves. In the final fight against Moss, Octavio had jumped sides, but she was well aware his allegiances were conflicted.

"You were a prisoner at HIDRA," she said.

Octavio looked away. "You call this being free?"

For a moment Sarah didn't know what to say. She turned back to the door, but paused before going inside again.

"After we leave the country, you can go your own way if you want," she told him. "If you think you'd be better off with Major Bright, you're free to go and find him. Until then, keep your opinions to yourself. I don't want the younger ones upset."

With that, she stepped back into the lounge and slid the door shut a little too quickly. It slammed loudly enough to make everyone inside look round.

Louise sighed as she went past. "He's a big baby."

Sarah gave no response as she walked through to her and Louise's bedroom. It was small and bare apart from a double bed, but less crowded than the room the four boys shared. In the far corner lay an object that looked like an Egyptian sarcophagus except for the fact it was made of smooth, white plastic and had a window in the front. Inside the casket was Sarah and Robert's father, Daniel Williams. He was one of the victims of the fall virus: he'd been on the plane with them when the meteorite hit and, like all adults exposed to the virus, had fallen into a deep coma for which there was no known cure. The casket was the only thing keeping him alive.

As always, Sarah went to the casket first and checked the panel on the side. The computer displays showed he was perfectly healthy, but still deep in a coma – no change. There was never any change. Sarah hated to see him in the machine, but it was better than the thought of him stacked in one of the HIDRA intensive care warehouses where so many thousands of other virus victims were stored. At least here, he was with his family. She sighed and stood up as Nestor appeared in the doorway.

"What about Daniel?" he asked. "If we're really thinking of flying out of Australia, he isn't exactly going to fit in the hand luggage."

Sarah shook her head. "I'm going to meet Rachel Andersen from HIDRA. Things have changed there. She'll make sure he's looked after when we're gone." From the bedside table she picked up a red box and placed it under her arm. Inside were blood samples from each of the children – much needed by Rachel and her team of scientists in their efforts to find a cure for the virus.

"I still don't trust her or HIDRA," Nestor said. "I should come with you."

"No. I need you here, Nestor. Just in case things kick off between Octavio and Louise again."

"It's not his fault, really," Nestor said, defending his brother. "We're all starting to get on each other's nerves. It's like we've been stuck in this place for ever."

"It's just for a few more days. Europe is going to be a big improvement, I promise."

Nestor nodded, but there was concern in his eyes. "Are you going to be okay out there?"

Sarah grinned and took a step back. With a moment's concentration she changed in front of his eyes, shielding herself in the image of the giant man again.

"I don't think anyone will mess with me," she said with a laugh as she walked through to the lounge. The Xbox was turned off and a news programme was playing on the TV now – something about a series of robberies in the city.

"...ongoing incidents of virus-related powers being used in criminal activity," the TV reporter explained. "This has raised fresh concerns about public safety in the aftermath of last year's meteorite strike..."

A middle-aged politician in a black suit appeared on the screen, surrounded by reporters.

"The fact is," he said, clearly used to the sound of his own voice, "we have a generation of superhuman delinquents loose in this country. They have been gifted powers that pose a grave threat to private and national security. Who knows how the fall virus has affected their minds or their morality? This is why I am presenting a bill to parliament to give police greater powers to arrest and detain minors suspected of being genetically or mentally...enhanced."

The camera cut back to a female newsreader. "That was Victorian Senator Anton Grey talking at the site of Monday's bank robbery in which criminals used what police are calling an *invisible mind shield* to disguise their activities. Have you ever wanted to be invisible, Bob?"

"Only when my mother-in-law visits," the male newsreader to her left replied and they both laughed as an advert came on. Louise blinked once and the TV turned off.

"What do you think?" Robert asked from the kitchen doorway, concern in his voice.

Sarah walked towards the door. "I think the sooner we get out of this country, the better. People are starting to get afraid of people like us. And that's dangerous."

5

Uncle Pete parked the car directly opposite the entrance to the bank and killed the engine. He looked round at his fifteen-year-old nephew, Alex, and gave him a big, fake smile that revealed two rows of crooked, nicotine-stained teeth.

"Okay, tell me what you're going to do, kid," he said.

Alex was a thin-faced kid and underneath his T-shirt it was possible to see that his body was just a little too skinny – as if he hadn't eaten a decent meal in a month. Which he hadn't. As Uncle Pete drummed his fingers on the back of his seat impatiently, Alex sighed and went through the routine he'd learned by rote. "I walk in the front entrance of the bank and make sure no one sees me. I smash the fire alarm with the hammer."

"Where's the hammer?" his uncle demanded. Alex pulled the metal tool, a toy no bigger than his hand, from his jeans pocket and held it up. His uncle nodded. "Go on."

"I move to the locked door near the tellers and wait for the manager to come out to start clearing the foyer. When he comes out the door, I slip through. By now the tellers will have left their stations, but I wait until the bank is evacuated before opening the drawers. I take the money from the drawers and put them in the bags – only the big bills – twenties and larger."

"You got the bags?"

Alex raised his jumper to show the wad of canvas bank bags tucked into his belt. His uncle nodded for him to continue.

"In the drawers I leave at least one note at the bottom of every tray," Alex continued. "I close the drawers after I've emptied them."

In the passenger seat, Stella, his uncle's girlfriend, frowned as she lit her third cigarette in half an hour. "Why's he got to do that, Pete?"

Alex's uncle snorted as if annoyed by the interruption, but answered anyway. "Because if you empty the trays or leave the drawers open for more than a minute a silent alert is sent to police HQ. A SWAT team would be kicking the door down in less than three minutes." He tapped his forehead. "Y'see? I've researched this stuff. It's all on Google."

Stella nodded her head, big earrings jingling. "But don't you think the cops are gonna start getting smart to this? I mean, I heard on the news they've linked the other robberies and…"

Uncle Pete stopped her dead with a dangerous look. "The cops haven't got a clue." He looked back at Alex. "I mean, how are they gonna catch the invisible boy? Huh?"

He reached over and punched his nephew in the shoulder.

"How many more times do I have to do this?" Alex asked. "Perhaps Stella's right. Maybe they've worked out what we've been doing."

His uncle looked at the woman, anger flashing in his eyes. "Now see what you've done. You've freaked out the kid."

Stella shrank back in her seat. "Sorry, Pete."

The man shook his head and looked back at Alex.

"Look, we just need some money right now. I didn't ask to have to look after you. But when I heard my sister's kid was going into a foster home, I stepped up, didn't I? Well, didn't I?"

Alex looked down at the floor of the car, dirty with discarded fast-food wrappers and empty cigarette cartons, and nodded. His parents had succumbed to the fall virus just a few days after the meteorite hit in the centre of Australia. Now, like thousands of others, they lay in comas – confined to intensive care facilities until a cure could be found. With no one to look after him, Alex had been headed for one of the new foster homes created for the kids of the victims. He'd been saved that fate when Uncle Pete – a man he hadn't seen since he was five years old – turned up to claim him. Alex had heard bad stories about the foster accommodation from the other kids at the emergency hospital, but in the four months he'd been in Uncle Pete's care, he often wondered if it would have been a better place for him.

"Hey, are you listening?" his uncle said, snapping his fingers rudely in Alex's face. Alex raised his head to show he was.

"I saved you from that home, didn't I?" Uncle Pete went on – a speech he'd given many times before. "Well, you've put a strain on our finances, son. Food, clothes, games…"

Alex couldn't remember receiving clothes, games or anything other than the most basic food to live on since he'd been in his uncle's care, but said nothing.

"When I was fifteen, I was out paying my way…"

Alex suppressed a smile, remembering a conversation he'd overheard between his mum and dad years before, back when they lived in Adelaide. His mum had received another letter from her brother asking for money… *He's never worked a day in his life,* his father protested angrily as she slipped a cheque into an envelope…

"Well, today it's time to pay your way, kid," Uncle Pete continued, placing a suntanned hand on Alex's shoulder. His gaze softened. "Come on, Alex. It's just until we have enough money to move back west. You don't know how much I hate Melbourne. Nothing's gone right for me since I moved here."

Alex looked through the window at the sunlight streaming down between the high-rises and wondered what was so bad about it.

"What do you say? Just a couple more jobs? Let's go for lucky number six and then grab a burger."

Alex nodded and tucked the hammer back in his pocket.

Uncle Pete grinned. "That's my boy. Now, let's see the magic."

Alex looked from his uncle to Stella and back again. Both had their heads turned to watch him like he was something in the zoo. *That's probably where they'll put me when we run out of banks,* Alex thought. Trying to ignore them, he closed his eyes and concentrated – thought about becoming nothing...

When Alex opened his eyes a few seconds later and looked down at his arms, he was already fading away. Up front, Stella swallowed loudly.

"This part still gives me the creeps, Pete," she whispered. The man jabbed her in the arm to be quiet.

"That's it, kid," he encouraged. "You're doing great."

Alex concentrated harder – imagined his arms, legs and body fading more, becoming totally transparent. When he looked down again, his body was completely invisible and he had the dizzying sensation of floating above the back seat of the car. Placing his hands where he thought his knees were, he took a couple of deep breaths and fought down the urge to be sick that sometimes came with the change.

"You okay?" his uncle asked. "You still there?"

Alex nodded, but laughed when he remembered there was no point in doing so – no one could see.

"Yeah, I'm okay," he said aloud.

"Then what the hell are you waiting for?" Pete demanded. "Get over there and get the money before we roast in this car!"

Alex pulled a face at his uncle, before opening the back door into the heat of the morning. He closed the door and took a step out onto the road... A motorcycle whizzed by, inches from his nose, the rider oblivious to the fact he had almost mown someone down. *They can't see you,* Alex reminded himself. *Careful.* Looking left and right, he ran across the street through a gap in the traffic.

For the sixth time in as many weeks, Alex was about to rob a bank.

6

The central branch of the Melbourne Savings Bank was already busy at noon that day – filled with shoppers and office workers on their breaks. Many were eating lunch on the go or drinking takeaway coffees as they stood in line at the counters.

Invisible, Alex slipped into the foyer behind an overweight man in a suit, dodging around the heavy glass door before it swung shut. Inside the high-ceilinged foyer the air was deliciously cool after the rising heat of the day. Sidestepping the man's bulk, he moved across the polished marble towards the far wall with the fire alarm point.

Weaving unseen through the crowd, Alex made the wall with relief and edged along until his shoulder was next to the glass-fronted box that read *In the event of fire break glass*. He reached inside his pocket, pulled out the hammer and raised it (a rather difficult operation because he could see neither the hammer nor his hand). *Here we go again,* he thought as he drew back the tool and smashed it down hard on the alarm.

An ear-splitting siren went off.

For a moment everyone inside the bank froze, looking around stupidly as if trying to work out what was going on. Then half the people decided the alarm was probably just some kind of practice drill, staying right where they were, while the other half started crowding towards the exit. Alex pressed himself into the wall as a woman walked by – close enough for her arm to brush him, but too preoccupied with getting out of the bank to notice anything strange.

The foyer started to empty quickly as the alarm continued, although some stubborn customers had taken the opportunity to move closer to the tellers as others left the line. Alex saw a gap in the crowd and ran across to the door beside the row of service windows.

Presently, the door opened and a suited man wearing a *Branch Manager* badge emerged to hustle slowcoaches towards the door.

"Move towards the exit," he said, shooing people away from the tellers. "Please, this isn't a drill."

Several of the people in line groaned, like they'd rather stay in a burning building if it meant getting served faster that morning. As the manager moved away, Alex caught the door and slipped through into the restricted area of the bank. The security door clicked shut behind him and he edged down the corridor, keeping close to the wall in case anyone came running in his direction.

A door to the left stood open and Alex went through, finding himself on the other side of the counter where the bank tellers sat. The bank employees were in the process of leaving in an orderly procession by the back door. Through one of the glass windows looking into the foyer, Alex saw the manager usher the last customer out, take a final look around to make sure the area was clear and then exit.

Now the interior of the bank was deserted apart from Alex. The only sound was the relentless drone of the siren. He waited against the wall for just a moment more (just in case some straggler came running through on his way out to the back), before pulling the rolled-up cash bags from his belt and going to the counter.

There were six swivel chairs – one for each of the tellers – and an equal number of cash drawers. Alex started at the farthest left, pushing the chair away and pressing the button to open the drawer. It slid out smoothly, revealing a tray of notes and coins. Alex opened the first bag and began to fill it with red twenty dollar notes, then yellow fifties and green hundreds. In each tray, he was careful to leave a couple of notes under each spring-loaded holding flap so as not to trigger the security alarm. When he'd taken all he could, Alex moved to the drawer on his right and repeated the operation. After half a dozen such jobs, he found that he was getting faster at opening and emptying the trays. What didn't change was the feeling of guilt – the realization he was stealing money, something that his parents would never have condoned.

But they're not here, Alex reminded himself. *Uncle Pete is.*

And Uncle Pete got what he wanted or there was hell to pay – Alex had learned that during the past few months. He had the bruises to prove it.

The bag was getting full, so Alex pulled the drawstring tight and tied it to his belt. The filled bag hung there –

invisible as long as it was in contact with his body. The ability to *fade out* (the name he had given to his power) had started to reveal itself just a few weeks after the fall virus hit and Alex was still learning how it worked. He'd tried to keep his invisibility a secret at first, instinctively realizing that it would not be a good idea for Uncle Pete or anyone else to know about it. However, it wasn't that simple, especially when he had a tendency to wake up in the morning semi-faded out.

Alex moved on to the next drawer, opening and emptying it in ten seconds flat. Looking up, he saw people moving around in the street through the main door. In the distance, the siren of a fire truck drew closer. Alex guessed that he probably had three or four more minutes. *Plenty of time,* he thought as he pressed the button to open the fourth drawer…

Whap!

Purple liquid exploded from the drawer, hitting him full in the face and chest and covering the rest of his body in a fine mist. Stunned, Alex stumbled back, dropping the bag in his hand as he did so. It immediately became visible as it hit the ground, spilling banknotes across the carpet. He looked down and realized that the bag wasn't the only thing not so invisible any more…

His upper body looked as if someone had thrown a

bucket of purple paint over it. He blinked the liquid from his eyes and examined the fourth drawer. Nestled where the money tray should be was the remains of a silver cylinder, split open to expel a dye-pack (Alex had read about those on one of the websites where his uncle had done the research – the cops put them in bags to mark money stolen by criminals). *Criminals. The cops.* A wave of panic swept over him as he looked down at his dye-covered hands and arms.

Go away, he prayed. *Disappear.*

Slowly, the dye began to fade out and become transparent. *Invisible again!* Alex had a brief moment of relief, before the fire alarm abruptly ceased. A terrible silence fell over the bank. Although he was fully faded out again, Alex crouched down – sensing that something was about to happen.

The front door of the bank crashed open noisily. Six men wearing helmets and body armour ran into the foyer, their boots screeching against the polished marble. Alex backed away from the counter, all the while keeping his eyes on the six cops in the doorway. It was plain to see from the body armour they weren't just normal police, but some kind of Special Forces. In their arms they held odd-looking rifles at the ready and crouched low to the ground as if expecting to be attacked at any moment.

Alex kept perfectly still – for a moment he didn't even breathe.

"We know you're back there!" the leader of the cops shouted into the bank, splitting the silence with his booming voice. "Come out now with your hands raised and you won't get hurt. This is the only warning you're gonna get!"

Alex wondered if Uncle Pete and Stella were still sitting in the car across the street, but instinctively knew they would have made a run for it the moment they saw the police go into the bank. He was on his own and would have to make his own escape. But he still had one advantage – the cops couldn't see him...

"Okay, kill the lights!" the leader yelled back through the door and instantly the bank was thrown into semi-darkness.

Alex blinked as his eyes adjusted to the gloom. The cops closed and locked the main doors behind them. Clearly they didn't want him slipping by them, which suggested they knew about his skill. *Perhaps they aren't so stupid, after all,* Alex thought with a sinking feeling.

"Activate the ultraviolet!" the leader commanded. The lights in the ceiling above the foyer flicked on again, but this time with a fluorescent purple hue. Alex looked down at his arms with shock – in the UV light the dye was completely visible once again. In fact, it glowed a fluorescent purple that stood out a mile. *I'm in trouble,* he realized, creeping further from the counter.

"Captain, back there!" one of the men shouted. "I've got movement!"

"Take him down!"

As Alex broke for the open doorway into the back of the bank there was a terrific sound of shattering glass. A hail of missiles tore through the teller windows and hit the walls around him. As he ran through the door, Alex had time to see a dart as long as his fingers embed itself in the frame of the doorway.

A tranquillizer dart.

Well, at least they're not trying to kill me, he thought as he stumbled headlong into the darkened corridor.

Yet.

7

Alex crouched under a desk in one of the office cubicles trying to control his breathing, which was coming in ragged, noisy gasps after his flight from the front of the bank. In the darkness at the rear of the building he was mercifully out of the ultraviolet glare and invisible again, but all the external doors seemed to be locked from the outside. *A trap,* Alex realized, and cursed his uncle's "foolproof" plan.

At the sound of a boot pressing into the carpet, he held his breath and peered round the edge of the desk.

Two of the armoured cops stepped cautiously through the main door and looked around the rows of cubicles.

"He could be anywhere in here," one hissed, loud enough for Alex to hear.

"Use the torch," the other said. "I'll cover the door so he doesn't slip through."

The cop who had spoken first nodded and removed something from his belt – an oversized lamp that emitted a UV beam. He advanced down the row of cubicles, a dart-gun held out in one hand and the lamp in the other, sweeping it left and right. Alex shrank back as part of the beam shone under the table, showing up droplets of fluorescent dye on the carpet. The cop went left, taking him away from the hiding place, but Alex knew it was only a matter of minutes before he was discovered.

Moving out from under the desk as silently as possible, he poked his head around the cubicle wall and checked out the burly cop guarding the only unlocked exit out of the room – he didn't fancy his chances. Worse still, that cop also had a UV lamp in his hand and was waving it around. *Got to get rid of the dye somehow.* Alex looked round and up for an alternative – and his eyes fell on something in the ceiling.

Set into one of the tiles was a metal nozzle that he recognized as a sprinkler fitting. Inside the fitting was a temperature sensitive cell designed to trigger the sprinkler system in the event of a real fire. The other cop's footsteps approached as he made his way back to cover the cubicles he hadn't checked. Not wasting another second, Alex carefully slid open the top drawer of the desk and instantly found what he needed – a cigarette lighter, the disposable kind Stella and his uncle used all the time. Taking the lighter, he stepped up onto the desk and raised it to the nozzle, aware of the table creaking under his weight.

"Hey, did you hear that?" the cop at the door yelled to his partner. "Over to your left!"

Alex struck the wheel on the lighter and held down the gas button. The flame flickered around the nozzle and within seconds he felt the heat burning his fingertips. Alex gritted his teeth. *Come on.*

"What's that light?" the nearest cop asked, flicking his lamp towards the ceiling.

The sprinkler spurted into life, spraying an arc of water in all directions. Simultaneously, six other nozzles around the room went active. Alex lowered the lighter and stood stock still as the water poured around him. The cops waved their lamps around in confusion and in one of the flickering beams Alex caught a glimpse of the dye washing away from his body. When he looked down he saw a pool of purple mixing with the water collecting on the carpet.

"What do we do?" yelled the cop nearest the cubicle over the sound of the water jets. The bulb in his lamp exploded in a shower of sparks. "Aren't these things waterproof?"

Taking advantage of their confusion, Alex put his hands on the flimsy cubicle wall and jumped into the walkway behind it. He ran for the door, aware of the water bouncing off his shoulders and head, creating an outline for the guards to see. Luckily they were too preoccupied with their exploding lamps to notice as he slipped through the door and into the corridor beyond.

Alex moved fast towards the back of the building – hoping to find some kind of exit that he'd missed the first time. Getting trapped in the office space was stupid, so no more mistakes. Rounding a corner, he found exactly what he was looking for – a set of double doors with an illuminated *Emergency Exit* sign above them. Splashing through the water pooling across the tiled floor, he ran full pelt for freedom...

He drew up fast as a figure stepped out of the shadows – the big cop from the foyer. The leader. In the darkness of the corridor Alex could make out the whites of the man's eyes and his hard gaze. Alex flattened against the wall, hoping he hadn't given himself away. The leader scanned the corridor ahead, as if sensing something, then raised a UV lamp. He swung the beam across Alex, but this time no dye was illuminated – the water from the sprinklers had done its job. Alex almost cried with relief.

Sweeping the lamp around again, the leader reached for a communicator clipped to his chest. "All units, report."

"Foyer, no movement, over," the comm barked back a second later.

"Office area, no sign," came a second reply. "But we've got dye residue on the floor here. Looks like the sprinklers washed it off the target's body, over."

The cop leader sucked his teeth in frustration and flicked off his lamp. "Okay, all units hold position. He's trapped in here and we'll get him if we have to wait till Christmas. Shoot anything that moves. I'm calling in back-up, over and out."

Alex edged along the wall, centimetre by centimetre, until he was almost level with the hulking cop. He was aware of the water splashing off his body – a dead giveaway for anyone paying enough attention, but the man's mind was elsewhere.

"Beta team," the leader said into his comm, "prepare

to move in. We've lost the dye-tagger. And someone shut off these damned sprinklers, over."

Alex moved past him and turned his attention to the exit at the end of the corridor. The doors were closed with a metal bar across the middle that pushed to open. Even with the sprinklers going full blast, the noise would be sure to attract the attention of the cop. He looked round at the man and the rifle slung over his shoulder, wondering if he could possibly be fast enough. Then his eyes fell on a dart-pistol tucked into the back of his trousers. *Dare I?* thought Alex.

Without warning the sprinklers shut off and the lights came up in the corridor.

"About time," sniffed the leader. Alex took a deep breath.

Don't think... Do.

Reaching out fast, he grabbed the handle of the pistol and fired at the area of the cop's body he thought most likely to hit – his backside.

The leader gave a cry that was an equal mix of shock and pain as he spun round, bringing his rifle up in the process. In his concentration on grabbing the gun, Alex had allowed his invisibility to slip. For a moment they looked one another in the eyes.

"Kid?" the cop said, before his eyes rolled up into his

skull and he crashed backwards, landing with a splash on the floor.

Alex dropped the dart-gun at his feet and threw himself at the emergency exit. Pushing the bar, he ran out into brilliant sunlight.

8

The two-bedroom unit owned by Uncle Pete was silent in a way that gave Alex the creeps the moment he stepped through the unlocked back door. Normally the place was filled with the sound of his uncle arguing with Stella, the TV blaring out a football match, or some of their no-good mates laughing and drinking. But not today. Alex walked through the kitchen, past the piles of dirty dishes stacked in the sink (his job to clean them, under normal circumstances) and down the corridor to the lounge room. It was empty and the giant LCD TV in the corner was turned off for the first time he could recall.

"Hello?" Alex called through to the bedrooms, but there was no response. The place felt abandoned – cleaned out. All that was left was the junk his uncle and Stella couldn't carry. *And me,* thought Alex as he slumped wearily onto the sofa and pointed the remote at the TV.

Getting back to his uncle's place had been easy enough. There were just a few cops covering the rear of the bank and he'd slipped past them and round to the front, just in case Uncle Pete was still there. The car was long gone, of course. He ran a few blocks before making himself visible again in a side street. The roads had been chaos, but he'd jumped in the back of a cab. The driver agreed to take him anywhere he wanted when Alex pulled a couple of hundred dollar bills from the bag still tied to his belt.

In the apartment, he flipped through the channels until he reached a station showing the local news. A reporter stood in front of the bank, talking about the massive police operation that was under way right in the centre of the city.

"They're bringing someone out," the reporter announced, turning back to the building as the camera focused on the door. Two medics appeared, wheeling a stretcher towards a waiting ambulance. "It seems as if one of the Special Forces team members has been injured."

Alex recognized the cop he'd shot, still unconscious on the stretcher.

The reporter looked back at the camera. "We don't know if the criminals are still inside the bank, but clearly they're not afraid to use violence to evade capture."

Alex had heard enough. With a shake of his head, he raised the remote to turn off the TV...

"*Wait, Alex!*" the reporter on the screen said urgently. "*You should keep watching—* ...the start of a city-wide manhunt for any of the robbers who might have escaped..."

Alex froze with his finger over the *off* button. Slowly, he leaned towards the screen, feeling more than a little stupid as he watched the reporter continue the story as normal.

"Did you just speak to me?" he asked finally.

Immediately, the screen flickered and crackled, making him jump back in surprise. The picture went to static for a split second before being replaced by a new image: a desert of snow that seemed to stretch on for ever. In the distance a skyscraper rose into the sky – out of place in the icy expanse. Shaking his head, Alex pressed the *channel up* button a few times, but every side seemed to be showing the same programme now. He lowered the remote as a tall, thin figure walked out of the snowscape towards the camera: a man in a dark suit that made him look like a silhouette against the glaring brightness of his surroundings. As he came closer to the screen, Alex could see his hair was pure white, although he only looked about as old as his uncle, perhaps in his early forties. The man stopped and smiled at the camera. Alex had the strangest feeling he was looking directly at him.

"Hello," the man said, "my name is Nikolai Makarov. If it's easier for you, feel free to call me Nicholas. It's so nice to finally get a chance to speak to you alone, Alex." His accent was Russian, but his English was perfect.

Alex sat back on the sofa and was silent for a moment. This had to be some kind of trick – a joke thought up by his uncle and his mates to make him look stupid. They loved to play their games. But the man on the screen – Nikolai Makarov – shook his head.

"Come, come, Alex," he said, as if reading his thoughts, "you know your uncle doesn't have the brains to set something like this up. In fact, he's busy selling you out as we speak. Take a look."

Makarov snapped his long fingers and the TV image abruptly changed to a shot of what looked like an interrogation room from a cop show. Uncle Pete sat at a metal table nervously smoking a cigarette while a suited man with a badge on his belt paced before him.

"It was the kid!" Pete whined. "I tell you, my nephew got these freak powers since he was exposed to that virus. Always sneaking around, all invisible like. He made me drive him to the bank – just ask Stella. He said he'd hurt us with some kind of mind control if we didn't help him rob the place!"

Alex stood abruptly and pointed at the screen. "Hey! He's making that up!"

The image snapped back to Makarov and the ice desert. He nodded sympathetically. "One of his so-called friends tipped off the police and they picked him up trying to escape the city. He's already given you up, Alex. In about three minutes the cops will be banging down the door of the house in which you're standing."

Alex shook his head. "How did you get those pictures of him? This must be..."

"Some kind of trick?" Nikolai Makarov finished for him with a wry smile. "Not possible? Please, Alex, I would expect someone who can make himself invisible to be a little more open-minded about such things."

"Then you're..."

"Like you," the man on the screen finished for him

once again. "Your gift is a by-product of your exposure to the fall virus, as I'm sure you've guessed. And so is mine."

Alex frowned. "You can control TVs?"

Makarov laughed. "And much more besides. I'd like to tell you all about it, but at the moment we have the small matter of the police to worry about. You shouldn't have gone back to the house, Alex. You're going to have to get smarter if you're going to stay free long enough for me to rescue you."

Alex looked around as a car screeched past outside. He turned back to the TV, deciding that the guy on the screen was his best bet at that moment. "What do I do? I haven't got anywhere to go."

"You've got about one minute," Makarov said urgently. "Just get out of there. Move!" The screen went dead.

Not hanging around, Alex ran straight through to the kitchen. Something crackled near the sink as he went past. Looking round, his eyes fell on Stella's iPod, lying forgotten near the window. The little white headphones were still plugged in and sound was coming from them, faint but audible.

"Take it, Alex!" Nikolai Makarov's voice commanded tinnily. "Go out the back door. They're already covering the front."

Hearing the sound of vehicles on the road, Alex grabbed the iPod from the window sill and ran out the back. (As he ran across the lawn he remembered that the player hadn't worked since Uncle Pete had thrown it at the wall during one of his and Stella's arguments – but he decided to think about that later.) From the house there was a crash as the front door was smashed open.

Alex jumped the back fence in one fluid movement and landed in the alleyway beyond, hitting the ground running.

He didn't look back.

Thirty minutes later, Alex walked onto the platform of a suburban train station with the hood of his jacket up to hide his face. Somewhere a police siren howled, but he didn't look round as he walked past the ticket office. It was tempting simply to fade out, but the run from Uncle Pete's house had left him too exhausted for that. For now he walked to the end of the platform, trying to keep out of people's way. The speakers announced that a train was due in two minutes.

"Well done, Alex," Makarov said in the headphone he had placed in his left ear. Alex looked down at the iPod. Now that he'd stopped running, the ridiculousness of taking orders from a broken MP3 player occurred to him. In the window, the playlist even read *Nikolai Makarov*. "No need to speak out loud. Direct your thoughts to me and I'll hear."

What now? Alex thought back, glad of the fact he wasn't going to have to speak out loud to the iPod in public. *I want to know what's going on here.*

Makarov sighed as if they were wasting time with questions. "Plenty of time to explain everything later, Alex. Right now you need to—"

I'm not doing anything until I get some answers, Alex answered firmly. *I've been chased, tricked and ordered around all day. I'm not going anywhere until you give me an explanation. Just who are you? And what do you want?*

The iPod was silent for a second, but then it sprang into life again.

"I'm just like you, Alex," Makarov explained. "Except I was exposed to the fall virus many, many years ago. Since then I've been able to cast my mind to distant places and control things remotely. My skills have given me riches and power, but now I have a different concern. I have a mission and I want you to be part of it."

Where are you? Alex asked.

"Far away," Makarov replied. "What's important now is that you find the others like you in Melbourne."

Why?

"Because people like us have to stand together," Makarov explained. "At the moment we're scattered, weak – you're going to help me bring us together, Alex. There's going to be a war and it's going to be us against them."

Alex shook his head, trying to process the information he was getting. *War? What war? Perhaps you're confusing me with someone else, because I'm just a kid—*

"Who has the power to make himself invisible," Nikolai Makarov interrupted. "I think that makes you pretty special, don't you? There are six others, Alex. They don't know it yet, but they're in imminent danger – I have sensed it. Go to them, help them and I'll get you all out of Australia."

Alex looked round as the train pulled into the station. He guessed he didn't have anything better to do – and there was nothing left for him in Melbourne.

Just tell me where to go, he replied.

The battered Range Rover drew to a halt at the crest of a hill overlooking the city. The driver's door opened and the equally battered Eco staggered out into the fresh air. He'd been driving non-stop for hours and now they were finally at their destination: *Melbourne*. Major Bright emerged from the passenger side and surveyed the city spreading out before them.

"It's bigger than I expected," Eco said. The city seemed to stretch on for ever into the distance. Most of Melbourne was a flat expanse of suburbs and highways, with the centre marked by a towering spike of skyscrapers huddled together. It sprawled away from them, shimmering in the heat of the afternoon. "How will we ever find the children you're looking for?"

During their flight from the desert, Bright had spoken about how the children in the city were essential to his plans. They were the key to his powers. But now Eco couldn't see how they could find them in a city of five million people. Bright, however, didn't seem concerned. He raised his hand to the view and splayed his fingers.

"I sense them in the north," he said quietly. "They cannot hide their thoughts from me. Six of them."

Eco looked to where he pointed. "What are we going to do?"

"Together they're strong," Major Bright replied. "But capture one of them and the rest become weaker."

"How do you intend to do that?" Eco asked.

Fire leaped around Major Bright's outstretched fingertips. In seconds his hand was aflame.

"First I'll divide them," he said. "Then they'll fall."

9

The sun hung low in the sky as Sarah entered the botanical gardens near the ANZAC shrine in the centre of Melbourne. She walked in the direction of the lake. The place was practically deserted, apart from a few people enjoying the last of the afternoon on picnic blankets laid out on the grass. From the way people had moved aside on the pavements as she walked from the train station, Sarah knew her giant-disguise was holding up – she projected it into the minds of the people around her in a five metre radius. However, the strain of maintaining the pretence was starting to give her a headache again.

Keeping to the shadows created by the trees and staying on the smaller paths through the park, Sarah allowed the image to slip away with relief. Although she was getting stronger, as they all were, using her powers for an extended period left her drained. She checked her watch and doubled her pace.

Dr. Rachel Andersen, the head of HIDRA in the region, was already sitting on the bench that overlooked the lake. She didn't look round, but Sarah knew that she sensed her presence. Sarah was also aware of at least four people stationed in the trees and bushes around the lake, hidden from sight.

"You didn't come alone," Sarah said as she took a seat on the end of the bench.

Rachel nodded. "Protection."

"For you or me?"

Rachel laughed. "For both of us. There are some dangerous people out there."

"Major Bright," Sarah said, seeing the scene from the desert playing out in Rachel's thoughts – the sandstorm, the crashing hovercopters.

"Hey, I thought you said you weren't going to do that mind-reading thing all the time!" Rachel protested with mock anger.

Sarah blushed a little. "Sorry. Sometimes it's difficult not to."

The woman nodded her understanding. They'd known one another since the original crisis with Colonel Moss and Major Bright, when Rachel had merely been the head scientist at HIDRA. When she found out about Colonel Moss's intention to turn Sarah and the others into super-soldiers, Rachel helped them escape and eventually took Moss's role as commander. Sarah well knew that Rachel's only interest was finding a cure for the fall virus, but she also knew she had to be cautious – as an organization, HIDRA was just too big, too complex, to read or predict.

"Have you considered Bright might come after you?" Rachel asked.

"I was hoping HIDRA would have caught him by now."

"We're closing the net," Rachel replied, a little shortly. "He's tougher than we anticipated."

"I know," Sarah replied. "I've fought him."

"We'll get him. He must be running very short of serum by now. With no fresh blood, he has no way to manufacture any more."

"Which brings us down to business," Sarah said. She held out the red box and Rachel took it. The woman didn't bother to open the lid, knowing that the insulated container contained six vials of blood extracted from the children. Each vial could contain a cure to the fall virus and bring the thousands of coma victims back to life.

"Thank you, Sarah," she said, holding the box on her lap. "You don't know how much this means to us. Of course, our research would proceed more quickly if you all came in—"

Sarah held up a hand. "Don't, Rachel. We're not returning to HIDRA."

Rachel sighed with exasperation. "But we can provide you with everything you need: food, shelter, education. What about the younger ones? How are Louise and Wei? When was the last time they went to school?"

Sarah looked away over the lake. As soon as they reached Europe, she intended to enrol Robert, Louise and Wei in the best private school possible. From the diamonds, they had enough money to last for years, now all they needed was new identities, which was where the new passports came in.

She looked back at Rachel, who was waiting expectantly for her reply, and felt a pang of guilt. She and her friends were planning to vanish off the face of the earth, safe for ever from anyone who knew their secrets. But as much as she liked the woman, Sarah realized she couldn't tell her – finding the viral cure would always come first with Rachel and they both knew it. And while Sarah desperately wanted to see HIDRA find a cure for the sake of her father and the parents of her friends, she also needed to protect the freedom of her group.

"They're doing fine," Sarah said firmly. "They'll be better when they know where their parents are." Both Louise and Wei had lost parents to the fall virus coma – and then HIDRA had "mislaid" their sleeper caskets. Her own father, Daniel, had only escaped the same fate because they had fled with him before he succumbed to the coma.

Rachel sighed. "Believe me, we're trying to find them. Colonel Moss deliberately lost the details of significant patients."

"Like the parents of children he wanted to control?" Sarah said bitterly.

"There's thousands of John Does among the sleepers," Rachel acknowledged. "We're DNA testing them all, but it's going to take time."

"Okay," Sarah said. She knew Rachel was trying her best in difficult circumstances.

"Is there anything we can help you with?" the woman asked, placing a hand on Sarah's arm. "Do you need food, supplies? How about Daniel – is he still stable in his sleeper casket?"

"He's fine," Sarah replied. "We're fine." The last thing she wanted was to become dependent on HIDRA. At the moment Rachel was in charge of things and her intentions were good, but she knew that could change without warning if another military man like Colonel Moss was put in control again.

"Just catch Major Bright," Sarah said, rising from the seat. A strange feeling passed over her as she did so – a sudden dizziness that came out of nowhere. She steadied herself against the bench. She sensed danger. Not for herself, but for the others back at the apartment.

"Are you okay?" Rachel asked with concern in her voice.

Sarah backed away. "Something's happening... Or something's going to happen." She frowned as she tried to understand herself. "Trouble. Don't follow me."

Rachel stood quickly. "Let me help!"

But Sarah was already gone, running into the darkness of the nearby trees.

Rachel's earpiece crackled. "Do you want us to follow her, sir?" one of the HIDRA agents asked from his hiding place. "We have men in position."

"No, stand down," Rachel ordered. "I promised her

before we wouldn't try to find their hiding place. And it's about time HIDRA started keeping its promises."

She looked in the direction where Sarah had gone and said a silent prayer for her safety.

Nestor was fixing dinner by the time his brother finally decided to come in off the balcony. Leaving the door standing wide open, he strode across the lounge. Louise gave a cry of annoyance as Octavio kicked past her, but he ignored it, grabbed a spare set of keys from beside the TV and went in the direction of the hallway.

"Where are you going?" Nestor demanded, blocking his way out of the apartment.

His brother sighed and jangled the keys in his hand. "I'm sick of sitting around here like a little kid. I'm going out to have some fun."

"Sarah said—"

Octavio laughed. "*Sarah said... Sarah said...* She gives the orders now, does she? Just like Colonel Moss used to. Get out of my way."

Nestor didn't budge. "That's not fair. I'm not going to let you put us all at risk."

"What's going on here?" demanded Robert, going to Nestor's side.

Octavio's face flushed red with anger. "All I want is get out of here for a couple of hours. And there's nothing you can do to stop me."

Isn't there? Louise said threateningly. The three boys looked round and saw her standing in the middle of the lounge, eyes locked on Octavio.

I'm not afraid of you, Octavio replied, swallowing heavily. *I'm not afraid of any of you!*

Louise gave no response, but a strange smile passed across her face, as if she'd been waiting for this moment for a long time. Her unusual eyes – one coloured blue, the other green – flashed with excitement, just like they did when she was playing one of her computer games. A deadly stillness fell over the room as the two faced one another.

"Hey! Look at this!" Wei's voice from the balcony cut through the silence. Everyone breathed again.

"I said come here!" Wei yelled a second time, real urgency in his voice. All four of them ran to the balcony, and looked to where the Chinese kid was pointing.

On the fifth floor of the tower directly opposite, one of the apartments was ablaze. Fire leaped at the window and black smoke was starting to drift upwards into the twilight. Seconds later there was an explosion that ripped out the window and a great chunk of the wall.

Bricks rained down onto parked cars below and the sound of people screaming in panic became audible.

Wei gave a whistle of amazement and everyone looked round at him.

"Why's everyone looking at me?" he asked indignantly. "Every time there's a fire I get the blame!"

Robert raised an eyebrow. "We're just remembering the last apartment you burned down."

Louise leaped to his defence. "That wasn't Wei's fault! The cooker was faulty."

There was a second, muffled explosion from the other side of the tower. The flames were starting to spread up through the decaying building to the floor above.

"It must have found a gas pipe," Nestor said quietly. "The entire tower could go up. What do we do?"

Robert shrugged, unable to tear his eyes from the terrible scene below them. From the seventh floor the sound of people yelling for help could be heard. A woman smashed a window and looked out desperately, but it was far too high to jump. Behind her it was possible to see the light of the spreading fire in her apartment. She shouted something they couldn't hear.

"What do we do?" Nestor said again, sounding helpless.

Octavio leaned casually against the balcony railing. "Sarah said we had to stay put. So let's just enjoy the show."

Robert looked at Octavio, anger flaring at his relaxed attitude to what they were seeing. On impulse he reached out and grabbed the boy's wrist with one hand. With the other he grabbed Nestor.

"You wanted to go out?" he said as Octavio's head jerked round in surprise. "Let's go!"

With that, the three boys teleported away, leaving Louise and Wei standing alone on the balcony.

10

The fire that had started on the fifth floor of the south tower was raging upwards, already consuming the sixth storey and spreading on to the seventh. The building had not been renovated in its thirty years' existence, so there were no modern safety features (such as fire doors or sprinkler systems) to halt the progress of the inferno. As in the other towers, the lift had not been in working order for months, so those residents above the fifth floor were piling into the stairwells and pushing their way upwards to escape the blaze. So intent were they at getting as far away from the fire as possible, no one seemed to notice as Robert, Nestor and Octavio appeared out of nowhere on the narrow landing between the eighth and ninth floors.

"Get out of the way!" a man yelled, pushing Nestor back roughly in his haste to get past.

The three boys pressed themselves against the wall to avoid being swept along with the flow of men, women and children heading for the higher levels. Octavio blinked at Robert, as if still uncertain what had just happened to them.

"Where are we?" he asked, a little stupidly.

Nestor nodded to the smoke rising up the stairwell. "Where do you think?"

Octavio rounded on Robert. "What did you teleport us here for? Are you crazy?"

Robert laughed. "I thought you said you were bored."

Octavio grabbed Robert's shoulders roughly and shook him. "Take us back! Right now!"

"No way!" Robert replied, pulling away. "We're going to help. Let's see if you can use your superpowers to do some good for once."

Take it easy, Nestor warned them. Even though people were most concerned about escaping the fire, their shouting was starting to attract some looks.

Why is everyone going up?

It was a good question. Robert pushed his way to the edge of the landing and looked over. The answer was three flights down – one of the explosions triggered by the fire had knocked out the lower levels of the fire escape, creating a stairless shaft below the fourth storey. Up was the only way to escape the fire, but judging by the sound of desperate voices from below, some people were still trapped on the sixth floor.

"There's no way out," Robert shouted back at the others. "I think there's still people down there."

Not waiting for their response, he started down the stairs against the tide of people, getting pushed and shoved in the process. Octavio shook his head and folded his arms.

"I'm not risking my neck."

Nestor grabbed his brother's arm and pulled him after Robert, who had already reached the next landing down. They followed down quickly, ignoring the warnings from various people that the lower floors were completely ablaze. At the landing of the seventh they caught up with the younger boy, who was standing in the doorway onto that level.

"There's still people below," he said urgently. "I'm going down to help them. You two check out this floor."

With that, he disappeared.

"I wish he'd stop doing that," Octavio said with a groan as he followed Nestor through the door onto the seventh.

They found themselves standing in an L-shaped corridor almost identical to the ones in their tower block. The only difference was that here the musty smell was overpowered by the acrid stench of smoke rising from the lower levels. At the end of the corridor a forgotten girl, no older than Louise, stood in an open doorway, her face frozen in fear. Nestor started forward, but Octavio caught his arm.

"No! There's danger!"

Before Nestor could protest, there was a muffled explosion and an apartment door to their right was ripped clean off its hinges. Flames leaped out of the open doorway and the boys hit the floor to avoid being fried. Thinking fast, Nestor raised his hands and using his aerokinetic power, directed a blast of air at the flames. There was a roaring sound and the fire grew in intensity, spreading along the ceiling above them.

"You're feeding it, you idiot!" Octavio cried.

Nestor clenched his fist, stopping the air blast. "Right. Bad idea."

The fire passed over them, igniting the ageing wallpaper along the corridor and spreading down.

Octavio looked round frantically. "It's surrounding us!"

"Okay, let me try this..."

Nestor blasted the flames again, only this time using a different concentration of air. Thick and white, it immediately drove back the fire above them. Octavio looked at his brother and nodded.

"It's working!"

"The oxygen fed the fire!" Nestor shouted above the howling air as he went to work extinguishing the flames around them. "I extracted the carbon dioxide from the air and used that instead."

"Thanks for the science lesson," Octavio said sarcastically. Nestor had succeeded in extinguishing the fire in the corridor and proceeded to blast CO_2 into the burning apartment. With the flames out, they could now see that a section of ceiling had been brought down in the blast, including a large iron support that blocked their path.

"What about the girl?" Nestor asked.

Octavio sighed and shook his head. "You deal with the fire. I'll do the heavy lifting."

He walked to the mass of debris blocking the corridor and peered through to the other side. The girl stood in the doorway of the apartment as if her feet were rooted to the spot.

"Hey!" Octavio shouted. "Get back! I'm going to move this stuff!"

If she heard him, the girl showed no sign, keeping her eyes fixed straight ahead, not moving a muscle.

"Great," Octavio sighed, taking a step back. He raised his hands and closed his eyes, visualizing the iron girder that blocked his way. Imagining it no heavier than a feather, he made it rise into the air and over to one side in his mind. There was a metallic grinding sound and he opened his eyes to see the girder floating near the ceiling. *Easy.* His first instinct was to send it flying down the corridor out of the way, but then he remembered the girl.

"Come on!" he shouted, turning his attention to where she stood. With the girder floating above, there was space for her to run through. "I said move!"

The girl looked at him and shook her head slowly. For the first time he noticed that tears were rolling down her cheeks. He was about to shout at her again, when the girder wobbled and he had to refocus to keep it in the air. *Not so easy.* A terrible pressure started to form at Octavio's temples, just like it always did when he overexerted his power.

"It's okay," he called, softening his voice. "I won't let you get hurt, but you have to come now."

The girl wiped her tear-stained cheeks and looked down at her feet, as if deciding whether she dared move them.

"Please," Octavio said, suddenly feeling the weight of the girder pressing down on his mind. "You'll be okay. Trust me."

At the other end of the corridor, the girl started to walk forwards, looking left and right as if she expected to be engulfed by fire at any moment. Octavio nodded encouragement to her.

"That's it. Keep coming..."

She passed under the floating girder, looking up as it started to tremble in the air. Octavio gritted his teeth.

"*Run!*"

The girl broke into a sprint, throwing her arms around Octavio as he lost his mental grip on the girder and it smacked down on the floor, sending a massive vibration through the building. Breathing a sigh of relief, Octavio patted the girl awkwardly on the shoulder.

"You're okay now," he said, but she showed no sign of releasing her grip around his waist.

With the fire extinguished, Nestor reappeared in the corridor and raised an eyebrow at the scene.

"Let's just get out of here, okay?" Octavio said shortly

as he grabbed the girl's hand and dragged her in the direction of the landing. "I've done enough hero stuff for one day."

Halfway to the end of the corridor, however, the three of them froze as the floor beneath them vibrated and a groan went through the building.

"That doesn't sound good," Octavio said.

Nestor nodded and they started for the stairwell at a sprint. Behind them there was a crash as the floor of the corridor collapsed under the weight of the girder. Safe on the landing, they looked back to see most of the sixth floor had fallen into the fifth.

"Robert's down there!" Nestor cried.

"Not any more," Robert replied, appearing beside them on the landing with his arms wrapped around two other people – an elderly couple who were barely able to stand. "Help me!"

Nestor moved to support the elderly man, who looked around in confusion at his change in surroundings.

"How did we get out here?" he croaked, his voice hoarse from smoke inhalation.

"It's okay," Robert reassured him. "We're going to the roof."

Even as he said those words, the stairs shook and debris from above fell down the shaft.

"This whole building is falling apart!" Octavio cried as the stairs down to the fifth floor collapsed. "Go!"

They started up the stairs, but the staggering movements of the old man and woman Robert had rescued made the going painfully slow. Nestor looked round at Robert as the stairs under them groaned.

"Get them out of here!" he cried, passing the man back.

Robert considered for a moment before nodding. "Okay. Keep moving up. I'll come back for all of you."

With that, he tightened his grip on the old lady, wrapped his free arm around the old man and all three disappeared. Nestor turned and followed Octavio and the girl up the stairs as a section of the wall collapsed.

"Nestor!" Octavio cried, looking back in time to see the stairs behind come away from the wall and pitch into the shaft. Nestor fell with them and the girl gave a scream. "No!"

Octavio rushed to the edge, fearing what he was about to see as he looked down. He jumped back as a shape rose up the shaft before him...

Louise floated a metre or two away in the middle of the stairwell, cradling Nestor in her arms like a baby. The brothers' eyes met, both too stunned to speak. Then they both looked at Louise.

"You didn't think I'd let you guys have all the fun, did you?" she said indignantly. Then she looked back at Octavio and her eyes flashed. "Race you to the top!"

With that, she zipped up the centre of the shaft, carrying Nestor with her. Octavio looked up stupidly for a moment.

"Wow, she can fly!" the girl he had rescued said breathlessly. "Can you do that?"

"She can float," Octavio corrected irritably and grabbed the girl's hand, leading her up the stairs the slow way. "And I'm still practising."

From the balcony opposite, Wei watched the fire spreading through the apartment block with frustration. It was bad enough that Robert and the other boys had left him behind, but then Louise had flown off to join the action. He always seemed to get forgotten. Well, when they got back he'd tell them exactly what he thought...

So caught up was Wei with his annoyance, that he didn't hear the door to the apartment click open and footsteps approach across the lounge until the stranger was standing right behind him. Finally sensing the presence of another person, Wei spun and came face-to-face with a skinny teenage boy. The boy's clothes were dusty and faded, as if they hadn't been washed in months, and his face was dirty. The boy smiled at him in a friendly manner, although it wasn't very convincing.

"Who are you?" Wei demanded, trying not to let the fear in his voice show. He wanted to get back inside the apartment, but the intruder was blocking the way through the door. The only escape route available was over the balcony and fifteen flights down.

"My name's Eco," the boy replied, fiddling with a bag slung over his shoulder. "Did they go out and leave you all alone?"

"My friends are coming back any minute now," Wei replied. "Who let you in here?"

"Oh, I've got a key," Eco answered, reaching into the bag. "Look."

In a flash, Eco removed an aerosol sedative and sprayed it in the younger boy's face. Choking on the fumes, Wei staggered backwards.

Robert, help! he managed to think as he collapsed against the balcony railings.

"Sorry, kid," Eco said as he pulled the unconscious Wei into the apartment. "Boss's orders."

As he moved Wei to the couch, however, a second boy materialized on the balcony – Robert. Eco dropped Wei and raised the aerosol again, spraying it at the doorway.

Robert was too fast, however, teleporting across the room in the blink of an eye. He reappeared by the kitchen and spun to face Eco.

"I don't know who you are," Robert said dangerously as Eco backed towards the balcony. "But you picked a fight with the wrong people on the wrong day."

A grin spread across Eco's face. "Did I?"

Robert heard movement behind him – too late. He turned in time to see a fist flying towards his head, followed by a jarring impact. As he hit the floor, he made out the looming shape of a man through blurred vision, and a voice he recognized.

"Hello, Robert," Major Bright said. "Good to see you again."

11

"What happened here?" Sarah demanded, trying to keep the emotion from her voice. She needed to keep it together for all of them. It was clear from their absence that Robert and Wei had been taken and, judging by the signs of a struggle, it had been done by force. Louise, Nestor and Octavio stood around the apartment, looking sheepish.

"There was a fire in the building opposite," Nestor said. "We decided to help."

He went on to recount the events of the last hour,

up to Wei's call for help and coming back to the apartment to find him and Robert gone.

"We found this," Octavio said, handing Sarah a scrap of paper.

She turned it over in her hands and read the handwritten message:

Sarah Williams – I have two of yours. Bring samples of all your blood to the ANZAC shrine tomorrow at dawn if you want to see them again. Come alone.

No HIDRA.

Major Bright.

She crumpled the note in her fist and looked out the apartment window. In the building opposite, smoke was still rising as a fire engine hosed down the burned-out floors. In the distance police sirens grew louder. Their hideout suddenly wasn't looking so *low profile* any more.

"What do we do?" Louise asked, her voice breaking. "He took Wei. I shouldn't have left him."

Sarah walked over and put an arm around the younger girl's shoulders as she began to cry.

"It's not your fault," Sarah told her, before looking round at Nestor. "The truck HIDRA gave us is still parked in the garage round the corner, right?"

He nodded.

"Get everything we need from here," she continued. "We take the truck and go within the next five minutes."

"What's the plan?" Octavio asked.

"The plan? We're going to get Robert and Wei back."

Octavio jerked his head at the door to the apartment. "The corridor is swarming with reporters since our adventure at the fire. One of the neighbours must have recognized us and given them the address. What do you want to do about them?"

Sarah gritted her teeth. "If they get in the way, we'll deal with them. Right?"

Louise wiped the tears from her eyes. "Right."

An hour later, Rachel Andersen stood in the middle of the decrepit apartment on the top floor of the block and wrinkled her nose. The place smelled damp, unhealthy. Sarah and the others were gone.

"How long did you say they've been living here?" Rachel asked Lt. Kaminski, her personal assistant at HIDRA.

The stocky, red-faced soldier checked his notes. "Landlord says the lease was signed three months ago. A big guy paid six months up front. Look at this place. It should've been torn down a decade ago."

Rachel walked out to the balcony and looked down at the car park. It was deserted now except for a few police circling the crumpled remains of a TV van.

"Some reporters attempted to follow them when they left the scene," Kaminski explained, appearing beside her on the balcony. "That's when the van imploded. They didn't try to follow after that."

Rachel smiled to herself. *Louise.* She walked back into the apartment and through to one of the bedrooms. Here Daniel's sleeper casket lay against the far wall. She checked the readout on the side, confirming that he was in a perfectly stable coma, before picking up the envelope taped to the lid. Her name was on the front. Inside was a sheet of paper with a message hurriedly written on it:

Rachel... Sorry we couldn't stick around longer, but things are getting crazy here. Perhaps we'll all meet again when this is over. Look after Daniel for us. Find a cure. Sarah.

Rachel patted the side of the casket. "Good to see you again, Daniel," she said. "I wish the circumstances were better."

Lt. Kaminski appeared in the bedroom doorway.

"Have this sleeper transported to the HIDRA base," she said, indicating the casket. "Make sure he gets the best treatment we can give."

* * *

Alex walked the edge of the car park between the apartment blocks, avoiding the police officers patrolling the area. Parked near the entrance to one of the buildings was a black military jeep with an insignia bearing the name HIDRA. As he watched, a tall woman and a soldier emerged from the building and entered the jeep.

"We're too late," Makarov told Alex via the iPod as the jeep pulled away. "The other children have gone, but I know where to find them."

What happened here? Alex asked, looking up at the burned-out wreck of the building opposite.

"A man called Major Bright," Makarov replied. "He seeks to steal the children's powers for himself. He's kidnapped two of them and the rest have fled. They need your help badly now."

Alex frowned. *If they're all so important, why are you talking to me? Why don't you help them directly?*

"Because they wouldn't believe what I say," Makarov replied. "They've learned to distrust the motives of others. But coming from another like themselves, they have a better chance of listening. I have foreseen it."

Alex gritted his teeth. *So, I'm just a way to get to them, right? You're using me. Just like Uncle Pete did.*

"No, Alex," Makarov assured him. "I can't do this

without you – I'm too far away and things are moving too fast. You're my man on the ground."

Right, Alex thought sceptically, but he had to admit, he wanted to trust Makarov. In the previous few months he'd lost his parents and then suffered with Uncle Pete and Stella. He needed someone to believe in.

"Trust me," Makarov said, and Alex wondered if the man had read his deeper thoughts. "When you are with the others I will bring you all to me. I have a place where people like us can live in freedom and use our powers for good. Maybe even find a cure for the fall virus. Wouldn't you like that, Alex?"

Use our powers for good. Find a cure. The phrases hit home with Alex. Uncle Pete had made him a criminal – now it was time to be one of the good guys.

Putting his head down as a police officer walked past, Alex headed off to continue Makarov's rescue mission.

12

Wei woke in a dark place with a start. Instinctively, he tried to rub his eyes and found that he couldn't move his arms. He was sitting on a steel chair with his wrists bound with rope behind the padded back. A metre away, Robert was tied to a similar chair. His head lolled on his chest.

Robert? Wei thought across to him. *Robert, are you okay?*

Robert gave no response. Wei looked around the darkened room. The walls were lined with benches and rusting tools. It was some kind of workshop, but it clearly hadn't been used in years. The atmosphere was cold, making him shiver through his thin T-shirt.

The door to the room opened, metal scraping on the concrete floor. Major Bright strode in, while his accomplice, Eco, hovered nervously by the doorway.

"What have you done to him?" Wei demanded as Bright put his hand on Robert's chin and raised his head. Satisfied that his prisoner was unconscious still, Bright allowed Robert's head to drop back down again.

"Just given him something to help him sleep," Bright replied. "We can't very well have him teleporting all over the place, now can we?"

Wei shivered again, from fear this time as much as from the cold.

"Chilly?" Major Bright asked with mock concern. He crouched before Wei so their eyes were level. "Well, in case you're thinking of heating things up in here – a word of advice. That rope binding your wrists has a non-flammable wire filling. It won't burn. And there's an added incentive not to use your pyrokinetic ability. Do you smell that?"

Wei sniffed and noticed for the first time the stench of petrol fumes. Looking down, he saw the concrete under his and Robert's chairs was wet.

"You're both sitting on petrol," Bright went on. "One spark and…boom!" He spread his hands to make his point. "So be a good boy now."

As the man stood, Wei clenched his teeth to fight back the tears that were forming in his eyes. He asked, "Are you going to kill us?"

Major Bright looked round on his way back to the door, as if surprised. "Kill you? *No, no, no.* I'm going to make sure you're very well looked after, Wei. I know that our present surroundings" – he waved his hand around the room – "are less than desirable. But I promise I'll find a better place to keep you when Sarah comes through with what I want. Somewhere you'll be safe, Wei, just like when we were all at HIDRA."

"Sarah will never give in to you!" Wei exclaimed.

Bright raised an eyebrow. "As long as I've got you and her brother, I'm betting she'll do whatever I ask."

With that, he walked out the door. Eco lingered just a moment longer, looking from Wei to Robert. Wei opened his mouth to say something – to plead with the boy for help – but Eco swung the door shut hurriedly.

Alone in the room apart from the unconscious Robert, an uncontrollable sob escaped Wei's lips.

* * *

"So, what do we do now?" Nestor asked. He sat on the edge of the bed in the motel room Sarah had checked them into half an hour before. They'd managed to slip away from the scene at the apartment block with the help of a diversion created by Louise.

"I thought that was obvious," Octavio answered from the faded armchair by the television. "We contact HIDRA. They're the only ones who can take on Major Bright."

Louise gave him a hard look. *You'd like that, wouldn't you? If you're a good boy, they might even give you your old room back. I bet all your toys are right where you left them—*

Don't push it! Octavio snapped back.

"Enough!" Sarah said. She turned from her place at the window and stole a look at the clock – midnight. It was dark outside now and the motel car park was deserted, but she wanted to keep a lookout anyway. Just in case they had been followed.

"We're not going to HIDRA," she said.

Nestor nodded in agreement. "Major Bright's note was clear – no outside involvement. Especially HIDRA. We can't put Wei and Robert at risk like that."

Octavio shook his head. "All this is Robert's fault anyway."

Sarah frowned, but controlled her anger. "What was that?"

"I said, all this is Robert's fault," Octavio persisted. "If he hadn't teleported us over to the fire, Bright wouldn't have been able to snatch Wei. Can't you see? The fire was a diversion. Classic military strategy: divide and conquer. And who do we know with military training? Well?"

For a moment they were all silent.

"My brother's a hero and he saved people's lives today," Sarah said finally. "You all did. If you hadn't rescued that girl, Octavio, she would have died in the fire. Do you really wish you hadn't been there?" She took a breath. "Now the main thing is to get Robert and Wei back."

"How do you intend to do that?" Octavio demanded.

"We beat Major Bright before, we can do it again," Louise interjected, still angry at Octavio's earlier comments. "We'll fight him together."

Sarah shook her head. "Not this time, Louise. Bright wants blood and he asked me to bring it alone. I'm going to give him just that."

The room erupted in protest. Nestor's voice cut through.

"We work as a team, Sarah!"

"Robert is my brother," she replied.

Nestor rose from the bed and walked towards her. "And he's our friend. So is Wei."

"It's too dangerous," Sarah said firmly. She was about to go on when a heavy knock on the door silenced them all. Holding up a hand, she moved to the peephole in the door and looked out. No one was standing on the other side.

Who's there? Octavio asked.

Ignoring him, Sarah flipped the lock and opened the door swiftly, sticking her head out and looking round the car park. The place was completely deserted. Her main concern was the truck, but looking over to where it was parked, she saw no one nearby. Taking a final look around, she closed and locked the door.

"Must've been the wind," she said with a shrug. "And the answer's *no*. I give Bright what he wants, free Robert and Wei and then we get out of here. He clearly needs more of the serum Colonel Moss created, but we still have the tickets and passports. We'll be on the other side of the world before Bright realizes we're gone."

A low chuckle came from the corner of the room, near the bathroom. "That's the stupidest plan I've ever heard," a male voice said.

Everyone looked around, eyes finally coming to rest on Octavio. He raised his hands.

"Hey! Not me!" he protested.

Sarah took a step towards the corner. "Say that again?"

"That's the stupidest plan I've ever heard."

Sarah looked at the others and could see the same thing in their minds. *Invisible.* She remembered the news story about the bank from earlier. They had an intruder in their midst. The only question was whether he was on their side or Major Bright's. Sarah decided to even up the chances of catching whoever it was.

Louise, turn off the lights! she snapped.

The younger girl jumped at the light switch, throwing the room into darkness.

"Go!" Sarah yelled. Herself, Nestor and Octavio piled towards the corner of the room, grabbing at whatever they could in the darkness.

"I've got him!" Nestor cried triumphantly.

"Okay, Louise!" Sarah exclaimed as she found what she thought was a foot and held it down firmly. "Lights on!"

When the lights came up, Nestor and Sarah were surprised to find themselves pinning Octavio to the floor. Nestor hastily removed his hand from his brother's mouth and Sarah let go of his ankle.

"Idiots!" Octavio snapped.

Nestor mumbled an apology, but was unable to suppress the smile forming at the edges of his mouth.

Sarah rolled her eyes and looked round. In the chair where Octavio had previously sat, someone was beginning to appear – a boy her age. At first he looked like a faded image in an old photo album, the kind her mum used to bring out from time to time when they were young. Gradually, the image sharpened, became deeper and fleshed out. The boy was brown-haired and his thin face was drawn, as if he was very tired or had been living hard for a while. Within twenty seconds he was as clear and visible before them as any normal person. In one hand he held an old-model iPod and had a white earphone stuck in one ear.

Octavio started forward to attack the newcomer, but Sarah caught his arm.

Easy, she said. *We know where he is now. No hurry.* She looked at the boy and said aloud, "Who are you and why are you here?"

"My name's Alex Fisher," he said. "I'm just like you. I'm a friend."

"Just because you're like us," Louise said, "doesn't make you a friend."

Alex looked at her. "If I wanted to hurt you, I wouldn't have made myself visible. Would I?"

Louise's eyes sparkled dangerously. "What makes you think you could hurt me either way?"

Louise, Sarah warned.

"Don't mind her," Octavio told Alex with a smirk, "she likes to fight with everyone she meets. Her way of getting to know people."

Sarah gestured for the others to relax. "Calm down, all of you." She rounded on Alex. "Make it good."

As the group turned their attention towards him, Alex swallowed heavily. Suddenly his mouth was dry.

"I know two of you have been kidnapped by this Major Bright guy," he said. "I can help. I know where you can find him."

"*We* know where to find him," Sarah replied. "The ANZAC shrine. Tomorrow morning at dawn."

Alex shook his head vehemently. "That's a trap. Go to that meeting and you'll never come back. I can lead you to Bright's hideout. You keep him distracted while I slip in the back and release Robert and Wei. With my powers, it shouldn't be a problem."

Sarah frowned. "How do you know so much about us?"

"You wouldn't believe me if I told you," he responded with a laugh, turning the iPod over in his hands as he did so.

Sarah put her hands on her hips. "Try me."

13

"Ouch," Louise said as Sarah inserted the needle in her arm. The plastic chamber of the sample-taker filled quickly with blood.

"Sorry," Sarah said as she removed the needle smoothly and wiped the insertion point on Louise's arm with a ball of cotton wool. "We need the blood to stop Bright from getting suspicious when I go in the hideout. Promise it's the last time for a while."

Sarah removed the vial and wrote *Louise* on the side with a black marker. Finally she placed it in a plastic box, along with the blood samples she'd already taken from Nestor and Octavio.

"Do you trust him?" Louise asked, looking through the bathroom door at Alex, who appeared to be dozing in the armchair.

Sarah looked round also and shrugged. His story about Makarov had been far-fetched and when he'd handed her the iPod, all she'd heard was silence on the earphones. However, after everything that had happened to them in the months since the meteorite strike, she wasn't about to judge anything as ridiculous. As he told it, Makarov was some kind of billionaire genius who wanted to help them. Something about a war coming and the suggestion he had some information about a cure for the fall virus. Whether that was true or not, she knew that Alex's ability to *fade out* would be invaluable to them against Major Bright.

"Right now he's probably our best bet to help Robert and Wei," she admitted.

Louise reached out and laid a hand on Sarah's shoulder. "We're going to get Robert back. He'll be okay."

Sarah nodded and stood up. "Make sure you get all your stuff out of here. One way or the other, we're never coming back to this place."

Louise went to the bed to check her bag as Nestor and Octavio walked in through the door to the motel room.

"The truck's ready to run," Nestor said. "We should get going. There's only a few hours until dawn."

Sarah walked over to Alex and kicked his foot. He snapped awake with a grunt.

"Time to go," she said. "Let's see if your story is true or not."

The sky was becoming light in the east as the truck pulled through a deserted industrial park. Nestor was behind the wheel again, managing to control the HIDRA truck like an expert – he'd had plenty of practice when they'd escaped from Major Bright the first time. Sarah sat beside him, with Alex to her left, anxiously listening to instructions from the iPod.

"Take a left here," he ordered and Nestor spun the wheel.

"How much further?" Sarah said. She was starting to feel nervous. Dawn was approaching now and the arranged meeting with Bright at the ANZAC shrine. If Alex's story about being able to find the hideout was a lie, they wouldn't even have time to make that meeting.

And she didn't want to think about what that would mean for Robert and Wei.

"We're here," Alex replied. "Stop the truck in this parking lot. We don't want to get too close."

Nestor manoeuvred the truck into the empty lot and killed the engine. Alex pointed across the road.

"That's the warehouse where Bright's holding your friends," he told them. "They're in a workshop area to the back. I'll go in that way." He turned to Sarah. "You go in the front and keep Bright distracted long enough for me to get them out."

Nestor sucked air through his teeth. "I don't like this plan. Why don't we all just go in the back way?"

"Haven't you ever heard of a stealth mission?" Alex replied.

"He's right," Sarah agreed, turning to Nestor. "You stay here with the truck. If we're not out in fifteen minutes, get to Tullamarine airport." She removed the envelope containing the passports and the tickets from under her seat and placed it on the dashboard. "You have all you need there. Get Louise and Octavio as far away from Bright as possible."

Hey! Louise protested, sticking her head through the window to the back. *We're not going anywhere without you!*

Sarah smiled at her. *You don't have a choice in this one, I'm afraid.*

With that, she gave Alex a nod and he opened the door. Grabbing the box of blood samples, she jumped out after him. The plan was to keep Bright distracted while Alex went in the back to rescue Robert and Wei. For that, she'd need the blood.

"Good luck!" Nestor said as she slammed the door.

Okay, let's go, she told Alex and they ran across the street, side by side. As they ran, he began to fade out and by the time they reached the pavement opposite he was completely invisible.

You'd better be right about this, she told the night where she thought he was standing.

Trust me, Alex replied out of thin air. His footsteps sounded on the pavement as he ran off.

That's the problem, Sarah thought to herself. *I don't.*

Alex skirted along the side of the warehouse. Although he was invisible now, he still had to be quiet as he squeezed through a gap in a chain-link fence and moved towards the workshops at the back.

"That's it, Alex," Makarov encouraged through the

iPod earphone. "You've earned their trust. Now you must bring them to me."

Alex crouched by the side of the building and paused a moment. *I don't think they trust me a bit,* he thought. *As for bringing them to you, that's not going to happen. They've already got their own escape plan.*

Makarov laughed. "Flying out of the country on a commercial airliner using forged passports? Even without the intervention of Major Bright, they would never make it."

You've got a better plan, I take it.

"There's a small airport just a few kilometres from your present location," Makarov said. "My private jet is en route to it as we speak. When you get out of the warehouse, direct the others to the airport and I'll fly you out of harm's way."

They'll never go for it, Alex replied with a shake of his head.

"They will," Makarov insisted. "Circumstances will demand it. Now – go and rescue the kidnapped boys."

The iPod went dead. Alex placed it in his pocket and looked round the edge of the building. The door to the workshops was just a couple of metres away and he moved fast. Trying the handle, he found it locked, but the window beside it wasn't. Sliding up the old wooden frame, he eased himself through. Thankfully, the room was deserted – from what he'd heard the others saying about Major Bright in the short time he'd known them, the man wasn't someone he was eager to meet.

Alex moved through the workshop and into a corridor with four doors. He went to the nearest one – Makarov had told him that was where Robert and Wei were being held – and looked through the small viewing window. Sure enough, he made out the shape of two boys bound to chairs in the half-light. This door was unlocked and he pushed it open gently to minimize the noise as it scraped against the concrete.

The head of the Chinese kid, Wei, snapped up at the sound. "Who's there?" he asked fearfully, straining to see.

Alex moved swiftly to his side. "It's okay. I'm here to help."

Wei looked around in confusion. Sensing the boy's fear, Alex reluctantly allowed himself to become visible again. There was no point in freaking the kid out any more than necessary.

"That's a cool trick," Wei whispered as Alex reappeared and began untying the rope around his wrists and ankles. "Who are you?"

"I'm with Sarah and your friends," Alex said. He

finished with Wei's bonds and moved on to where Robert was slumped in his chair. "What's wrong with him?"

"He's been drugged."

Alex crouched before Robert and gave his shoulders a shake as Wei ran round to untie the ropes. Robert's eyes flickered open and he mumbled something unintelligible. Wei released Robert's bonds and he flopped forwards. Alex caught him and hoisted him onto his shoulders in a fireman's lift.

"This is going to make getting out of here tough," Alex told Wei as they turned to the door.

"And it just got even tougher," Eco announced from the doorway.

Alex and Wei froze. The skinny kid had a gun in his hand.

14

Sarah shivered in the cold, early morning air as she walked through the front door of the warehouse. The building was a wreck, with holes in the ceiling and rusting pieces of metal strewn here and there in the massive, empty area. It looked as if it hadn't been used in many years. In the far corner stood a Range Rover with a dent in the front. There was something sad and lonely about the place. Sarah hated to think that Robert was being held somewhere within the building, but she kept her mind focused.

"Sarah, you're early," the unmistakably deep voice of Major Bright echoed from the darkness at the back. "And at the wrong meeting place. But I forgive you."

She looked ahead and saw his hulking figure emerge out of the shadows. He was dressed in his HIDRA uniform still, but it was ragged in places, as if he'd been in a fight recently.

"I sense you've brought what I requested," he said, stopping beside one of the crumbling concrete pillars that held up the roof.

Sarah raised the box of blood samples.

"That's good," he said, producing an object from his pocket and tossing it on the ground between them – an empty syringe gun. "Because I'm all out of super-juice."

Sarah jumped back as Bright teleported from the column to within a metre or so without warning. Close up, she could see his red-tinged pupils and the sheen of sweat standing out on his closely cropped hair. It reminded her of the last time she had faced the major and how the serum had driven him into an insanely violent rage. Reaching out, he snatched the box from her hand and opened it eagerly.

"Why are there only four samples?" he demanded.

"Because there's only four of us," Sarah replied. "You kidnapped Robert and Wei, remember?"

Major Bright laughed and banged the side of his skull with his palm. "Right. Right. I get confused. The serum can do that."

Sarah took another step away as he closed the box.

"It won't do you any good," she said, trying to keep her voice calm and in control. She needed to keep Bright busy while Alex got to Robert. "The untreated blood won't give you our powers again."

Bright grinned. "You underestimate me, Sarah. Colonel Moss left the research files from *Project Superhuman* in an online storage dump. Any fool with a basic knowledge of chemistry and a centrifuge machine can recreate the serum mix. All I need is a constant supply of blood and that's where you come in. From now on you're going to keep me stocked with samples from your friends if you want to see your brother again."

Listening to him made Sarah's skin crawl. "That wasn't the deal you promised. I want Robert and Wei back now."

Bright sneered at her. "Do I look like the kind of guy who keeps promises?" He cocked his head to one side. "No. Of course I don't. That's why you're here and not the ANZAC shrine, right?"

Sarah could sense his mind scanning hers and then searching beyond the walls of the warehouse.

"Also, you didn't come alone," he added. "The other three are sitting across the road in a truck. You're the one who's broken the deal."

Sarah glanced in the direction of the entrance. "You've got what you wanted, Major," she said. "Now let my brother and Wei go. You know you can't take us all on."

Bright's eyes blazed with anger and his thoughts invaded her mind.

CAN'T I?

His anger was like an invisible force, driving Sarah backwards onto the ground. She hit the concrete and crawled away as Bright advanced towards her.

MY DEFEAT IN THE DESERT WAS A FLUKE. I'M MORE POWERFUL THAN THAT NOW.

His words screamed through Sarah's brain. She raised a hand in a futile effort to shield herself from him. Reading his thoughts, she sensed only a tumbling stream of hate-filled images.

Alex, she cried out with her mind, *have you got Robert and Wei?*

A door at the back of the warehouse screeched open and Bright paused to look round as Alex and Wei emerged, supporting Robert between them. Sarah pushed herself up. Alex looked at her and shook his head.

Sarah, I'm sorry.

Eco appeared behind them and gave Alex a push into the warehouse with the end of the gun. The gangly boy circled his captives with the weapon raised, looking over at Major Bright as he did so.

"I caught the intruders, sir," he said.

Bright nodded at him approvingly. "You're a good soldier, Eco. Keep watch on them while I deal with this one." He turned back to Sarah and removed two objects from his pocket: a tiny bottle of liquid and a syringe. "You'll soon learn that cooperating with me is the only way forward, Sarah. Until then, I think it's best if you sleep this one out with your brother."

Sarah rose into a crouch as Bright slid the syringe through the bottle lid and filled it. He advanced again, the needle pointed towards her like a weapon.

"When you wake up, we'll be one big, happy family," he said just before he lunged at her. Sarah tried to sidestep, but he caught her arm, yanking her round.

"Robert," she yelled desperately, "get them out of here!"

At the other end of the warehouse, her brother lifted his head fractionally and gripped Wei and Alex's arms. A split second later the three of them disappeared. Eco gasped in shock and lowered the gun. Major Bright cursed and turned back to Sarah, eyes narrowed.

"Very clever," he hissed. "But *you're* not going anywhere."

Sarah cried out as he jabbed the needle into her upper arm. However, before he could depress the plunger, the front door of the warehouse exploded, as the truck smashed through at high speed. Behind the wheel, Nestor drove headlong towards them. Bright looked round in surprise as the vehicle came at him. Sarah slipped from his grasp and ran. At the last minute, Bright teleported across the warehouse and reappeared at Eco's side.

The truck ploughed on, clipping one of the decaying concrete supports and toppling it. As Nestor sent the truck round in a tight turn, a massive section of the roof crashed down at the back of the warehouse, sending Bright and Eco running for cover. The vehicle's wheels screeched as it headed back for Sarah. The passenger door flew open and Alex threw out his arm.

"Sarah, grab on!" he cried as the truck approached.

Moving fast, she ran for it and caught his hand. With all his strength, Alex pulled her into the cab as the truck sped out of the warehouse. It flew through the gap in the door and hit the road, not slowing for a second.

YOU CAN RUN, Major Bright's mind-scream echoed after them, *BUT YOU CAN'T HIDE!*

Sarah collapsed on the seat as the passenger door

swung shut beside her. Looking into the back of the truck, she saw Robert lying on one of the seats along the side beside Wei and Louise. Octavio looked round and nodded to show her brother was okay.

"Hold still," Alex said beside her. He grabbed the syringe that was still sticking in her arm and pulled it out smoothly. The liquid sedative inside had not been delivered. He grinned at her. "Do you always cut it that close?"

"Usually," Sarah replied, breathing heavily after the ordeal with Bright. Composing herself, she reached into her pocket and removed the mobile phone her father had given her months before. She'd only turned it on a couple of times since leaving HIDRA, having heard that phone signals could be easily traced – almost like carrying a homing beacon around with you. Whether that was true or not, she needed HIDRA now. Bright wouldn't be far behind.

"Turn left here," Alex said to Nestor. "We'll never make the main airport, but I have another way out of the country."

"Let me guess," Sarah said. "Makarov."

Alex shrugged. "Do you have a better plan?"

"He's right, Sarah," Nestor said. "We don't have a choice."

Sarah nodded, but gave Alex a look. "This Makarov guy had better be everything you say he is."

Not waiting for Alex's response, she turned on the phone and speed-dialled the emergency number Rachel Andersen had given her. It went through to an automated message and Sarah said the code-word – *sleeper*. The line connected. Rachel picked up after two rings.

"Andersen," she snapped.

"If you want Major Bright," Sarah said urgently, "you'd better come get him now."

"Got company!" Nestor announced. In the side mirror the lights of a speeding Range Rover appeared.

Bright was giving chase.

15

"Sarah, where is Major Bright?" Rachel demanded down the phone line, not wasting a second. In the background there was a commotion, as if people were springing into action all around.

"Right now, he's following us in a four-wheel drive," Sarah said, checking the side mirror as the Range Rover sped towards the back of their truck. "Getting closer by the minute. We're heading south—"

"It's okay," Rachel interrupted. "Our satellite has already locked onto your mobile signal. We're tracking you. Just keep that phone turned on."

Sarah was suddenly glad she'd been cautious with the mobile all those months.

"A Special Forces team with be with you in five minutes," Rachel continued as the Range Rover rammed the back of the truck. Nestor struggled to control the wheel, but managed to keep the truck on the road.

"We might not have five minutes!" Sarah exclaimed. "Got to go."

She killed the line and placed the phone in her pocket.

"We're about a kilometre from the airport," Alex said. "We're going to make it!"

"You sure about that?" Nestor said, nodding towards his window. Sarah and Alex looked over and saw that the Range Rover had drawn level with them. Major Bright looked across, red eyes blazing with fury. He twisted the wheel and slammed the Range Rover against the side of the truck. The truck juddered but was too large to be put off course by Bright's smaller vehicle. The Range Rover pulled away again, its passenger side crumpled from the impact.

"Just keep your foot on the accelerator," Sarah ordered Nestor. "He's doing more damage to his vehicle than ours."

"What's he up to now?" Alex asked, craning his neck to see into their pursuer's vehicle. Eco had reached across to take the wheel. In that instant, Major Bright disappeared and the teenager jumped into the driver's seat, managing to keep control of the Range Rover somehow.

"He teleported!" Nestor exclaimed. "Where did he go?"

A thud from the top of the truck answered their question.

"Something's on the roof!" Louise cried from the back.

Sarah looked round sharply at a sound of tearing metal. Through the open hatch in the back wall of the cab she could see into the rear of the truck. Louise and the others cowered as a metre square section of the roof rolled back like the lid of a sardine tin. Major Bright looked through the gap with an insane expression on his face.

SURPRISE!

"Wei!" Sarah yelled through to the back. "Light him up!"

After his ordeal at the warehouse, the Chinese kid didn't need telling twice. Raising both hands towards the roof, Wei let loose a stream of fire that engulfed

Bright. With a howl of pain, the major reared backwards as his clothes caught alight. Then he threw himself off the side of the truck. Sarah stuck her head out the window and watched him rolling across the road to extinguish the flames. Finally he came to a smoky rest as the truck sped away. The Range Rover braked and came to a stop beside him.

"Wei, you did it!" Louise cried, throwing her arms around her friend.

Wei blew on his fingers. "Payback."

Alex pointed to the right. Beyond a chain-link fence on the side of the road were runways and hangars. "There's the airport. Go through that gate. Don't stop!"

Nestor gunned the accelerator. The truck hit a set of double gates plastered with *Danger: No Entry* signs and sped through onto the tarmac. Although the airport was small, designed only for the light aircraft that were parked in the distance near the traffic control tower, the runway itself seemed a massive, empty area. Nestor scanned the space before them as the truck thundered on.

"Where to now?" he asked. From the direction of the buildings a warning siren sounded. "We seem to have drawn attention to ourselves."

"Keep going," Alex replied. "Our lift is here."

Sure enough, the roar of a jet engine became apparent as they hit the runway. Looking towards the breaking dawn, Sarah saw the shape of a plane approaching. It was sleek and black, with strangely angled wings that gave it the appearance of something between a small passenger jet and a stealth bomber. As it came lower, Alex pointed ahead.

"It's going to land over there," he said.

Nestor followed the path of the jet as it touched down on a runway heading diagonally away from them. The plane continued to roll for several hundred metres before slowing to a halt.

"Put your foot down, Nestor," Sarah said. "We're almost—"

That's when something thudded against the roof of the truck cab. All three in the front looked up and then at each other with one thought: *Bright*.

A split second later the major's hand smashed down on the windscreen, shattering it. Grasping the glass with his fingers, the major pulled out the entire pane and threw it to one side. Bright twisted his head down to look into the cab. His face was red from the fire and his closely-cropped hair burned away at the front, making him look even madder than before.

DID YOU THINK YOU'D LOSE ME THAT EASILY?

Nestor slammed on the brakes and their attacker had to hold on to stop from being thrown off the truck again. As Nestor stepped on the accelerator again, Bright was thrown in the other direction, completely off balance. It was only a momentary reprieve, however, as he started pounding the top of the cab with his fists and feet. Sarah and the others ducked as the frame crumpled around them and the remaining windows imploded.

"We're not going to make it!" Alex cried, looking at the jet through the open front. It was still a few hundred metres away. "He'll tear the whole truck apart before we get there!"

"If he doesn't roll us first!" Nestor replied, struggling to control the wheel. As Bright smashed the top of the truck to pieces, the vehicle rocked right and left, becoming dangerously unstable.

"*Roll us,*" Sarah said. "That's not a bad idea."

Nestor shot her a look.

"Everybody hold on back there!" Sarah yelled through to the rear, before turning back to Nestor. "When I say, pull the wheel to the right as hard as you can."

Nestor shook his head. "That doesn't sound like a very good plan, Sarah."

Sarah put on her seat belt and grabbed the handbrake. Bright's fist ripped through the top of the cab and his arm snaked in, reaching blindly at them. Alex reared back in his seat away from the grasping hand.

"No time!" Sarah yelled. "Just do it, Nestor! Now!"

Nestor wrenched the wheel round. Sarah pulled the handbrake on full. The truck wheels locked out with a deafening squeal and the vehicle went into an uncontrollable spin. As the brakes stopped the wheels, the conflict of forces flipped the truck onto its top and the momentum sent it rolling along the runway. Sarah held on for dear life as the remains of the cab shattered around her and the world tumbled round and round. Through the window she saw Major Bright thrown from the roof and dashed against the tarmac. He disappeared from view as the truck rolled on.

Then, just as Sarah thought they would all be crushed by the seemingly unstoppable tumbling of the truck, it ended. With a groan of twisting metal, the machine came to a rest, right way up, in the middle of the runway.

"Are we alive?" Nestor asked quietly from the other side of the cab.

Sarah looked round, still stunned. The top of the cab was pushed down at a diagonal angle, obscuring the view ahead. To her right Alex was unclipping his seat belt. His nose was bleeding, but he seemed otherwise unharmed. Nestor was white as a sheet and staring forwards with his hands locked to the wheel.

"We have to get out of here," she said, reaching past Alex to give Nestor a shake. "Wake up!"

The Colombian boy came to his senses and pushed open the door. Sarah found her own door jammed shut, so she slid across the cab and exited after the others. As they ran round the back of the truck, she took a moment to survey the damage the roll had inflicted. The vehicle was a battered mess and looked roughly half the size it had when they'd started out – as if it had been through some kind of compacter.

"We really trashed this ride," Alex said with a low whistle.

"Get the back open!" Sarah commanded, but Octavio and Louise were already jumping out. To Sarah's relief, Robert followed after, still dazed but unharmed by the look of things.

"We need to get out of here," Alex said urgently, holding out a hand to help Wei down.

Sarah looked at the plane sitting on the tarmac just a hundred metres from where the truck had come to a stop. Then she looked back in the direction from which they had come. In the middle of the runway Major Bright lay motionless, face down, one arm twisted round at an unhealthy angle. In the distance, the Range Rover approached at high speed with Eco behind the wheel.

"Is Bright dead?" Nestor asked at her side.

As if to answer his question, the major stirred, pushing himself onto all fours with a howl of pain. Sarah winced as he wrenched his dislocated arm back into its socket and rose to his feet. His head jerked round at them.

"Run!" she yelled.

The group broke in the direction of the plane. Alex scooped up Wei and threw him over his shoulder while Nestor helped Robert along. Looking back, Sarah saw Bright gaining on them inexorably. The plane was still fifty metres away. The back door was open, steps leading up – but she knew Bright would catch them before they got there.

"Wait," she cried, grabbing Louise and Octavio's arms. "We have to slow him down!"

As the others ran on, Louise and Octavio stopped and turned. Major Bright charged towards them like an enraged bull, head down. Exchanging a quick glance, Louise and Octavio had the same idea at the same time. Holding out their arms, they projected an invisible shield dead ahead. Bright ran headlong into the force and bounced off – almost as if he'd smashed into a brick wall.

"Yeah!" Louise screamed, jumping up and down as Bright landed on his back, stunned. "Let's finish him."

Octavio caught her arm as she started forward. "Let's just quit while we're ahead, huh?"

"Good idea," Sarah agreed and the three started running to the plane. The engines were howling and the jet was already moving. From the back steps, Nestor pointed to the sky.

"HIDRA!" he cried.

Sarah looked over her shoulder and saw the shapes of three hovercopters approaching from the east, the red-tinted dawn sky at their tails. Reaching inside her pocket, she removed the mobile and tossed it as they reached the back of the moving jet and ran up the steps.

The pilot of the lead hovercopter scanned the scene below as the windshield HUD automatically picked out various targets: the speeding four-wheel drive, Major Bright, the private jet. He glanced at the image of Commander Craig at the HIDRA base on the screen.

"We've got a Range Rover moving along the runway, sir," he said.

"That's a confirmed hostile," Craig responded. "Take it out."

The pilot touched the trigger on his joystick and a burst of tracer fire flew at the wheels of the vehicle. The tyres exploded and the Rover flipped several times. Satisfied, the pilot turned his attention back to the jet, which was picking up speed towards the end of the runway. Directly behind it, Major Bright was giving chase again, arms outstretched as if he planned to grab the rear fins and physically stop the plane.

"The jet is approaching take-off speed," the pilot informed command. "Shall I target the engines?"

There was a five second pause before the response came – a long time when things were moving fast. The pilot's finger hovered over the trigger impatiently.

"Negative," Craig finally replied. "Bright is the primary target. Take him down alive if you can."

"That's a go," the lead pilot answered, pushing down on the joystick. The hovercopter swept in low until it was travelling just a few metres above the runway. The other two pilots followed suit.

As Major Bright desperately tried to latch onto the back of the plane, the lead pilot let loose with a volley of bullets that ripped up the tarmac around his feet. Bright stumbled and hit the ground as one of the rounds almost went through his ankle. Before him the jet sped away, lifting gracefully into the air at an incredibly steep angle.

Bright clambered to his feet, but did not move forward – the jet was airborne now. His powers finally spent after the successive teleports, he watched it rise into the distance helplessly.

The hovercopters drew closer.

"Let's try out the squirt guns on him," the lead pilot said, switching weapons on his console. The *squirt guns* were a new HIDRA technology fitted to all the hovercopters – each was linked to a tank of concrete foam that could be sprayed on a target to subdue it non-lethally. Major Bright looked round. The three hovercopters circled him with a speed and agility impossible in normal helicopters.

"Let him have it!" the lead pilot ordered and all three guns fired at once, dousing Bright in waves of grey foam that smothered his arms, legs and body. The big man struggled madly against the liquid mass, but his movements slowed as the concrete mix snap-dried in the air. Within seconds he was encased in a mound of concrete that was as solid as rock. Trapped from the neck down, his powers spent during the pursuit of the children, Bright threw back his head and screamed in impotent rage.

"Major Bright is ready for collection by the ground team," the lead pilot said into the comm with a chuckle. "Just tell them to bring a hammer and chisel."

* * *

The jet climbed fast, engines roaring as it gained altitude. The interior was all plush leather and mahogany – more like the inside of a hotel room than any plane Sarah had been on before. In the middle of the carpet, an *M* for Makarov stood out in gold thread. Finally off the ground, the group slumped in the plush seats.

"That was *too* close," Nestor said breathlessly.

"Cool," Octavio commented, looking around the cabin as he put his feet up on the seat opposite. "Look at the size of that TV. Do you think they've got Blu-ray?"

"Definitely Blu-ray," Alex replied with a nod, dabbing at his bloody nose with a tissue. "This place has everything. Told you this guy is mega-rich."

Sarah rose and stood before him. "Where's Makarov?" she demanded. "Where are we being taken?"

Alex held up the iPod and shrugged. "It's gone quiet."

Sarah grabbed it from him and put one of the earphones in her ear – nothing.

"Calm down," Alex said, trying to placate her. "He'll be in touch. The main thing is we escaped Major Bright, right?"

"But escaped to what?" Nestor said.

Sarah moved along the cabin towards the front of the plane, fighting the angle of ascent. Determined to get some answers, she grabbed the cockpit door and threw it open. What she saw made her gasp in surprise.

The cockpit was empty. The joysticks moved as the jet began to even out, but there was no one in the pilot or co-pilot's seats. The control panels were a mass of blinking lights and computer readouts. Ahead was empty sky.

"How's that possible?" Nestor asked, appearing at her side.

Before she could venture an answer, Louise gave a yell from the back of the plane. Sarah looked round to see yellowish gas pouring out of the air vents around the cabin.

"Cover your mouths!" Sarah commanded, but it was no use. Louise and Wei had already fallen to the floor unconscious. Octavio was succumbing too, sliding out of his chair to the floor. Sarah ran over to Alex, holding her breath to stop from breathing in the gas.

We're being drugged! she cried. *I thought you said Makarov was a friend!*

Alex shook his head helplessly. "I don't understand—" His eyes rolled up into his head and he slumped back in his chair before he could finish the sentence. By the cockpit Nestor hit the floor. That only left Sarah and Robert. Fighting the urge to inhale, she stumbled to her brother, who was still half-asleep from the drugs Bright had given him earlier.

You have to teleport out of here, Robert, she said. *Do it now while the jet is still over the ground.*

"No way, Sarah," he replied dully. "We stay together. Right?"

Sarah grabbed her brother's shoulders and shook him. *I said, go!*

Robert shook his head. "Not leaving you."

Before Sarah could protest any further, his eyes closed. Grabbing one of the cushions from Robert's seat, Sarah moved to the nearest vent and tried to block it. For a second it seemed to work, but then the gas billowed round the edges of the cushion in a great cloud that enveloped her face and made her choke violently. Dropping the cushion, Sarah staggered back and placed her hand against the side of the cabin. All around, her friends lay unconscious – helpless. Her head spun as she took another breath of gas-filled air.

As Sarah leaned against the wall and slid down into a sitting position, an old saying ran through her mind:

Out of the frying pan, into the fire.

Her eyes closed.

16

By mid-morning a heavy summer downpour had started in Melbourne and showed no sign of stopping. HIDRA operatives sheltered under umbrellas around the airstrip and looked for excuses to get inside the airport buildings.

Rachel Andersen's staff car pulled up by the terminal, which had been taken over as a temporary base of operations. She emerged before her driver could get the door and ran through the rain to the lobby of the building, where Commander Craig was waiting for her.

In the corner of the room, a scrawny kid in his late teens sat in a chair, with his left hand cuffed to the armrest.

"We got him, sir," Craig said with obvious pride, referring to the capture of Major Bright.

"Who's this?" Rachel asked, referring to the sorry-looking kid.

"One of Bright's lackeys," Craig responded, looking round at Eco.

"He made me do it!" Eco protested, his voice strained, as if he was about to cry. "Bright said he'd vaporize me if I didn't drive the car for him."

"Shut up and speak when you're spoken to," Commander Craig said, before leaning in to speak to Rachel confidentially. "He's been whining like that since we pulled him out of the wreck of the Range Rover. We'll question him and then transfer him to the local authorities. Records show he's got a juvenile rap sheet as long as your arm."

Rachel sniffed. "Sarah and the other children?"

Commander Craig looked embarrassed. "They were picked up by an unidentified jet seconds before our copters got here. We couldn't stop it without putting their lives at risk."

"Where did it go?"

"North. We managed to track it for about three hundred kilometres, but then it just disappeared. Where it headed after that is anyone's guess."

Rachel frowned. "It flew under the radar?"

"No, sir," Craig said decisively. "It was at high altitude when it vanished. We think the jet was fitted with some kind of stealth device. The airport security cameras picked up these shots."

He handed her a series of grainy printouts showing the mystery jet on the runway. "That doesn't look like any private plane I've ever seen," she said. "Any leads on who it belongs to?"

Craig shook his head. "There's no obvious registration mark on the side. The control tower didn't even know it was here until the plane was on the ground. The only marking is that logo near the wing. We're still following up on that."

Rachel held one of the photos closer to her face and made out the shape of an *M* set inside a circle. "Makarov," she said quietly.

"You know what that is, sir?" Commander Craig asked with interest.

"I could be wrong, but it looks like the logo for Makarov Industries. It's a Russian company that manufactures scientific equipment. The director, Nikolai Makarov, developed the sleeper caskets we use to keep the victims of the fall virus."

"That's quite a coincidence," Craig said pointedly.

"Or no coincidence at all. His name also came up in connection with the meteorite strike in Russia six months ago. Makarov owns the region in which the object hit – which was one of the reasons why our people weren't allowed access to the strike site. Follow up on that and inform me the moment you find anything. We need to locate Sarah Williams and the others." She handed the photographs back. "Now, where's our prisoner?"

Commander Craig nodded to a door flanked by two HIDRA commandos. "We're holding him in the airport manager's office."

Rachel started in that direction, but paused when Craig gave an embarrassed cough. "What is it, Commander?" she asked impatiently.

"Forgive me, sir," he said, "but we have a HIDRA interrogator being flown in from the Pacific Mobile Base. Bright isn't going to be as easy to question as that kid. He's a dangerous criminal and should be handled by a professional—"

Rachel held up a hand to silence him. "Your concern is noted, Commander," she said. "But time is of the essence. Do you have a sidearm?"

Craig patted the pistol on his hip by way of a response.

"Very good," Rachel replied. "If Bright tries anything, you have my permission to shoot him."

Commander Craig looked at his boss, trying to work out whether she was joking or not. Rachel turned and strode across the room past Eco, whose face had drained of all blood and who was staring at her with an expression of sheer terror. Craig gave him a wink as he followed Rachel into the office and closed the door.

Bright sat in the middle of the room, wrists and ankles cuffed to the legs of a metal chair. Tape had been placed over his mouth. His blue eyes flashed in silent fury as Rachel walked over to him and inspected the bandaged burn marks and cuts on his skull. She nodded at the HIDRA commando stationed in the corner of the room to leave. The man went without a word. Rachel turned back to Bright, gripped the edge of the tape and ripped it away from his face.

"Hello," she said.

Bright grinned at her. "Long time, no see, Dr. Andersen. I heard General Wellman put a *scientist* in charge," he said with a contemptuous sneer. "What a joke."

"I'm sure you'll have a good laugh with Colonel Moss about it," Rachel said, leaning close to him, "when you see him in the prison yard after your court martial."

Bright rattled the cuff against his chair mockingly. "Do you really think you'll be able to hold me?"

Rachel smiled grimly. "I hear you've run out of serum. I think our prison walls will do just fine."

Bright closed his eyes.

Rachel stood over him. "Face it, Bright, you lost," she said with a hardness in her voice that made Commander Craig look up in surprise. "Your war is over. If you don't want to spend the rest of your life in solitary confinement, you'll tell me everything you know about what happened to Sarah Williams and the others."

Bright's eyes snapped open. He looked at Rachel with a new interest and laughed unexpectedly.

"What's so funny?" she demanded.

"You know," he said, relaxing a little, "when I saw those kids lift off in that plane I was convinced it was HIDRA whisking them off. But now it turns out you don't have them either. So who does?"

"That's what I'm trying to find out," Rachel said coldly.

Bright shook his head. "All these months you've had them right under your hand and you let them slip away. The scientific find of the century and you lost it. All that precious research grabbed by someone else."

"All I care about is their safety," Rachel asserted.

"Help us find them and I'll make sure you get some consideration for it at your trial."

Bright held her eyes. *"Please.* I'd have more respect if you just admitted that we both want those children because of their powers. Whether it's for war or science, what's the difference?"

"I'm not like you."

"Really? I don't see you crying over any of the other orphans running around this country. Well, I guess someone else is looking after Sarah and the others now."

"You're not going to help us," Rachel said through gritted teeth.

Bright stared blankly at her and said nothing.

"Then you can take a nap." Rachel reached inside her pocket and removed a syringe-gun. Before Bright could react, she jammed it against his neck and pulled the trigger. A second later, he slumped forward in the chair, unconscious. Rachel turned and walked to the door.

"Prep him for transport," she ordered Commander Craig. "The interrogation can continue at the Pacific Mobile Base. I want him out of this country. He'll tell us what he knows whether he wants to or not."

Craig signalled for the commandos outside to help him with Bright. As Rachel exited the room and crossed the lobby, her personal assistant, Lt. Kaminski, ran into the building and gave a hasty salute.

"Sorry to interrupt, sir," Kaminski said breathlessly. "Our space observatory in the Philippines just sent through an initial report of an object headed towards earth."

"Another meteor?"

"That's what they think, sir," Kaminski replied. "It seems to originate from the same quadrant of space as the Australian and Russian strikes. Their initial projections suggest that it will come down somewhere in the Pacific North American region. They're working to improve that estimate."

Rachel nodded. "Okay, I want to be ready for this one. All HIDRA personnel are to be put on full alert. Get my plane ready for transport to the Mobile Base. Wherever that meteor comes down, I want to have our people ready to move in within the first few hours. Our best chance of finding a cure for the fall virus is getting access to an infected meteorite shortly after impact."

"I've already summoned your jet, sir," Lt. Kaminski replied. "It's waiting for you on the runway."

Rachel smiled at his efficiency. "Very good, Lieutenant."

Kaminski produced an umbrella as Rachel strode out of the building towards the private jet sitting on the runway.

"The *Ulysses* has been notified you'll be arriving, sir," he yelled above the crash of the rain and the roar of the jet engines powering up. "They're currently crossing the Date Line on the same latitude as Japan. You'll be on deck within eight hours."

The HS *Ulysses* was HIDRA's mobile base of operations in that part of the world – a decommissioned US aircraft carrier designed to provide response to any event that happened in the Asia–Pacific region. There was just one problem: Rachel hated ocean travel almost as much as she disliked flying.

"I forgot to ask," she said to Kaminski as they approached the jet. "What's the estimated time until the next meteorite strike?"

"It's a best guess at the moment, sir," Kaminski replied, "but the Philippines station is saying four days."

"Then we've got four days to find out where it's going to hit, evacuate the area and get our scientists on the ground. This is the big one, Kaminski, I can feel it."

"Yessir."

The meteor had crossed light years of space. In the great vacuum, the rock appeared to be stationary. In fact it was travelling at high speed – almost twenty kilometres a second. Ten metres across and irregularly shaped, it was practically invisible against the black curtain of space – an insignificant speck in the vastness of the universe.

This meteor, however, was the subject of great debate on a blue planet circling a sun several million kilometres away.

Scientists in an observation station near the equator of that planet had designated it a PHO – a *Potentially Hazardous Object* – and were busy giving it a name and a number. The meteor was large enough that if it hit the planet it would create an explosion with the force of several nuclear bombs.

They were worried.

The scientists would have been a lot more worried, however, if they'd known that the meteor wasn't alone. Their sensors had not yet detected that it was one of many – one of almost fifty, ranging in size from less than a metre across to thirty. They travelled in a ragged pattern scattered across hundreds of thousands of kilometres of space, but they were all going in the same direction.

The storm was coming…

And it was headed directly for earth…

17

Sarah Williams awoke and noticed two things. Firstly, she was no longer in Makarov's jet, but lying in a bed in a white-walled room with a window that stretched from ceiling to floor. Secondly, she had a splitting headache – probably the result of the gas she'd inhaled on the plane.

With a groan, she pushed herself into a sitting position and took a better look around. The room was anonymous; its bare walls were clean as if they'd been freshly painted and there was a brand-new smell to the carpet. It was like being in a building that had been recently renovated. The contents of her pockets – a few coins, the keys to their apartment in Melbourne, the envelope containing the passports – had been laid out on a small table beside the bed. Her clothes were neatly folded on a chair in the corner and looked as if they'd been washed. Throwing back the bedcovers, Sarah touched the soft material of the gown she was now wearing. On the right shoulder an *M* set into a circle was sewn in gold.

M for Makarov, Sarah thought with a shake of her head.

Slightly unsteadily, she got out of the bed, walked to the window and looked out. An expanse of blue sky greeted her. In the distance there were mountains on the horizon, but looking down she saw only flat, snow-covered plains – an empty landscape devoid of buildings. The vision was bright and hard and clear, bringing to mind an exceptionally cold winter's day. It was like looking at the view from a plane window. One thing was for sure – she wasn't in Australia any more.

"Welcome, Sarah."

She jumped away from the window and looked round to see who had spoken. The voice seemed to come from all around. A section of the window lit up with images, as if a projector had been turned on it. The head and shoulders of a woman appeared on the glass – she was blonde and attractive, although her face had a strange quality to it. There was something about the skin – a little too smooth, maybe. Or the features – a little too perfect.

"I trust you slept well," the woman continued. "If English is not your preferred language, say *speech options* or touch the glass to customize."

As an alphabetical list of languages began to scroll up the window, Sarah leaned closer. She now saw that the woman projected on the glass was a computer generated image, albeit an incredibly realistic one. An avatar.

"My name is Lucy," the image continued. "I have been assigned as your personal concierge during your stay. Say *concierge options* or touch the glass to customize my attitude and appearance."

"Where am I?" Sarah asked, feeling only a little self-conscious at talking to a window.

"The Chukotka Autonomous Zone, Russian Federation," the woman replied. An animated map of the world appeared, zooming in towards the Asian continent. The image expanded further, towards the far north-eastern corner of Russia.

"Chukotka is located on the Chuckchi Peninsula and is

one of the most remote and sparsely populated areas of the globe," Lucy continued as a stream of geographical data began to scroll. "Total area: 737,700 square kilometres. Population: 83,987. Main industries: gold, coal, copper and lead mining. Current local time: 11.36 a.m. Local temperature at ground level: -10°C..."

Sarah held up a hand. "Woah, stop!"

Lucy immediately ceased talking and the data stream on the window froze. Sarah took a deep breath and tried to process what she'd just been told.

"What is this building?" she asked.

"Makarov Tower 7," Lucy replied as a line drawing of a skyscraper replaced the data on the screen. "153 floors tall, the tower is one of seven positioned at major locations around the world, including Hong Kong, Mexico City and Berlin. Each tower is identical in height, design and building materials. Because of their distinctive tapering shape, many of the Makarov Towers have attracted the nickname *the Spire*. You are welcome as one of the first guests at the newly constructed Tower 7."

Sarah moved to the door. "If I'm a guest," she said looking for the handle and not finding it, "I guess I'm free to leave this room whenever I want. How do I get out of here?"

"Guest services have been informed you are awake," Lucy said with a calmness that was starting to grate on Sarah. "Please wait for one of our operatives to escort you to brunch."

"Sure," Sarah said, moving away from the window. She grabbed her clothes from the chair and started dressing hastily, scanning the room for some other way out as she did so. It didn't take long to find: an air vent located in the wall above the bed.

Robert, she called to her brother. *Robert? Nestor? Anyone?* There was no response from him or the others. Either her power had failed or there was something blocking her communication with them. The sensation was strange, accustomed as she was to the easy psychic connection with her friends. Putting aside her unease at this development, she decided to use more conventional means of locating them.

"That is not necessary," Lucy said from the window, not a hint of emotion in her voice, as Sarah stood on the bedside table to reach the vent.

Running her fingers over the raised screws that held the grille-covering in place, Sarah bent to retrieve a coin from the table and set to work unscrewing them one by one.

"I really think it would be better if you waited for

your escort, Sarah," Lucy continued. "Perhaps you would like to do some yoga or other wake-up exercises in the meantime."

"Thanks, but I don't like waiting," Sarah said as she ripped the grille away and cast it across the room. Makarov had drugged them on the plane – she wasn't about to wait around for his minions to collect her from the room. Placing both hands on the edge of the vent, she pulled herself up and squeezed through into a narrow metal shaft. She slid forwards with her elbows and knees. A couple of metres ahead, another grille was set into the floor of the shaft. Reaching it, she looked down into corridor on the other side of the bedroom door.

"Sarah, can you still hear me?" Lucy called from the room. "This really isn't necessary."

"Oh, shut up," Sarah replied. With all her might, she pushed down on the grille and it popped out, landing with a clatter on the floor a couple of metres below. Manoeuvring round, she lowered herself through the gap, hung for a moment and then dropped. Landing deftly, she went into a crouch and surveyed the corridor in both directions. The walls and floor were pristine, featureless and white, just like those in the bedroom. The entire place had the look of somewhere newly made.

The sound of footsteps moving down the corridor sent Sarah running in the other direction. She rounded a corner and pressed herself into the wall, sneaking a look back as she did so. A woman in a plain blue uniform bearing the Makarov logo approached the door to her bedroom. The door slid open automatically and the woman looked inside. Sarah expected her to react to finding the room empty, but surprisingly the woman merely stood there, staring blankly ahead as if waiting for some kind of command.

Sarah pulled her head back. Her movement triggered a sensor and a door slid up beside her, revealing a larger chamber beyond. Checking the area was deserted, she moved into the semicircular room. Lift doors were set into a central column, but she ignored them for the moment, opting instead to move to the massive windows that were along one side of the room. They showed another angle of the ice desert outside and she took a moment to scan the view – little different from what she had seen from the bedroom window. In the distance stood something that looked like buildings – maybe a small village or a factory, but that was about it.

Bleak. As much of a desert as the outback of Australia.

On the other side of the room, a computer terminal

set into the wall caught Sarah's eye and she walked over. As she touched the screen, a welcome message flashed on, followed by a series of icons. *General Information. Local Environment. Guest Services.* Tapping the final option, a new screen opened up and she tapped *Guest List*. The names of the others appeared on the screen:

Louise Bates

Alex Fisher

Nestor del Fuentes

Octavio del Fuentes

Sikong Wei

Robert Williams

Sarah Williams

She hit the option next to her brother's name: *Locate.* The screen changed to a spinning 3D map tracing a path from the area in which she was standing to a room several floors above.

"The guest you have requested, *Robert Williams*," a computerized voice from the terminal announced, "is currently located on the 153rd floor. The central express lift has been called for your convenience."

With a hiss, the lift doors slid open. Sarah hesitated, but decided she had no option but to take the lift, as more footsteps approached from the direction in which she'd come. As she stepped into the lift, the doors closed and the car began to rise swiftly. Seeing a small fire extinguisher set in the wall under the lift control panel, Sarah removed it, thinking it might make a useful weapon against whatever awaited her on the 153rd floor.

Seconds later the lift came to a halt and the doors opened. Weapon raised, Sarah jumped through and into a crouch, finding herself...

In a garden.

Blinking in confusion, Sarah took in her unexpected surroundings. The lift appeared to have taken her to the very top of the Spire. The walls were sloping glass, angled to a point high above – like being inside a transparent pyramid. The room itself was a large open space, clearly intended as a kind of viewing platform. The unusual thing about the place was that the entire floor was covered with grass. Around the edge of the area stood rows of trees through which a gentle breeze blew – no doubt artificially created. It was like being in an indoor park.

In the centre of the room, on a gentle incline, was a long stone table around which Robert and the others sat. They looked in surprise at Sarah's sudden entrance. She straightened up and slowly lowered the extinguisher. Her friends didn't seem like they were in danger. They seemed like they were having lunch.

"Sarah!" Louise cried as she ran over and threw her arms around her. "It's okay!"

"What is this?" Sarah asked, looking over at the others. She allowed the extinguisher to drop from her hand onto the grass.

"Come on," Louise said, taking Sarah's hand and leading her towards the table.

As they approached, a tall man got up from the head of the table and walked towards them. The first thing Sarah noticed about him was his hair – which was completely white. The second thing she noticed was his eyes – deep, black irises that seemed to swallow you up as you looked into them. The man stopped before her and extended a slender hand to shake.

"Greetings, Sarah," he said with a lilting Russian accent. "I'm Nikolai Makarov. Welcome to my world."

18

"You arrived just in time to save us, Sarah," Octavio said sarcastically as she approached the stone table. "Lunch was getting cold."

Ignoring him, Sarah took a seat between Robert and Louise. The table was a single slab of polished stone and covered with a feast of food – bacon and eggs, chips, hamburgers, ice cream, chocolate. A woman in a uniform identical to the one Sarah had seen on the floor below, approached the table and laid a plate in front of her. Sarah noticed the vacant, expressionless eyes with interest, remembering the way the other woman had stood there uselessly in the corridor after going to her room. There was something robotic about them both.

"Thank you," she said, but the woman gave no response. She merely walked back to where two similar attendants stood, off to the side of the table, waiting to serve should they be needed. Sarah's stomach rumbled at the smell of the food – she hadn't eaten in hours – but she refused to take anything until she had some answers about what was going on.

At the other end of the table, Makarov resumed his chair, laying a napkin across his lap with a flourish. "I hope you forgive us for starting the meal without you," he said, pouring tea from a silver pot. He offered some to Alex, who was sitting to his right. "You were in such a sound sleep, we didn't want to disturb you. It seems you inhaled a stronger dose of the sleep agent than the others. Probably when you tried to block the vents in my plane."

Sarah held his gaze. "Yes. Just why did you do that?"

"Gas you?" Makarov replied, taking a sip of tea and putting the cup down. "When you opened the cockpit door I was worried you were going to tamper with the controls. My autojet is a prototype. The instrumentation is very sensitive and emotions were running high after your escape from Major Bright. It would have been easy to cause a fatal crash. It was absolutely for your own protection."

Around the table the other kids nodded, as if his explanation made perfect sense. Sarah shook her head in exasperation. It was like she'd fallen asleep and woken up at the Mad Hatter's tea party.

"Excuse me," she protested, rising from her seat and placing her hands on the stone table. "But am I the only one here who finds this all a little strange? I mean, look at where we are." She indicated the grass and the blue sky above them through the pyramid. "Yesterday we were in Australia and now this guy" – she waved a hand at Makarov – "whisks us off to somewhere in Russia. I really don't know what to say."

"*Thank you* would be a start," Alex said. "Or perhaps you're forgetting it was Nikolai who actually saved us from Major Bright."

Sarah turned her attention to him. "Of course, you would say that. You're his right-hand man."

Sarah, Robert thought at her side. *Take it easy.*

Take it easy? she said. *Didn't you hear me calling you down there? I thought something had happened.*

Sarah, we're fine, Robert reassured her. *It must have*

been the after-effects of the gas blocking your psychic communication.

*Right, or some*one *blocking me,* she said, casting a sideways glance at Makarov.

Why would he do that?

I don't know, but I'm going to find out... She trailed off as she saw Robert's expression becoming increasingly worried. Looking round the faces of the others turned towards her, Sarah realized she wasn't achieving anything by losing control. Taking a breath, she took her seat again and reached under the table to give Robert's hand a squeeze.

"I'm sorry," she said. "I was being rude."

"Your concern is quite understandable," Makarov replied, pressing his fingertips together as if he were about to pray, "as are your questions. I apologize for using the sleep gas on you and the others, Sarah. I thought it was for the best. Do you forgive me?"

Sarah gave Robert a reassuring look and then nodded. The tall man smiled as if satisfied with her response. Carefully, she reached out with her mind, testing the edges of Makarov's consciousness, trying to work out what he was really thinking. She sensed nothing. It was like looking into a cloudy lake, impenetrable and unfathomably deep. For whatever reason, Makarov was shielding his thoughts from her and, more to the point, he had the power to do so.

"I know being brought to such a remote part of the world must be disconcerting," he continued, giving no indication he had sensed Sarah's effort to probe, "but it is my home and normal to me. My personal jet is at your disposal to fly you to any location around the globe. Even back to Australia, if that's what you want."

"Not likely," Octavio snorted. "You should've seen where we were living. This place is a *big* improvement."

Louise turned to Sarah, unable to control her excitement. "He's right, Sarah! Wei and I have been up for hours and we went exploring. There is so much cool stuff here. There's a pool on the 128th floor."

"And a cinema," Wei added. "And a games suite."

"And there's a park even bigger than this one," Louise continued. "We can stay a while, can't we?"

Sarah looked around the group, realizing that everyone was looking at her. Including Makarov.

"I was hoping you'd stay a few days, at least," he said. "You've all been running so long. Don't you feel tired? Wouldn't it be nice to rest here just for a short time?"

Sarah thought there was a hypnotic quality to the way he spoke – so measured and calm. *Was that what he was trying to do – hypnotize them?* If so, the others didn't seem to realize it. Once again they were looking at her, awaiting her response. She threw up her hands in exasperation.

"All I want to do right now is eat!" she said and the tension broke.

Robert and Louise began piling her plate with breakfast items: bacon, eggs, sausage and mushrooms. Her stomach rumbled uncontrollably and she realized that it was probably over a day since she'd last eaten. She picked up a fork and took a bite of bacon – it was just about the best thing she'd ever tasted and it was all she could do to stop herself from devouring the whole plate in one.

"Don't mind us," Nestor told her. "We've all been pigs."

Sarah started tucking in. She might not trust Makarov yet, but his food was great.

"Now, where were we?" the Russian said as she proceeded to clean her plate.

"You were going to tell us about how you got your powers," Octavio answered.

"Yes, quite right," Makarov said with a nod. "I was exposed to the fall virus, just like all of you have been. As you know, exposure causes the development of special abilities in a very small number of people."

"But only in children," Wei interrupted.

Makarov waggled a finger at him. "Excellent point, and you're quite right, I was a child at the time. This was many years ago, of course. I would say that I was one of the very first humans to be affected by the fall virus – eight years old and living with my father in a central area of Russia near the Tunguska River. I was getting ready for school when the meteorite hit less than thirty kilometres from our house."

"What was it like?" Louise asked, leaning forward. Makarov really had everyone's attention now – even Sarah stopped eating.

"The blast wave from the impact broke every window in our home and knocked my father off his feet. There was a sound like a hundred thunderclaps and the sky went dark as night." Makarov stopped abruptly, as if considering something. "But perhaps it's easier to show you. Everyone close your eyes for a moment. Please."

Around the table the children did as he asked, including Sarah. Slowly, an image began to form in their minds...

Makarov – young now, only eight – runs across a swaying field of wheat towards a line of trees. In the distance the sound of something like thunder rolls and a shadow falls across the sun. Makarov turns to look back towards a farmhouse in the distance. A cloud of dust is rising behind the building, covering the sky. There is red light in the cloud – a wall of flame the height of a tree.

A bearded man – his father – runs across the field as the fire engulfs the house. "Nikolai, run!"

The boy turns and continues to flee as the wheat catches alight. The sky is black as night now and ash is falling all around. His father grabs Makarov and pulls him along. Before them, fire sparks amidst the trees and in seconds they are ablaze.

"Where can we go?" Makarov asks as they draw up short.

"The river," his father replies, dragging him off to the side as the flames race across the field at an alarming rate.

They reach an incline and clamber down towards the sound of running water. The air temperature is increasing rapidly and the atmosphere is clogged with smoke now. The ground is muddy and steeply sloped. Makarov slips as they descend, but his father holds firmly onto his wrist.

"Into the river!" the man orders. "It's our only hope!"

Makarov plunges into the water, which feels icy cold after the heat of the field, and his father follows afterwards. Behind them, a wall of fire forms along the top of the ridge, sending searing waves of heat in their direction.

Red hot embers from the trees fall all around, sizzling against the surface of the water as they land. Makarov screams as one of them touches his neck.

"Get to the middle!" his father cries, pushing him forward in the water. On the other side of the river, people are running down the bank to escape another wall of fire. One man is burning and plunges into the water with a sickening hiss. Smoke rises where he hits, but the man does not surface again.

Almost in the middle of the river now, the current begins to take hold and Makarov finds himself being carried downstream. He turns, arms outstretched, but his father is fighting his way across the river to help a younger child struggling to keep her head above water.

"Father!" Makarov yells.

"Swim against the current, Nikolai!" his father calls back, not looking round. "I have to help them."

Makarov yells at him again, but he's being carried too far away now for his father to hear above the roar of the fires from either side of the river. For a moment he tries to fight against the current, but it's no use. Giving in, he allows himself to be swept away as all around him the world burns...

The vision ended and they opened their eyes. For a few seconds, no one around the table spoke, shocked by the vision of hell they'd been shown. Makarov still had his eyes closed. His face looked suddenly drained, as if from the effort of showing them his memory.

"What happened to your father?" Nestor asked finally, breaking the silence.

"I never saw him again," Makarov replied, opening his eyes. "I can only assume he died in the fires."

"He was a hero," Robert said.

Makarov raised an eyebrow. "Was he? I would have preferred he survived rather than sacrifice himself for strangers." He made no effort to disguise the bitterness in his voice.

"What happened to you?" Louise asked.

"I floated further along the river," said Makarov. "I was carried past burned farmland and entire forests that had been flattened by the impact. That one meteorite caused the same devastation as an atomic bomb. Finally, I was picked up by a group of priests who were fleeing the destruction. My entire family died in the Tunguska event, so they took me in and raised me. I guess I owe them my life."

"What about the fall virus?" Nestor asked.

"There were victims," Makarov answered. "As I'm sure you know, the virus is extraterrestrial in origin: carried across the universe on lumps of rock and debris.

The ruling powers of the time would not entertain stories of an alien disease. So, it was covered up."

"That's quite a story," Sarah said, laying her knife and fork down.

Makarov turned his gaze on her. Sarah sensed his mind reaching out, trying to read her thoughts, but she put up a mental wall and blocked his attempt to probe, just as he had done to her earlier. A smile flickered across Makarov's lips and he gave the slightest nod, as if acknowledging the power of another psychic.

"I'm sure the story of your brush with a meteorite is equally amazing, Sarah," he replied. "But I'll find out all the details soon enough."

"Only if I let you," she answered, aware that the rest of the table was regarding their exchange with interest.

Makarov laughed and clapped his hands together unexpectedly. "Well, enough of all this morbid talk. If you've all had your fill, let me show you my home!"

"Yeah!" Wei exclaimed. "I want to see the computers again!"

Beside him, Louise was almost bouncing out of her chair in excitement. As Makarov rose from his seat a shape appeared from the trees at the edge of the park. Sarah's eyes widened – for a moment she was convinced a wolf was walking across the grass towards them. Then she saw that its body was metallic. The "animal" was in fact a robot.

"What is it?" Louise asked in wonderment as the robot moved to Makarov's side and stood there. It was indeed doglike – designed around the body shape and size of a wolf, although instead of fur and skin, it was covered in dark, polished steel. Two ears atop its angular head were permanently pricked and looked as sharp as razor blades. Its eyes were slits that pulsed rhythmically through various shades of red. Along the side of its body a distinctive slash of white stood out against the dark metal.

"Meet Balthus," Makarov replied, indicating the machine. "I suppose you could call him my pet. He's in fact one of a line of robots I created to replace huskies in the harsh Chukotkan environment. They're much better suited to the cold and never get fatigued. I call them robowolves."

"Can I pat him?" Louise asked, moving forward.

A low electronic noise that sounded very much like a snarl came from Balthus. Louise froze.

"Balthus, behave!" Makarov chided the robowolf, walking over to reassure the girl. "I'm sorry, Louise. He's designed as a work dog, so his manners aren't always the best." He leaned towards her conspiratorially. "I'll reprogram him to fetch a stick. Now, let's have our tour."

With that he started across the grass towards the lift, Balthus padding along at his side. The others got up from the table and followed. Alex hung back to walk beside Sarah.

"There, I told you he was one of the good guys," he said to her quietly.

"Right," she replied. "Too bad his meteorite story doesn't add up."

Alex looked at her questioningly.

"Haven't you ever heard of the Tunguska event?" she went on, unable to keep the smugness from her voice. "It was a meteorite that hit Siberia, Russia, last century. I read all about it on the web when we were in Melbourne."

"So?"

"So, it struck in 1908," she replied, popping a last piece of toast in her mouth. "Which would make Nikolai Makarov..."

"Over a hundred years old," Alex finished for her.

They both looked over at Makarov as he stepped into the lift and beckoned for the others to follow him in.

"But I'm sure there's a very good reason why he would lie to us," Sarah said as she walked ahead. "Right?"

"Right," Alex replied, a feeling of unease beginning to stir in his belly.

19

Sarah had to admit, the Spire was impressive.

Their bedrooms were located between the 129th and 131st floors, which seemed designed solely for guest accommodation. Above this, on the 132nd floor, was a fitness level, featuring a gym and a swimming pool as big as Sarah had ever seen. Floor 148 was packed with enough computer, audio-visual and games equipment to keep Wei and Louise entertained for the next twenty years. A museum stocked with relics from antiquity as well as items from twentieth century history stretched across the 80th floor. Then there was the library (146th floor), the indoor tennis and squash courts (145th) and the ballroom (143rd).

Makarov led them through successive levels, delighting in showing off his toys. At every *ooh* and *aah* from the group, he would give a satisfied laugh and assure them that they hadn't seen anything yet.

"The Spire has the best of everything," he said. "The best the twenty-first century has to offer in terms of technology, knowledge and leisure. I like to think of it as a repository for everything humankind has achieved up to this point."

"A repository?" Nestor asked, with a glance at Sarah, as they approached the lift to another level. "You make it sound as if you're preserving things here."

"Yeah," Sarah pressed, "are you expecting something to happen?"

Makarov waved his hand through the air. "I learned from my childhood experience that civilization is fragile. Who knows when something is just going to fall from the sky and wipe out everything we've achieved? I want to make sure that can never happen. Each of my towers is designed to withstand any extreme event that is thrown at it. Whether that be an earthquake, a nuclear explosion or even a meteorite strike."

He looked round at them on the threshold of the lift and smiled. "Nothing will bring this tower down. I'd bet my life on it." He let this sink in for a moment, before nodding towards the waiting lift. "Come on, let me show you the jungle."

The park inside the pyramid on the 153rd floor had been something to see, but there was an even more impressive one across the 140th and 141st floors – a simulated rainforest environment filled with exotic plants and birds.

"How does anything grow in here?" Robert marvelled as they walked along a grassy avenue under the trees. The atmosphere was humid, tropical. "There's no windows on this level."

"Tungsten bulbs in the ceiling work as sunlight simulators," Makarov replied, strolling up ahead. Beside him the robowolf, Balthus, moved along almost silently despite its size. "The temperature is regulated by the Spire's central computer. There's even a rainstorm every day at 4 p.m. It's the closest you'll get to a rainforest without going to the Amazon."

Sarah watched a green and yellow parrot fly through the trees above their heads. "It's amazing. I'm just trying to work out why you need it."

Makarov looked at her as if the question was a stupid

one. "Why? Why not? The Spire is designed to be a completely self-contained environment. A person could spend his life within its walls and never feel the need to step outside."

"Wow," Sarah replied. "That's kind of a weird idea."

Octavio piped up, "Sarah doesn't feel comfortable living in all this luxury, Nikolai. Slums are more her speed."

"Octavio," Nestor warned.

"My hope is that one day all people will live like this," Makarov continued. "I grew up in poverty. It is my belief that everyone should live like kings. And one day, with the help of my technology, we all will."

One of the uniformed women appeared through the trees and whispered something in Makarov's ear. With a sigh, he turned to the group.

"Business calls. This is going to keep me occupied for the rest of the day, I'm afraid. Please explore the rest of the upper levels of the Spire to your hearts' content. Catch a movie. Go for a swim. Relax. After everything you've been through, you've earned it."

He started towards the exit, but turned after a few steps.

"Oh, I almost forgot. I only have one rule – please don't venture below the 90th floor of the Spire."

"Why?" Sarah asked. "What's down there?"

"Just the administrative areas of my empire. Offices mainly. Some research labs. Boring to young persons such as you. I think you'll find the upper levels of the tower much more fun. Is that acceptable?"

Makarov held Sarah's gaze as he asked this.

"Sure," she replied. "We'll try to keep out of trouble."

The Russian gave them a little bow. "Until later."

As he departed, Alex looked at Sarah. "Why do I get the feeling you don't mean that?"

Rachel Andersen groaned as the intercom on the other side of her cabin blared. Pushing herself off the bed she had collapsed into less than an hour before, she staggered across the gently swaying floor and pressed the *speak* button.

"Andersen."

"We've got Nikolai Makarov on the line, sir," Lieutenant Kaminski answered through the speaker. "Online link-up in the communications room."

"I'll be there in five," Rachel replied, cutting the comm.

She dressed quickly and exited her cabin, taking the stairs up three levels. Halfway to her destination, however, she felt her stomach turn over and a wave of nausea rise. She dashed to the nearest exterior door and threw it open. Steeling herself against the blast of cold air, she rushed out onto the deck of the aircraft carrier. Finding the railing at the edge of the deck, she leaned over and looked down at the dark, swirling water of the Pacific Ocean, over thirty metres below. Thankfully, the feeling of seasickness that had plagued her since her arrival on the HS *Ulysses* began to subside.

"Are you okay, sir?" a concerned voice asked. She turned to see a kid in an orange jumpsuit – a member of the flight deck crew. He looked barely old enough to drive a car, let alone service fighter jets.

"Fine. Just getting a little fresh air. Carry on."

The kid saluted and walked off towards the double row of hovercopters sitting on the edge of the deck. Taking another deep breath, Rachel looked back across the wide expanse of the deck, which formed a massive, seaborne landing strip. Currently the *Ulysses*, HIDRA's mobile base in the Pacific, was heading through quiet waters, but Rachel still hadn't found her sea legs. With one final breath of briny air, she headed back into the ship and carried on down the corridor to a door marked *Communications Room*.

Kaminski stood as she entered the room – which was

wall-to-wall computers and comm gear. He indicated a computer showing a blonde woman in a link-up window – Nikolai Makarov's personal secretary.

"Mr. Makarov is ready to speak to you now, Colonel," said the blonde woman as Rachel took her seat. She had a strange, flat way of speaking that Rachel found a little disconcerting. But she soon forgot about that when Makarov appeared on her computer screen. Even through the slightly pixelated link-up image his eyes were magnetic.

"So good to finally speak to you, Dr. Andersen," he said with an accent like syrup. "Or is it Colonel?"

"Colonel officially," she replied, "but I prefer Dr. Good to speak to you too, Mr. Makarov. It's a shame you never answered my calls when the meteorite struck in your region six months ago."

Makarov held up his hands apologetically. "Forgive me. As you can imagine, I was busy at the time, coordinating the clean-up efforts. Although the meteorite was small, it caused considerable damage to one of our copper mining operations. Thankfully there were no casualties."

Rachel raised an eyebrow. "And no trace of the fall virus either?"

"Luckily, no," Makarov replied.

"Well, our tracking station suggested that the meteor entered our solar system on the same trajectory as the virus-infected Australian and South American meteorites. That's why HIDRA was so eager to get access to the site—"

"I am quite happy to allow you access to the area," Makarov interrupted, much to Rachel's surprise. For six months HIDRA's requests to visit the strike site had been rebuffed – first by Makarov's spokespeople in Washington and then by the Russian government. He had friends in powerful places.

"When would your people like to arrive?" Makarov went on, his dark eyes showing some animation for the first time. "I could have the area ready for your inspection in say…three days?"

Rachel gave no reply. She had the distinct feeling that the man was mocking her. More than that, after months of evasion, his sudden decision to let them in was perplexing. *Three days.* The estimated time until the next meteorite strike. *Is it possible he knows?* she wondered.

"Well?" Makarov pressed. "Don't tell me you have something more important to do."

Somehow he knows about the new meteor, Rachel thought. It was just an instinct, but she was absolutely certain she was correct. In the video window, a smile flickered across Makarov's lips and she had the same feeling she did around Sarah Williams – that her thoughts were an open book to this person.

"I'll prepare a research team," she lied to him – at such a critical time she had no intention of wasting resources on a strike site that was over half a year old.

Makarov bowed his head. "Very good. I'll be pleased to host your people during their stay in Chukotka. Please talk to my PA about the arrangements. Now, if you'll excuse me—"

"There's just one more thing," Rachel said, clicking her mouse to send the image of the jet from the Melbourne airport to Makarov's computer. "Have you seen this plane before?"

A micro-expression of annoyance flashed across Makarov's face, before he shrugged his shoulders casually. "I can't say I have. However, the picture quality is rather poor. Why is it of interest to you?"

"It's a private jet fitted with stealth technology," she continued. "It was involved in the suspected kidnapping of several virus-altered children in Melbourne yesterday."

"Kidnapping?" he exclaimed. "How awful."

"The logo on the side looks like yours," Rachel said. "That's the Makarov Industries *M*, isn't it?"

"Hard to see, really. You're not suggesting that jet

belongs to me, are you? I admit that I have the know-how and means to build such a plane, but why would I put my company logo on the side? Not very...*stealthy...* is it?" He chuckled at his own joke.

Maybe because you're a complete show-off, Rachel thought to herself, but said, "We just wondered if you might have developed such a jet for a third party."

Makarov shook his head sadly. "Afraid not. Were these children under your care?"

"You could say that," she replied.

"Then it's a shame you didn't keep a better eye on them, isn't it? There are plenty of unscrupulous people out there who would just love to get their hands on a bunch of kids with superhuman powers." A smile flickered across his lips. "Some of them used to work for HIDRA, or so the papers say."

Rachel ignored the reference to Major Bright. "So, you don't know anything about the children or the plane?"

"No," Makarov sighed, as if the conversation was getting boring. "But I do have contacts in the aerospace industry. Why don't I ask around and get back to you in—"

"Three days?" Rachel interrupted, anticipating his words.

Makarov grinned. "You read my mind, Colonel. It was a pleasure to finally speak to you. I hope we get the chance to do so again."

"Oh, you can be sure of it," Rachel replied as she killed the video feed and looked across the table to where Lt. Kaminski sat at another computer. "Well?"

"The voice analyser shows a stress spike when you sent him the image of the plane," the lieutenant replied, "but apart from that it didn't pick up any unusual patterns. He's a pretty cool customer, sir."

"Too cool for someone who was just told he's suspected of kidnapping," Rachel replied.

"Are you really going to send a scientific party as he suggested?" Kaminski asked.

"No. We have more important things to worry about right now. What's the news on the new meteor?"

"The current estimate is it's going to come down somewhere on the west coast of America, possibly in the Los Angeles area," Kaminski said. "However, the Philippines station is reporting something strange about the meteor signal. Some kind of interference surrounding it, like there's a larger mass out there. They're running scans."

"All we can do is get close to ground zero when it hits," Rachel replied. She didn't want to think about the destruction that would be caused if the meteor did indeed strike in the middle of an urban area – it would be like detonating a nuke. "Keep me updated on any developments. Makarov can wait."

Rachel knew that heading east was the right thing to do, but she couldn't shake the feeling that Makarov was connected to the disappearance of the children. And she was sure he knew about the new meteor somehow. Her stomach turned again and she closed her eyes with a groan.

"I'll get the bucket, sir," Kaminski said and went running.

20

The next morning, Sarah sat on a couch positioned in front of the east-facing windows on the 150th floor. She had her knees drawn up to her chin and she was deep in thought, staring out over the empty expanse of snow. A couple of times through the morning haze she fancied she saw a flash of blue on the horizon – the sea – but perhaps it was just her imagination. Her mind was full of thoughts about what they had left behind in Australia: their father, Daniel…Rachel Andersen and HIDRA…Major Bright. The thought that Bright was most likely in custody was the only thing that brightened her mood.

So engrossed was she in these reflections that she didn't sense Alex approach from the lift until he was standing right behind her.

"Did you want something?" she asked, without looking round.

"Nestor and the others are going to the pool," Alex replied. "We wondered if you wanted to join us."

"No thanks."

Alex gave an exaggerated sigh. "Just what is your problem? Are you so disappointed that Makarov turned out to be one of us?"

"That's yet to be seen," Sarah answered sharply.

"Oh, you'd just love him to be the bad guy, wouldn't you? That's why you want to go sneaking around on the 90th floor, to try to find something incriminating."

Sarah looked round at him for the first time. "You and the others might be prepared to accept Makarov's story at face value, but I'm not."

"Will you listen to yourself?" Alex said firmly, moving round to block her view. "You're so desperate for a fight. No one says we have to stay here for ever, but at least the others haven't forgotten how to enjoy themselves."

"I have to look after them," Sarah snapped back, rising

from her seat to challenge him. "They might have forgotten what happened at HIDRA, but I haven't. I'm—"

She stopped talking as the lift doors opened and the tall figure of Makarov stepped out, closely followed by Balthus. The red eyes of the robowolf scanned the room intently as it entered.

"Oh, I'm sorry," Makarov said, placing a slender hand on his heart. "Have I disturbed your privacy?"

"It's okay," Sarah said, shooting a look at Alex. "We were just talking about you, in fact. Back in Melbourne you told Alex something about a war coming. And about a cure for the fall virus."

Makarov nodded seriously as he approached them. Balthus hung back, but never got more than a few metres from its master.

"Well?" Sarah pressed.

Makarov smiled at her. "I do admire your directness, Sarah. Six months ago, a meteorite contaminated with the fall virus crashed several kilometres from the Spire. It was too small to cause any serious damage, but several of the workers at my mining operation in this area were infected. Luckily the Spire has advanced medical facilities and I ensured they received the best possible treatment."

"They're still here?" Alex asked.

"Oh, no, no," Makarov said. "Sent to a specialist hospital in Moscow, along with their families. I did, however, obtain several samples of infected blood before they were shipped out. I have been analysing these samples and am confident I am on the verge of a breakthrough."

Sarah and Alex exchanged a glance. "You mean, you've almost found a cure?" she asked. "Why didn't HIDRA tell us about this?"

Makarov chuckled and shook his head as if the statement was ridiculous. "HIDRA! They're still stumbling around in the dark, I'm afraid. After some of the mistakes they've made, I'm surprised you trust them at all, Sarah. I don't know what Rachel Andersen has told you—"

"You know Rachel?" she interrupted, but Makarov ignored the question.

"—but she is nowhere near finding a cure. I, on the other hand, am only days away from producing a serum that will awaken all of the sleepers."

Sarah looked at Makarov. The thought of bringing Daniel back, along with the parents of the others, made her heart leap. Suddenly, more than anything in the world, she wanted to believe in Nikolai Makarov, but something in her heart just wouldn't let her do it.

"We need to tell the world about this," she asserted. "HIDRA has to know."

Makarov's face darkened. "I will not hear of it until I am completely ready." He forced a smile that was more like a grimace. "Just a few more days. Then we will give this gift to the world. It's not like we're in any rush, are we?"

Sarah shrugged. "I guess not."

"Besides," Makarov continued, "you still haven't seen all the surprises my home has to offer."

"I call this the training zone," Makarov announced as they stepped out of the lift onto the 117th floor of the tower later that day. It was part of his ongoing tour of the Spire and the entire group was assembled. "You all have unique abilities, but I'm sure each of you will find something here to test your powers."

The room consisted of various cubicles and stand-alone rooms, marked with signs such as *Mind-reading Development* and *Psionics*. Wei ran over to a room marked *Fire Zone* and looked in through an observation window.

"Cool," he whispered, casting a look over the assembled items within – boxes, sofas, stacks of hay. All eminently flammable. The walls were lined with heat-resistant padding.

Makarov walked over and patted him on the shoulder. "Everything to keep a young fire-starter amused for hours."

"Can I—" Wei began, but was interrupted by a *slam* from the far side of the room. As the group looked round, the sound came again. And again. *Slam. Slam. Slam.* A thirteen-year-old boy approached across the floor, bouncing a basketball expertly in his right hand. He was dressed in the uniform of one of the tower servants and had a thin, angular face framed by jet black hair swept back in a ponytail.

"Ah, Ilya," Makarov said. "Ilya is the only child from the Chukotkan meteorite strike to develop special abilities."

Sarah shot him a look. "You're keeping him here? What about his family?"

Makarov waved his hand dismissively. "Victims of the virus. I've been made Ilya's guardian. I see so much of myself in him."

"Why didn't you tell us about him before?" Sarah said.

"Oh, so much to tell, so little time," Makarov answered. He stopped speaking as Ilya broke into a run towards them, ponytail flying. The boy threw the basketball with both hands. It arced through the air, dropped cleanly through a hoop set into the wall high above their heads and bounced back into the boy's hands. With that, he turned and walked casually over to where they were standing. His blank expression did not change one iota as he looked over the newcomers.

"Say hello to our guests, Ilya," Makarov ordered.

"Hello, guests." His voice was flat. The uniform wasn't the only thing he shared with the tower workers – the emotionless demeanour reminded Sarah of the women.

"What's his special power?" Octavio asked, looking over the kid's ponytail with a sneer. "Hair styling?"

Ilya narrowed his eyes at the other boy and held up the spinning basketball on a single finger, showing some life for the first time.

"Now, now, there's no need for that," Makarov warned the boy gently, placing a hand on his head. "Octavio has telekinetic powers like you – he can move things with his mind alone. Why don't you show him what you can do, Ilya?"

The Russian kid turned his blank eyes from Makarov to Octavio and smiled for the first time. "Let's try some target practice. If you think you can handle a little competition."

"Do your worst," Octavio hissed in reply as the pale-skinned kid led the way to a rectangular building in the far corner of the floor.

"We can watch from above," Makarov announced as Octavio and Ilya entered through a set of sliding double doors. He took a set of steps up the side and the others followed. At the top they found a clear roof, designed for observation of the area below, which looked like an indoor tennis court. A rectangular playing area was marked out on the floor and divided into two halves, coloured red and blue. A yellow line divided the two sections from one another. Around the area, metal barriers about a metre in height stuck out of the floor, slanted at forty-five degree angles. The sides of these barriers bore impact marks, as if objects had been thrown against them repeatedly.

Sarah leaned over the railing and looked down as the two boys entered the court and took places at either end of the room – Ilya in the blue zone, Octavio in the red.

"What is this?" she asked Makarov.

"A testing ground for psionics like Ilya and Octavio," Makarov replied. "A kind of target practice game."

"You built all this for Ilya?" Sarah asked, looking around the other training areas.

Makarov shook his head. "Of course not. I always knew there would be more people like me in the future, such as you and your friends. I guess you could say this is the very first school on earth for people such as ourselves." He touched the communicator on his shoulder. "Computer, give us fifty discs. Random dispersal."

In the room below, Ilya bounced from one foot to another and rubbed his hands together as if in anticipation of action, although his blank eyes showed little sign of excitement. Octavio looked up at the others from his group and shrugged. In the centre of the room a black cylinder rose out of the floor and began to spin rapidly, emitting a whirring noise.

Makarov raised his hand and called out, "Computer, release on my mark!"

As he lowered his hand, a clay disc the size of a plate flew out of a slot in the spinning cylinder at high speed. It shot across the court towards Ilya. The Russian boy was expecting the projectile, however, and threw out his hand. The disc stopped and hung suspended in the air about a metre from his head, completely under the control of the boy's mind. On the other side of the court, Octavio watched in fascination as Ilya drew back his arm and punched his fist forward in a violent motion. Although no physical contact was made with the disc, it flew across the court at high speed towards Octavio.

"Watch out!" Nestor yelled as the missile hurtled towards his brother.

At the last possible moment, Octavio raised his hands and projected a shield. As the disc hit the invisible barrier, it exploded in a puff of white clay. Octavio staggered back as shards from the disc flew around him. On the viewing platform, Makarov clapped his hands together and gave a childish laugh of excitement.

"Excellent start!" he exclaimed as a second disc was spat from the cylinder in a random direction across the court. This time it headed straight for the wall, but Ilya pointed a finger at the missile and swept his arm towards his still-stunned opponent. The disc whipped round at frightening speed and Octavio had no choice but to throw himself behind one of the metal shields dotted around the court. As the disc smashed against the barrier, a mighty clang echoed around the area.

Another disc ejected the cylinder and Ilya sent it flying against the shield even faster and harder, followed by another and another. Trapped, Octavio ducked and covered his ears against the clanging of the discs against the metal.

Makarov shook his head sadly. "This isn't much sport for Ilya, I'm afraid." He touched the communicator again. "Computer, increase the disc firing rate to medium."

Immediately the discs began to fly from the cylinder at the rate of one every four seconds. Each disc was mentally snatched from the air by Ilya and sent flying towards Octavio's hiding place. Behind the barrier, the Colombian boy was beginning to resemble a plaster statue, so thoroughly covered was he with clay powder from the exploded discs. He looked up desperately at the others, watching from above.

What do I do? he thought desperately to Nestor, who was watching from above with concern.

Louise answered for him. *Get out there and fight like you mean it!*

Spurred on by her words, Octavio threw himself out of cover as another disc ejected from the cylinder, heading straight for him. He held out his right hand, stopped the disc in mid-air and pushed his palm forwards. The disc flew towards Ilya's head. The Russian boy casually leaned to one side and the disc shattered against the wall behind him.

Keep it up! Nestor encouraged his brother, who had already snatched a second disc from the air and sent it flying across the court into the blue zone. The disc came closer to Ilya this time and the Russian had to throw up a shield to stop it from hitting him in the chest. As the disc exploded, Octavio pushed another in his direction as it ejected from the cylinder. Ilya had anticipated the move, however, and held out his hand as the missile approached. The disc slowed enough for him to catch it in his hand. Ilya twirled the disc on his index finger as he walked forward to the edge of the blue zone.

He's too good! Octavio thought with a little awe as he backed away. Ilya was starting to spin the disc ever faster, creating a humming sound that filled the air as it picked up speed. With a lightning fast motion, Ilya threw out his arm and the missile flew forwards. Octavio had to hurl himself back to avoid it. The disc smashed against the wall centimetres from his head.

"Excellent," Makarov breathed as he touched the communicator again. "Computer, fast release."

As the discs started to fly out at the rate of one every couple of seconds, Ilya was free to pluck each one from the air with his mind power and send them hurtling towards Octavio, who had no option but to cower against the wall as they exploded around him. Ilya was clearly aiming around him, but the discs seemed to be hitting closer and closer.

"That's enough," Sarah said to Makarov, but the Russian didn't seem to hear her – so intent was he on the spectacle below.

"Make him stop!" Octavio yelled out as another disc smashed into the wall beside his head.

Sarah moved towards Makarov and grabbed his arm, pulling him round. "I said, that's enough!"

He waited a second, before speaking leisurely into the communicator. "Computer, stop."

Immediately the sound of discs hitting the wall ceased as the cylinder slid back into the floor. Nestor flew down the stairs towards the entrance to the court. Sarah and the others looked down to where Octavio was huddled, unmoving. On the other side of the room, Ilya stood impassively, showing no excitement at his victory. Nestor ran down the steps of the viewing platform.

"What kind of game do you call that?" Sarah demanded, rounding on Makarov again. "He could have been hurt."

"You are all just beginning to realize the full potential of your powers," he replied, speaking to the entire group as much as to her. "The only way for you to get stronger is to be pushed, as I'm sure you've learned from the battles you've fought already."

In the room below, Nestor crossed to where Octavio was still huddled. "Are you okay?" he asked with concern as he helped his brother to his feet.

"Fine," Octavio muttered, brushing the clay dust from his body. "I think I twisted my ankle."

"Let me help you."

As they moved towards the exit, someone else entered the court – Louise.

"What do you think you're doing?" Nestor asked as she walked onto the court, but Louise looked only at Ilya, waiting motionless in the blue zone.

I want to have a go at this game, she announced.

Above, Makarov looked questioningly at Sarah, as if asking her permission. "Well, well. It seems I'm not the only one around here who likes games to be a little... *challenging.*"

Sarah looked down at the younger girl, who met her gaze with determination in her eyes.

"Do it," Sarah said and Makarov clapped his hands.

"Computer, a hundred discs."

As the cylinder rose from the floor again, Octavio limped past Louise with his arm around Nestor's shoulder for support.

Take his head off, he said as they exited the court.

Makarov brought his hand down. "Computer, release!"

The first disc flew from the cylinder and was caught in mid-flight by Ilya. As he moved to send it in Louise's direction, she threw out both her hands and it exploded right in front of him, showing him with fragments. Taking advantage of Ilya's surprise, she snatched up the next disc when it was barely out of the cylinder and sent it arcing towards him. Ilya destroyed it less than a metre from his head.

On the viewing platform, Makarov moved closer to the edge and looked down, a flicker of annoyance passing over his face as Ilya staggered back.

"Bit more of a *challenge* for your boy?" Sarah asked with a smile as Louise sent two more discs flying into the blue zone.

"Defeat her!" Makarov yelled down to the court, his voice suddenly a rasp. "Computer, maximum speed!"

The discs began to whip out of the cylinder at an alarming rate. Louise and Ilya wheeled their arms frantically, picking missiles from the air and sending them across the court, whilst simultaneously blocking ones coming at them. From the viewing platform, the others watched wide-eyed as dozens of discs flew back and forth across the court, creating a dizzying blur of motion, punctuated by explosions of clay. Makarov leaned against the rail and let out a heavy breath. Sarah tore her eyes away from the action below for a second and saw that his eyes were narrowed and his face lined with effort – almost as if he were involved in the battle.

"What's she doing?" Robert cried out.

Sarah looked round and saw that Louise had dropped her hands to her side and closed her eyes. On the other side of the court, Ilya sent a wave of missiles directly at her. The discs did not reach their target, however. As they approached the girl, they changed course and spun around her, beginning to orbit her body as if caught up in some kind of gravitational pull. Within a few seconds there were at least twenty discs circling Louise, gradually picking up speed. The cylinder in the centre of the court had dispensed its last missile, so Ilya lowered his hands and stood, watching the discs fly around Louise.

Then the girl's eyes snapped open. *You'd better duck.*

One of the orbiting discs flew out at amazing speed, hurtled across the court and hit the ground at Ilya's feet, driving him back. Another followed, pushing him back further. And another. And another. As his back hit the wall, Louise started throwing discs towards him like bullets from a machine gun, peppering the area around him with broken shards of clay. The Russian boy had no option other than to crouch down with his hands over his head.

"Stop!" he cried. "You win!"

The remaining discs clattered to the floor. Louise stood triumphant in the red zone. Waving to the cheering members of her group, she walked across the court and extended a hand to her crouching opponent.

"It's okay," she said. "You can get up now. I'm finished."

Ilya raised his head, blinking the dust from his eyes and stood uncertainly. A cut from one of the flying shards was starting to bleed on his right cheek. Blinking in confusion, the boy touched his face with his fingertips and looked down at the red liquid on them.

"My blood," he murmured, shaking his head.

"It's just a scratch," Louise said, but she could see from the look in the boy's eyes that he was completely confused. The blank assuredness from earlier had gone completely. "Are you okay, Ilya?"

He looked at her. "Where am I?"

"Get away from him!" Makarov snapped, half-running across the court. He pushed Louise to one side and bent over the boy.

Ilya began to ask something else, but Makarov held a hand in front of his face.

"Enough," Makarov said softly. The boy's eyes went instantly blank again.

"What's wrong with him?" Louise asked as Sarah and the others approached across the room.

Makarov chuckled, trying to make light of it. "Ilya's a big baby. Afraid of the sight of a little blood. Go back to your quarters and get a plaster."

Ilya obeyed silently, walking wordlessly through the other children. Sarah and Louise exchanged a look, but said nothing.

"What an amazing demonstration," Makarov went on, turning his attention to Louise. "I thought Ilya was unbeatable, but it seems we have a new champion."

"Yeah, you did good," Octavio said unexpectedly. "The thing with the discs spinning around you was cool."

Louise shrugged. "I can show you how to do it sometime."

Octavio nodded and looked at his feet. Sarah gave Louise a wink, but then turned her attention to Makarov. The man looked as if he had aged twenty years in twenty minutes – his skin had lost its lustre and his entire body, tall and strong before, seemed suddenly frail. Makarov seemed to sense her scrutiny, because he pulled himself a little taller and started back across the court.

"Hey!" Sarah called after him. "What about the virus research you promised to show us?"

"Forgive me, but I grow tired," Makarov said over his shoulder. "A side-effect of my enhanced powers. I must leave you until the dawn. Remember, my home is yours."

With that, he left the court. Louise looked at Sarah and Alex in surprise.

"He's going to bed?" she asked. "It's like, only three o'clock."

Sarah moved forwards and went through the door after him. She still had plenty of questions to ask their host, and she wasn't going to let him run out on them that easily. However, outside the room he was nowhere to be seen. She ran round the side of the court. Makarov had vanished into thin air.

"Looks like we're on our own again until the morning," Alex said, appearing at her side.

Sarah nodded. "It's time to find out what's happening below the 90th floor."

21

Sitting on the grass of the open area on the 153rd floor, they held a council of war.

"Okay," said Nestor, who was chairing the discussion, "let's try to list good things about our present situation."

"Nobody's trying to kill us," Alex suggested with a grin.

"At the moment," Sarah said under her breath.

"This place is warm and dry," Octavio said. "Which is more than can be said for our last apartment."

"Food is good," Louise added.

"Food is *great*," Wei corrected. "And the swimming pool. And the computers. And the games stuff…"

"Okay, okay," Nestor said, holding up a hand to stop the endless list. "Things we don't like."

"Makarov's story about the Tunguska meteorite doesn't make sense," Sarah said firmly. "If he was really there when it happened he would have to be over a hundred years old."

"The vision he showed us felt real enough," Nestor replied. "But did you see him this afternoon? He *looked* a hundred years old."

"Whatever," Sarah said dismissively, "his story stinks."

Nestor nodded. "Others?"

"The workers are creepy," Louise said. "And that Ilya kid was just like them. As if he was sleepwalking. When I hurt him in the game, he seemed to change, but then Makarov got to him."

"Anything else?"

"His idea of skills training isn't fun," Octavio said, rubbing his ankle.

Louise giggled. "Speak for yourself."

"And?" Nestor went on.

There were murmurs around the group, but nobody offered any other evidence against their current home.

"This whole place feels wrong and Makarov's hiding something," Sarah said vehemently. "Can't you all feel it? Something under the surface? The Spire looks amazing and has everything we could ever want, but it's a prison. If we stay here too long, we'll end up prisoners just as much as we ever were when we were held at HIDRA. I dare anyone to say they don't feel it as well."

For a moment the group was silent, each member lost in their thoughts. Sarah could tell her words had hit home.

"Makarov claims he's found a cure for the fall virus," Sarah continued. "I'm not going to sit here doing nothing until he decides it's time to let us in on the secret. While we're having fun in paradise, our families are lying in sleeper modules. We owe it to them to find out everything we can, whether Makarov is ready to share it or not."

There was agreement around the group.

"Okay," Nestor said finally, "so what about the lower levels of the tower? Robert, what did you find out?"

"I teleported down to the 90th floor," he said. "There's nothing much there. The central lift doesn't go any lower, but I found another one. I saw a group of the tower workers get in, but there's a scanner and camera. We won't be able to get past without alerting Makarov, I'm sure."

"Couldn't you just teleport further down the building?" Nestor asked, but Robert shook his head.

"No. There's some kind of block. Almost like an invisible barrier that won't let me teleport past the 90th. It's weird."

"It's Makarov," Sarah asserted. "I've tried to read what's going on down there and come up blank. He's using his mind to shield the lower levels of the tower from us."

"Please!" Alex said with a laugh, but became serious when he saw the others' expressions. "I mean, why would he want to do that?"

"That's what we need to find out," Nestor said. He turned to Sarah. "I take it you've got a plan?"

She nodded. "I'm going to sneak into the restricted levels, access the central computer and get the information about the fall virus cure. There has to be some way to get it to Rachel Andersen at HIDRA. She'll know what to do with it."

"Sounds risky," Octavio sniffed.

Sarah raised an eyebrow at him. "Since when did you get so cautious?"

"How do you think Makarov is going to react when he finds out we've been trying to break into his restricted area?" Alex asked.

"I don't know," Sarah shot back, "but something's going on down there. I can sense it, even if I can't see it."

Nestor nodded. "Sarah's right. However, we should take a vote on this. It affects all of us. Okay?"

There was murmured agreement around the group.

"Okay," Nestor said. "All those in favour of Sarah checking out the lower levels?"

Sarah, Robert, Louise and Nestor all raised their hands. After a moment, Octavio reluctantly raised his also. Louise looked at Wei, who shrugged at her apologetically.

"It's good here, Louise!" he whined. "I want to stay!"

Louise glared at him. Finally, the Chinese kid raised his arm with a roll of his eyes.

All eyes fell on Alex, who folded his arms.

"Looks like I'm outvoted anyway, so what's the point?" Alex said to Sarah. "But if this is the way it's going to be, I'm coming with you. I want to make sure the group gets a fair report of what's down there."

A smiled passed across Sarah's face as she rose from the grass. "That's good, because I'm going to need your help getting into the restricted levels." She looked round the others. "The rest of you, just act normal. Well, as normal as any of you can manage."

With that, she strode away towards the lift entrance.

Nestor gave an embarrassed cough. "Uh, meeting adjourned."

Alex rose with a shake of his head, unable to escape the feeling that Sarah Williams had just got exactly what she wanted.

The war room on the HS *Ulysses* contained a circular table with a giant computer screen in the centre. Currently it displayed a map of the Pacific, showing the location of the ship – heading towards the west coast of the USA. Rachel Andersen, Commander Craig and five of the highest ranking officers on board were gathered around the illuminated communications table. The head of HIDRA, General Wellman, and several of his staff were participating in the meeting from the HQ in Paris via a link-up window on the screen. The grey-haired general poked his wire-framed spectacles back on his nose expectantly.

"Good morning, General," Rachel said as she stood from her seat to address the meeting. "Gentlemen. I'm going to bring you all up to date on the latest report from our meteorite early-warning facility in the Philippines. It's not good. In fact, it's the worst possible scenario."

The tension in the room was palpable as she brought up a series of black and white images on the big screen. They showed a misshapen object floating in the midst of the darkness of space.

"We picked up this object two days ago," she explained. "Meteor P163. A ten-metre-wide object heading towards earth. Estimated strike time is just two days from now. Unfortunately, it's not alone."

She brought up a new set of images from the Philippines observatory. These showed many such objects – irregular specks travelling through the void. A series of gasps and murmurs went around the room from those who hadn't yet seen the images.

"The new data shows a series of objects headed towards us," Rachel went on. "We've detected thirty so far, ranging in size from ten to thirty metres across. Our astronomers think there might be more out there."

"They're meteors?" General Wellman asked and Rachel nodded. "How far away are they?"

"The first should hit within the next forty-eight hours."

Commander Craig shook his head. "How is that possible? Why didn't we pick these up sooner?"

"We're still trying to work that out," Rachel replied. "Perhaps some kind of radiation from the lead meteor shielded the rest from our sensors. If it's any consolation, all the other monitoring stations missed them too, including NASA's. It's almost like they were hidden from view until they reached a certain distance."

"Is it safe to assume these objects originate from the same source as the Australian and South American strikes?" General Wellman asked. "That they are probably infected with the fall virus?"

Rachel cast a look at their resident astrophysicist, Dr. Fincher, who was one of the few scientists in the room. He was a beanpole of a man, two metres tall, with a permanent shadow of stubble around his face. He stepped towards the central area so that he could speak.

"Their current trajectory suggests they come from the same quadrant," Fincher affirmed. "Except they're significantly larger than those meteors and the number suggests a greater threat of contamination. Of course, when they hit earth, the fall virus will be the least of our problems."

General Wellman raised an eyebrow. "How so?"

Fincher coughed nervously, aware all eyes in the room were turned towards him. "The Australian meteorite was about fourteen metres across and threw thousands of tonnes of dust into the atmosphere, General. This affected the temperature and weather patterns of the entire southern hemisphere for weeks afterwards. The result of thirty or more meteorites hitting the globe in quick succession would be devastating. The amount of material thrown into the sky would block out the sun for months, maybe years. Earth would spiral into a prolonged winter, shutting down food production, global communication and causing the biggest extinction event since the dinosaurs died out. Millions of people would die, perhaps billions."

The room was silent as Fincher's words sank in.

"Can we stop them from hitting us?" Rachel asked. "What about the American defence satellites? Can they be turned against the meteors?"

Commander Craig shook his head. "The US missile shield doesn't come online until next year. It's just not ready. Maybe if we had a few months, some of our nukes could be used to deflect the storm. But not with only two days' notice."

"Are you saying," the general said, "there's no way we can stop these meteors from hitting the earth?"

Everyone looked at Fincher again. He closed his eyes and replied, "If we're lucky, a few of the objects might pass on by. But, yes, sir. We're going to get hit badly. There's nothing we can do to stop it."

On the screen, General Wellman had gone a shade of white, as had most of the people around the room. "I'm initiating Operation Shield," he announced finally.

The name, *Operation Shield*, sent a chill through Rachel Andersen, much like it had when she'd first read about HIDRA's top secret emergency protocol shortly after taking command. Like everyone else in the room, she knew that over the next few hours the families of all HIDRA personnel – hers included – would be transported to a network of underground bunkers located around the world. In these bunkers they would wait out the worst of the devastation in the hope of being able to rebuild the world at some time in the future. *Shield* was designed to be activated in the event of an imminent nuclear war or a massive virological outbreak, but it seemed that they were facing a different threat. The governments of every nation would be notified as well so they could put their own emergency procedures into effect.

"This information is to be kept absolutely confidential until we're ready to announce it," General Wellman continued, his voice brittle. "The last thing we need is panic on a global scale. This is damage limitation, people. Over the next forty-eight hours we're going to save as many people as we can. Go to it! Dismissed."

The room cleared out. Only Rachel, Commander Craig and Dr. Fincher remained behind.

"Was there something else, Colonel Andersen?" Wellman asked.

"There's some more data we'd like to show you, General," Rachel announced, giving Commander Craig a nod. He tapped the central screen and a global map opened, showing the estimated meteorite strike locations around the globe. Each of them related to a major urban area: London, Tokyo, New York, Beijing – the list went on. The largest cities of the world were going to be hit.

"We've plotted the most likely impact sites based on the speed and trajectory of the meteors," Craig explained. "General, this looks like a premeditated series of strikes to me. I'd say our cities are being deliberately targeted."

"Amazing," General Wellman gasped. "It can't be chance. Can it, Dr. Fincher?"

Fincher shook his head slowly. "There's about as much mathematical probability of these meteors accidentally falling on every major city in the world as there is of a blue elephant appearing in this room right now."

The general snorted and rubbed his chin. "This throws a whole new light on proceedings. Are we saying what I think we're saying?"

Rachel nodded. "A coordinated attack on the earth from an extraterrestrial source. Would you agree, Commander?"

"It looks like we're at war," Commander Craig affirmed. "We just don't know who – or what – with."

"Unfortunately we don't have the luxury of speculating on that matter at the moment," General Wellman asserted, regaining his composure. "For the next forty-eight hours all our resources have to be directed towards making sure our people are safe. Colonel Andersen, I want you to turn your ship towards the HIDRA base in Hawaii. There's a bunker there. Get your people to it at any cost."

Rachel coughed, a little nervously. "That's what I wanted to speak to you about, General. I want permission to turn the *Ulysses* around and head for the Chuckchi Peninsula in Russia."

Wellman frowned. "The site of the last meteorite strike?"

Rachel nodded and told him about her previous conversation with Makarov and the abduction of the children. "He knows something about the meteor storm. I can feel it."

"Forgive me, Colonel, but I need something a little more than your feeling to go on," the general replied curtly.

Fincher stepped towards the table. "We had our satellite run a scan of the Chukotkan wilderness, General. Makarov has a skyscraper there – built in the middle of nowhere. We picked up a strange energy signature." He touched the table screen and a satellite photo of the Spire appeared. "It's like nothing we've ever seen before, but it seems to be beaming a signal into outer space."

"Guess where that signal is pointed," Rachel said. "Right at the meteor storm."

Wellman rubbed the bridge of his nose, as if suddenly tired. "First you tell me that it's the end of the world. Now you want to point a warship at one of the most influential businesspeople in the world. For god's sake, Makarov plays golf with the president. He—"

"General," Rachel interrupted, "the end of the world?"

Wellman sighed. "What do you intend to do when you get to Russia? Sit off the coast getting a tan while the meteorites fall all around?"

"No," Rachel replied, "I intend to investigate that signal and level that skyscraper if necessary."

Wellman laughed. "And start a war with Russia at the same time?"

"I think the Russians will have better things to worry about than Makarov, don't you, General?"

Wellman stared at her for a moment, before finally relenting. "Okay, take the *Ulysses* to Chukotka. Investigate the signal and then get your people to the bunker in Hawaii. I didn't listen to you once before, Andersen, and Colonel Moss made me look like a fool. I'm not going to make the same mistake again."

Rachel smiled. "You won't regret this, sir."

"I sincerely hope not," he said.

The video screen died. Rachel looked across the table at Commander Craig.

"Turn this ship around," she ordered. "We're going after Makarov."

22

Three a.m. Sarah moved as silently as possible along the corridor on the 144th floor. Ahead walked one of the workers, apparently oblivious to her presence. But as Sarah approached the bend in the corridor, something unseen grabbed her wrist.

Alex.

Don't sneak up on me like that, Sarah thought as he took her hand in his. Almost immediately, she saw her arm begin to fade out and become invisible. *I can't believe it,* she told him as she became transparent. *This is a weird feeling.*

Well, get used to it fast, Alex replied, pulling her along the corridor. *We have to keep up with that woman or we won't be getting onto the lower levels tonight.*

Sarah nodded, although she knew there was little point when you're invisible. It was a strange sensation to be moving forward when you can't see any part of yourself. Almost like your eyeballs were floating along with no body. *Strange.* She tried to concentrate on the job at hand.

Running as silently as possible, they reached the central area of the floor, where the woman was waiting for the lift to arrive. She stared directly ahead, completely unmoving.

They really are like robots, aren't they? Alex thought.

Before Sarah could offer her opinion, the lift doors opened and the woman stepped through. Moving on tiptoes, Alex and Sarah slipped inside and pressed themselves against the side wall. The woman stood stock still in the centre of the car as it began to descend the fifty-four storeys down to the 90th floor, the lowest level that it could access.

The lift doors opened and the woman walked out. Before they closed, Alex and Sarah darted through and followed a few paces behind. The corridor into which they'd stepped ended at another lift, marked *Floors 11–*

89: Restricted Access. The woman placed her hand against a palm-print scanner and the doors opened.

Now, let's see what Makarov is really up to, Sarah thought as they went in after the woman.

The lift descended just five floors, to the 85th, before opening again into a deserted kitchen area. Rows of industrial-sized cookers and work benches gleamed in spotless chrome – clearly designed to cater for hundreds of people if necessary. The woman walked out of the lift and headed across the kitchen in the direction of a set of double doors.

Oooh, sinister, Alex thought as they stepped out of the lift. *Perhaps Makarov's planning on setting up a restaurant or something.*

Shut up, Sarah replied. They watched the woman disappear through the doors. Sarah's eyes fell upon an emergency exit. She led Alex over.

"Let's take the stairs," she whispered.

They started down the stairwell. Glancing over the railings they saw that the shaft stretched down hundreds of steps to the very ground level.

What are we looking for? Alex complained as they passed one landing after another.

Makarov's lab, Sarah snapped back, keeping a mental note of the signs they'd passed at each level: *Kitchens 2,*

Housekeeping 6, Maintenance 3 – nothing of immediate interest. Then Sarah stopped as something caught her eye.

Sleeper Modules.

She pushed open the door carefully and they slipped into the area beyond, which was a massive chamber. There were no external windows and the only light was provided by the flashing readouts of the technology that the room housed – rows of squat, white caskets that resembled Egyptian sarcophagi.

"Are those what I think they are?" Alex asked.

"Sleeper caskets," Sarah confirmed as she scanned the room – she counted at least thirty of them. Sensing they were alone, she released Alex's hand and became visible again.

"But what are they doing here?" Alex asked, appearing also. "I thought Makarov said all the virus victims from the last strike were shipped out to a hospital in Moscow."

"Good question," Sarah replied as they approached the nearest casket. "Let's see if we can find the answer. They look different to the ones used at HIDRA."

The modules were indeed bigger and bulkier with more complex data readouts than the one that housed her father, Daniel. The entire top of the casket was transparent, domed plastic, rather than having a single window. Inside the casket lay a dark-haired woman in her twenties. As with the sleepers Sarah had seen at HIDRA, the woman had sensors attached to her forehead and chest. However, this sleeper also had a metal cap placed on the top of her head. A single thick cable extended from the cap into the top of the casket. Fibre-optic wires pulsed rhythmically within the cable in time with the rise and fall of the woman's chest as she breathed.

"What's that on her head?" Alex asked.

Sarah shook her head. "I don't know. Perhaps some kind of monitoring equipment. It looks as if Makarov has modified the original design for the casket."

They moved to the next one. It contained a boy of about ten and he wore a skullcap identical to the woman's. Sarah pressed a button on the side of the casket and the lid swung up with a hydraulic hiss.

"What are you doing?" Alex demanded, catching Sarah's wrist as she reached inside.

"Don't you want to take a closer look?" she replied, pulling her hand free. "Or did we break in here just to wander around?"

Alex sighed. "Just be careful."

With a nod, Sarah gingerly touched the cap on the

sleeper's head. It didn't move, so she gripped the cable and gave it a wiggle.

"It's on firm," she said. "Maybe held by some kind of suction."

She pulled harder and the cap came away in her hand.

Alex leaned in. "But what's it for—"

Without warning, the sleeping boy's arm shot out and grabbed his shoulder. Alex cried out in surprise as the boy's eyes flicked open wide and stared wildly.

"где – я?" he demanded.

"It's okay," Alex replied, gritting his teeth as the boy's fingers dug into his shoulder. "We're friends."

The boy looked at him in confusion for another second, clearly unable to understand his words, before his eyes closed again. Alex laid his hand back down again and looked round at an equally shocked Sarah. Hastily, she replaced the cap on the boy's head.

"Is that normal?" Alex asked.

Sarah shook her head. "No. The coma should be deep. If these people are victims of the fall virus, then it's different to anything I've seen before. Did you understand what he said?"

"Sounded Russian to me. Why didn't Makarov tell us he was caring for them here?"

"Perhaps because he *isn't* caring for them," Sarah

suggested, indicating a readout on the side of the casket. "That looks like a power meter."

"What are you saying? That it's draining their energy?"

Before Sarah could respond, there was a clang from the other side of the room and a huge set of double doors swung open. They both ducked beside the nearest casket as the main lights in the chamber flicked on full. Alex immediately began to fade out as footsteps approached. As he went invisible, he took Sarah's hand in his. Looking round, she saw her arm go transparent, followed by the rest of her body.

Good job you came, Sarah told him with relief.

Just keep a hold of my hand, Alex replied. *If it's Makarov, he'll be able to detect our thoughts even if we're faded out.*

Sarah indeed sensed the man's presence in the room and the power of his mind probing every corner. She threw up a psychic wall around herself and Alex, hiding them from Makarov's thoughts just as effectively as their invisibility.

I'm shielding us, Sarah told Alex. *Let's see what he's up to.*

Hold on a minute, he said as she began to move after the footsteps. *Perhaps we should just get out of here.*

You do what you like, Sarah replied tersely, *but I'm going to get some answers. Come with me or go, just don't get in my way.*

Shaking his head, Alex allowed her to lead him from behind the casket out into the open. Makarov walked down the central aisle that bisected the circular chamber towards a wide flight of stairs leading up to another room. A metre behind him the hulking shape of the robotic hound, Balthus, padded along.

Moving quickly through the rows of caskets, Sarah and Alex followed Makarov as he reached the bottom of the stairs and started up. In his right hand he now held a cane that he leaned heavily upon, as if having difficulty walking. Sarah remembered how he had started to look drained towards the end of their time together that day. Now he moved like a much older man – slow and stooped as if every step was made with great effort. It wasn't difficult to catch up.

At the midpoint of the stairs, Makarov held out a hand to Balthus. "Stay," he commanded and the metal beast stopped in its tracks. Makarov continued on up.

Leading the way, Sarah started up the stairs with her hand still in Alex's. They stuck to the very edge, giving Balthus a wide berth. As they passed, the robowolf's head darted round in their direction. The red slits that were its eyes looked directly at them. Sarah and Alex froze, not even breathing for a terrible moment. Balthus tilted its head slightly and raised its nose, as if smelling the air. Then the robowolf turned and sat down on its haunches with a metallic clang. Its eyes dimmed as if it was going into some kind of low power mode. Sarah and Alex moved forward again.

Nice doggy, Alex thought as they edged past.

The stairs ended at an archway that led through to another circular, windowless chamber, roughly the same size as the last. However, this room had no sleeper caskets and was empty save for a raised area in the centre upon which a beam of light shone down from the ceiling. Every part of the walls was covered with computer components: LCD readouts, drives, access terminals and ports. One section of wall was taken up by a giant world map with red lines pointing towards various locations, like arrows heading towards targets.

Makarov stumbled towards what looked like a main terminal, the *tap tap tap* of the walking cane punctuating every step he took. Sarah and Alex slipped into the chamber, but hung back in the shadowed area near the wall and watched as the man examined data on the screen.

"Computer," he said hoarsely, "status report."

"Sleepers are in perfect stasis," the machine replied. "Psychic energy levels are stable. I detected a power fluctuation in sleeper module 22, but energy harvest has been restored."

The sleeper we awoke, Sarah thought to Alex. *I told you the modules were draining their power somehow.*

"Have the pod checked for glitches," Makarov ordered. "We cannot afford any disruption at this stage. Was the beacon affected?

"The beacon is fully functional. No contact was lost with the meteor storm. Estimated time until first impact, 46.27 hours. Meteor trajectories remain within a 0.01% range of accuracy. All fifty meteors are on course for their targets."

Satisfied by the answer, Makarov turned and walked to the middle of the chamber.

He's bringing more meteorite strikes! Sarah exclaimed. *Why?*

I don't know, Alex replied as he turned his attention to the map on the wall. Cities around the globe were highlighted. *They look like targets! He's going to hit the cities!*

Sarah turned to the light in the middle of the room. *What's that in the beam?*

They strained to see, eyes adjusting to the brilliance

of the light beam. There was something floating there – a dark, irregular shaped object about two metres in length. The surface of the object was smooth, almost like glass. It rotated slowly, polished sections catching the light as it turned.

It looks like a piece of rock, she thought. *Or a meteorite fragment.*

Makarov stopped before the rock and went down on one knee, an operation that was clearly a strain for him. As Sarah and Alex crept closer, it was possible to see that his skin was as thin and crumpled as ancient paper. Now he really did look a hundred years old.

What happened to him? Alex asked.

I think we're about to find out, Sarah replied as Makarov raised his head to the rock, eyes glinting in the light.

"Master," he croaked, still breathless from the effort of his ascent to the chamber.

A deep voice sounded in reply. It resonated around the chamber, at once seeming to originate from the rock and come from all around. Sarah felt the presence of something incredibly powerful – the owner of the voice was ancient… intelligent…

Evil.

"I am the Entity," it replied. "I am the beginning and the end. My power spans galaxies; worlds are my playthings. Who disturbs my thoughts?"

The Entity. With her enhanced mental powers, Sarah sensed that the voice came from a long distance away. It was not of the earth. The voice spoke across light years of space.

"Your servant, Nikolai Makarov," he replied. "What is your bidding?"

"Ah, the earthling," the Entity answered. "Are the children contained?"

"I have them at the tower, master," Makarov said, his eyes fixed on the rotating object in the light. "Their fate is at your whim. I will have them killed before dawn if it is your wish."

Sarah gripped Alex's hand even tighter, resisting the urge to cry out. She thought of Robert and the others sleeping innocently at the top of the Spire.

"No," the Entity said. "We need them alive if we are to discover the limits of their power and control it. After my meteor storm brings the virus to the entire world, there will be many more of their type. Such organisms have thwarted me before on other worlds."

"They will not stand in your way," Makarov assured the alien. "I sense that some of them will join our cause, given the correct pressure."

"What of the girl who leads them?" the voice asked.

Makarov shook his head. "Sarah Williams is already powerful and difficult for me to read. I sense she will not turn. It would be better to eliminate her—"

"The girl is of interest to me," the Entity replied. "You will not harm her yet. Her weakness is her devotion to her friends. As long you have them, she is at your mercy."

A flicker of annoyance passed across Makarov's face, but he bowed his head. "You are infinitely wise, master."

"Is everything else prepared?" the Entity went on.

"The sleepers continue to power the meteor beacon at the top of the Spire," Makarov said. "The storm draws near."

"Excellent," the Entity said. "You humans have proved to be an amazing source of psychic energy – one of the best I have ever found. How ironic it is that this energy will be used to guide my meteors to their final targets on earth – the bringers of humanity's inevitable enslavement."

Makarov nodded. "When the meteor storm hits, the virus will be carried to every part of the globe. Those infected will become your slaves. Earth will be yours, master. All humankind will be subsumed into your consciousness. No one will stand in your way."

"You have served me well these hundred years, Makarov," the Entity said approvingly. "But I see you grow weak again. Touch the beam and drink of my power."

"Thank you, master." Makarov extended his arm and placed his hand in the light. As he did so, the beam glowed red. Makarov threw back his head as he was engulfed by the light.

He's changing! Alex exclaimed. Sure enough, the lines on Makarov's face began to fill out and disappear. His hunched body, which had previously looked so frail and bent, now straightened and became strong again.

"To join me is to live for ever," the Entity said as Makarov stood, young again. "Wait. I sense the presence of others. You are not alone!"

Makarov looked round the chamber in confusion. "I sense nothing."

"Fool!" the Entity bellowed. "You have been tricked by a mere girl!"

Time to get out of here, Alex suggested, pulling Sarah back towards the chamber entrance.

"Show yourselves!" the Entity's voice boomed from the light beam. "You cannot hide!"

Sarah and Alex, however, were already running down the stairs past the sleeping Balthus. They hit the bottom and carried on through the lines of sleeper caskets as Makarov's voice echoed across the chamber.

"Balthus, awake!" he commanded. "Hunt them down! Bring them to me dead or alive!"

23

What was that thing back there? Alex thought breathlessly as they made it to the other side of the chamber and ran into the corridor. In their haste to get away, he'd lost concentration and they had become visible again.

Some kind of alien intelligence, Sarah replied. *It's behind the fall virus – and there are more meteorites on the way. We have to warn the others. We have to stop this.*

Behind them, a lumbering figure leaped from the sleeper chamber. The robowolf was coming after them.

Hitting the stairwell door, Sarah and Alex flew through and ran to the edge. Below them, stairs stretched down vertiginously towards the bottom of the Spire.

"Up or down?" Alex asked as something slammed against the door behind them – Balthus.

"Up!" Sarah exclaimed at the sound of footsteps approaching from below. They ran up three flights, taking the steps two at a time. They stopped at the sound of another robowolf coming down the stairs.

"In here!" Alex said, pulling Sarah through the nearest door. Slamming it behind them, he shot the lock on the door and stepped back. Breathing heavily from their dash, they both looked round.

They were standing in another circular chamber, but the ceiling was even higher here – at least three storeys. The area appeared to be empty except for a single, massive shape sitting right in the middle. As they walked into the room a sensor triggered and lights set into the floor and ceiling came on automatically. Now they could clearly identify the shape in the middle – the stealth plane that had picked them up in Melbourne. It looked strangely out of place in the room, like some kind of squat, black sculpture.

"It's the jet!" Alex exclaimed as they circled the machine. "How did it land in the Spire?"

Sarah walked to a control panel and ran her hand over the screen. "I don't know, but we have to find a way out of here."

She pressed a button and the entire left wall split open delivering a blast of ice-cold air into the room. As the wall continued to slide open, a wide ramp began to extend outwards off the edge of the building.

"A landing strip!" Alex marvelled with a shake of his head. He walked to the very edge of the room and looked over. The side of the Spire sloped downwards – over seventy storeys to the snow-covered ground. He looked up. Above them, framed against the night sky, he could see the penthouse levels – a sheer climb on the glass windows of the building. The landing strip finished extending with a clang. It stuck off the side of the building over fifty metres – an insane feat of engineering. Alex thought of the Entity and realized they'd found the explanation for Makarov's incredible machines and robots – alien technology.

Robert! Nestor! Sarah called out with her mind, but immediately sensed that her message had not reached her friends. The same power that had prevented Robert from teleporting to the lower levels of the Spire was now blocking their telepathic communication. Without her link to Robert and the others, Sarah felt suddenly cut off, isolated. "We have to get out of here," she said, looking around the chamber in desperation.

"Maybe we can escape in the plane!" Alex called over to Sarah, who had opened up a store cupboard on the far wall. She produced two heavy coats and ran across to him.

"Who's going to fly it?" she said, throwing a coat at him. "Put that on."

Alex slipped his arms into the coat, glad of the protection from the sub-zero breeze blowing into the room. "What are you planning?"

"We're going to climb up to the penthouse and warn the others," Sarah said. She walked to the edge and looked up.

"Are you joking?" Alex said. "We'll never make it! There's nothing to grip on to." A blast of freezing air buffeted them back. "The wind would blow us off the side of the building even if there was."

"Have you got a better idea?"

"We surrender and wait for another chance to escape," Alex suggested as something thudded against the fire escape door. A second later Balthus smashed clean through the metal door. The robowolf stepped into the room, head scanning left and right, eyes glowing a deeper shade of red as its gaze fell on them. Balthus gave a low growl and advanced slowly, extended claws scratching on the floor. Its jaws fell open, revealing two rows of metal teeth like razor blades.

"Think it's going to let us do that?" Sarah asked as the wolf approached. They retreated, until they were standing at the very edge of the landing strip. Balthus tensed its back legs as if preparing to leap at them. Desperately, Sarah looked round and down – at the sloping side of the Spire.

"Let's jump," she said.

"Huh?" Alex replied, looking at her as if she was crazy.

"It's okay," she said, grabbing his arm. "We'll make it."

"Sarah, no—" Alex began, but the sound of Balthus running at them had already spurred her into action. Moving forward, she went over the edge, pulling Alex with her.

For a split second they fell...

...before hitting the side of the building and sliding down. The glass was covered in a thin layer of ice that cut down resistance. Alex let out a cry as they slid, picking up more speed by the second. Before them the side of the building stretched down at a seventy degree angle, a plain of glass whizzing past ever faster.

"Grab something!" Alex yelled as they slid along side by side. He reached out a hand and tried to slow their descent, but his skin burned as it contacted the speeding ice.

"It's coming after us!" Sarah cried.

High above them, the robowolf had gone over the edge and was also sliding down the side of the building, legs splayed to control its descent. Suddenly Alex was glad they weren't slowing. He looked down and saw the ground growing closer. He judged they'd slid down almost two-thirds of the side of the building at that point.

"We're slowing down!" Sarah said, grabbing his arm. At the lowest levels of the Spire, the angle of the walls changed dramatically towards forty-five degrees and then to an even gentler angle. Within a couple of seconds they came to a stop on a massive pane of glass that was practically horizontal. It formed the roof of a large open area containing vehicles that looked like small aircraft. Painted on the floor below them in massive letters – *Level 10*. They'd almost reached the bottom of the tower.

"I can't believe we made it!" Alex gasped as they rested on the glass.

"It's not over yet!" Sarah said, pointing back at the massive shape of Balthus sliding towards them at alarming speed. She pushed Alex to one side and rolled in the other direction just in time as the robot barrelled past them, carried by its own momentum towards the edge of the building. For a moment it looked as if it would shoot over the side, but then Balthus extended its claws. With a screech of metal against glass, the robowolf found purchase and came to a stop.

"It's coming back!" Alex said as Balthus began to claw back towards them. A cracking sound filled the air as it moved across the glass. Splinters began to form all over the pane on which they were sitting, caused by the weight of the machine and the scratches its claws had made.

"We're all going to fall through," Sarah said urgently, looking round. A metal beam separated the pane they were lying on from the next. "Get to the support!"

They pulled themselves across the surface of the glass towards the edge of the pane as Balthus approached. The robowolf came within a metre of Alex and raised its massive front foot. A set of claws as sharp as butcher's knives gleamed in the moonlight.

"Look out!" Sarah screamed as the claws descended, centimetres from Alex's leg. He pushed himself back as Balthus hit the glass, shattering the pane completely. The robowolf let out a howl. At the last moment,

Sarah grabbed Alex's arm and pulled him onto the adjacent pane.

Balthus wasn't so lucky.

The robowolf hurtled down, crashing into one of the vehicles below a couple of seconds later. Its body spun in the air and went hurtling across the floor, finally coming to rest in a tangled heap. Sarah and Alex looked down, waiting for the robot to get up.

It didn't.

"Thanks," Alex said with relief. "You saved me."

Sarah looked up towards the penthouse levels of the Spire, nearly half a kilometre above them now, and shook her head. "Makarov will send more of his machines when Balthus doesn't return. We've got to keep moving."

"Moving where?" Alex demanded.

"Anywhere but here."

Alex nodded and looked round. His eyes fell on the top of a ladder at the edge of the glass roof. "Some kind of access point by the looks of it."

"Let's get to ground level," Sarah replied.

Avoiding the massive gap created by the shattered pane, they slid carefully along the roof of level 10 towards the top of the ladder. Alex climbed on first and started down the side of the building. Levels 11 to 153 of the Spire were made of sloping glass, but floors 1 to 10 had vertical walls. The ladder led down the side all the way to the ground. Ignoring the biting cold of the metal against his skin, Alex made good progress downwards, closely followed by Sarah.

A couple of minutes later, they both jumped down onto the snow at the side of the building. The ground level of the Spire extended away in either direction – an unbroken wall of concrete rather than glass. Wind howled along the edge of the Spire. Alex's fingers and ears were so cold they felt as if they'd been cut with a knife.

Sarah pressed her hands against the side of the building. "How do we get back inside?"

"I don't think we do," Alex replied, indicating the shape of another robowolf prowling in the distance. "One of Makarov's machines on sentry duty. We should get out of here."

Sarah nodded, pulling her coat tight against the bitter chill of the night air. "But where?"

"No time to worry about that!" Alex took her hand as the robowolf turned in their direction. They ran into the snow, trying to put as much space between themselves and the base of the tower as possible. After some distance, they stopped and crouched down in the snow. Looking back, they saw the robowolf walk the perimeter of the Spire, seemingly unaware of their presence. Another appeared, patrolling the building in the opposite direction.

I can't see any way back in, Alex thought to Sarah. *And I bet there's more wolves on patrol.*

If we can't get back inside the Spire, Sarah replied, *then perhaps there's somewhere we can find help. Or at least some way to contact the outside world. HIDRA needs to know about the meteor storm. It's less than two days away! We need to find a phone or something.*

Alex looked at her incredulously. *What, in this wasteland? In case you hadn't noticed, there's nothing out here but snow for hundreds of kilometres.*

I saw some buildings to the east from my bedroom, Sarah suggested, indicating the lightening sky on the horizon. *That way.*

Where are you going? Alex demanded as she got to her feet and set off towards the rising sun. *How do you even know there's anything out there?*

Sarah stopped and looked round at him. *I don't,* she replied flatly, *but it's our best hope at the moment. Makarov and the Entity are bringing more meteorites to earth – we have to stop them.*

How do you propose to do that?

Sarah shrugged. *I don't know, but there has to be*

someone out here who can help us. Also, Makarov has answers about the virus. The Entity uses it to control people – so they must have a cure. I intend to get it from them.

With that, she turned and carried on into the wasteland. Alex clambered to his feet. *Okay, okay,* he called. *I'm coming!*

Makarov paced the chamber in front of the Entity's light beam, impatient for the return of Balthus. Although his master had fallen silent, the meteorite fragment continued to spin slowly, suspended only by the mighty psychic energy of the alien force.

The rock was the largest surviving piece of the meteorite that had exploded over Tunguska in the year 1908. Makarov gained his psychic powers that day, but even as an eight-year-old had been smart enough to hide them from the Siberian priests who rescued him. He could already sense their superstitious beliefs that the meteorite strike was a punishment from God. If the priests discovered he could read their minds, Makarov knew he would have been denounced as a devil.

So as he grew, he kept his power hidden.

All the time his abilities were developing, however:

mind-reading, thought control, extrasensory perception. In his dreams he saw things that had not happened yet, visions of a future where earth was ruled by an alien mind of unimaginable strength – the Entity. He instinctively knew that this force was also the source of his own hidden power and he began to formulate a plan to make contact.

As he grew older he began to use his secret abilities to amass a fortune: gambling money on horse races and games of chance where he always knew the outcome. He fled to Europe after the communist revolution and bought factories and land – *Makarov Industries* was born. By the age of thirty he was already a millionaire many times over. Within a few decades he was one of the world's first billionaires.

But he never forgot his dreams of the powerful force from the meteorite. Makarov had grown to hate the people who surrounded him, those from whom he had to forever hide his secret. Meanwhile, the meteorite called to him in his dreams – promising contact with the one being in the universe who could understand him.

So Makarov returned to Russia.

Making friends with the communists was easy with the technological secrets he brought from the West. Their space programme never would have got off the ground without his knowledge or money. And that's when he began his search for what remained of the meteorite in earnest, buying up vast tracts of land across Siberia and mining them for any trace, any piece of the alien artefact.

It was a long search, taking over twenty years and hundreds of thousands of man-hours to complete, but finally, he got his reward. The meteorite fragment was found at the bottom of the Tunguska River. The same waterway that had swept him away from his father that day in 1908 now yielded the object that would change his life for ever. As he had suspected, the rock was a transmitter – a way of communicating directly with the alien intelligence that had thrown it towards the earth.

The Entity existed light years from earth and its power was immense. In psychic communion with the alien, Makarov learned that it spread across the galaxies by means of the virus, taking its consciousness wherever it went. A hundred thousand intelligent civilizations on as many worlds had succumbed to the power of the Entity and now earth was in its sights. As Makarov communicated with the alien it began to show him visions of the future: a storm of virus-infected meteorites hitting earth and blackening the sky, the survivors infected by the virus first going into the coma and then becoming part of the great alien consciousness, little more than puppets under its control.

The vision would have been terrifying to most people: the end of life on earth as humankind knew it and the beginning of a new era of existence. However, Makarov was not most people. He'd learned to hate his life on earth: always having to keep his power a secret, never being able to trust another person. The Entity offered a release from all that. The chance to reveal his powers to the world. To use them to rule in a way he had never dreamed possible. Why did the alien need him? Makarov had learned from business that however powerful a company might be, when it wanted to take over another, it helped to have someone on the inside.

The Entity was no exception.

So, he became the alien's representative on earth, preparing the way for the coming storm. He built the Spires: seven fortresses that could survive the coming apocalypse. Among them, the one in Russia was the most important, containing the beacon that would guide the Entity's meteors to strategic points around the globe: Washington, London, Delhi, Beijing – every major metropolis would be hit.

But more important than that, he tracked down the children.

From what Makarov could tell, the Entity feared only one thing: those few individuals, like himself, who were immune to the virus and developed powers as a side-effect. Such individuals had fought and defeated the Entity before, on other worlds in other galaxies. By Makarov's calculations, based on the infection rates from the trial-run Australian strike earlier that year, the eventual rate of immunity would amount to 0.02% of all those infected. Worldwide, that was a significant number of people.

A significant number of people that would eventually be his to rule.

"I sense your thoughts, earthling," the Entity's voice boomed around the chamber unexpectedly. "You cannot hide your desires from me."

Makarov bowed his head slightly. "Then you will see I serve only you, Master."

The Entity's laughter filled the room. "I know your ambitions."

Ambitions. Makarov sensed the powerful brain-scan of the Entity searching out the darkest, most hidden recesses of his mind. His dreams of ruling as a king over the immune 0.02% were laid bare. The Entity would have its billions of slaves to control and he would have his own race to command – on a peaceful little enclave somewhere far from the rest of the world. Somewhere warm.

Australia, maybe.

"You will need someone to control the humans with immunity, master," Makarov ventured, as he had many times before. "Who better than your first servant on earth? Those who will not accept your rule will be... disposed of."

"You know this arrangement pleases me," the Entity replied. "Appeasement has worked on other worlds. But in light of recent events, I wonder if humans are so easily controlled, or if you are the one to control them. If you cannot contain a few children, how will you command the thousands to come? Perhaps there is a better candidate – this Sarah Williams, for instance. She has proven herself most resourceful."

Makarov's expression darkened. "Sarah Williams is a child. She does not have a tenth of my abilities."

The Entity sighed. "For now. I sense she will become a great power."

Before Makarov could reply, Balthus appeared at the door of the chamber and waited respectfully, head bowed. There was a dent in the side of its body – as if it had taken a blow.

"What happened to them?" Makarov demanded of the robowolf.

The robot raised its head and its synthesized voice responded, "INTRUDER CHILDREN > ESCAPED > OUTSIDE > PRESENT LOCATION UNKNOWN."

Makarov clenched his fists and took a slow, deep breath. He turned back to face his master and went down on one knee before the beam.

"Forgive me, master," he said softly. "They will be found and destroyed. Surely these are the type of dissenters who have no place in our new world order."

"The boy is of no interest to me," the Entity replied. "However, I want the girl brought back alive. Is that clear?"

"Abundantly, master," Makarov said with a bow as the beam dimmed, indicating that the Entity had broken contact. Rising slowly, he turned to face the robowolf, who stood ready for action.

"Assemble the wolf pack, Balthus," Makarov commanded as he walked over to his robotic servant. "Find them and kill them." He paused for just a second before adding more quietly, "Kill them both."

24

"I can't feel my feet any more," Alex complained as they trudged through the snow. The sun was rising ahead of them, bringing with it a biting wind that cut across the plain. While the thickly padded coats Sarah had picked up in the tower were doing an excellent job of insulating them against the sub-zero temperature, their trainers were highly ineffective at keeping out the cold and damp.

"How long does it take to get frostbite?" he went on, looking across at Sarah, who was walking alongside him. "People lose their toes, you know."

Sarah gritted her teeth. "Maybe if you stopped talking about it, it would be easier."

Alex fell silent for a moment, but then shook his head. "Nope. That's not helping at all."

"Well, it's helping me," she replied tersely. "You haven't shut up in the last hour."

"Just trying to stop my teeth from freezing shut. You know they're probably having breakfast in the tower right now. Bacon and eggs. Beans on toast. Sausages—"

"Will you be quiet?"

They trudged on in silence, struggling as the ground inclined towards a ridge. Alex skidded as his foot went through to the permafrost beneath the fresh snow. Pulling himself up, he ignored Sarah's outstretched hand and staggered on.

"Don't help me," he muttered. "You've done enough, thanks."

Sarah stomped after him. "What, this is my fault? You're the one who led us to Makarov. I never should have listened to you."

"If it wasn't for me, Major Bright would still have you trapped in Melbourne," Alex shot back. "You had to go sneaking around, didn't you? We were living in a paradise, but you just couldn't accept it. I guess you're happy now we're going to die of exposure out here."

Sarah shook her head as the slope increased. "You heard him talking to that...*thing* in the Spire. Makarov would have killed us all eventually if we didn't become its slaves."

"Whatever. You just had to prove me wrong about him, didn't you?"

Sarah laughed bitterly. "Well, you *were* wrong about him."

"I saw where you were living in Melbourne," Alex went on. "Practically a slum. With your powers you could have lived much easier."

"We had to keep a low profile. People were after us."

"I don't think you know how to enjoy the gifts you've been given."

"What, like robbing banks?" Sarah demanded and grinned as she saw Alex's face redden despite the cold. "That's right, I watched the news."

"I was forced to do that. You don't know how it was."

"Well, don't judge me either."

They fell silent as they reached the top of the incline. On the other side, the ground sloped down onto another massive plain. In the distance, a group of industrial buildings stood out against the flat wastes.

"That's not a village," Alex said breathlessly.

"No," Sarah said, "it's better. Those factories are sure to have communications gear."

She looked back across the ground they had covered. The Spire rose like a giant, gleaming stalagmite behind them – a surreal sight in the midst of the desolation. It was as if the building had been plucked out of the centre of a large city and deposited in the middle of the ice desert. She shielded her eyes against the snow that was beginning to fall with the coming of the dawn and squinted to make out a series of black shapes moving out from the base of the tower.

Robowolves.

"What is it?" Alex asked, following her gaze.

"Hunters," she replied. "Let's keep moving."

The snow grew in intensity and within a few minutes a full scale blizzard was lashing the plain.

Balthus loped forward, claws extended for extra grip on the snow and ice, distinguished from the other robowolves by its larger build and the streak of white along its side. A few paces behind, the rest followed, red eyes scanning ahead. The wolf-leader drew to a halt and the pack followed suit. The snow had effectively obscured the tracks of the children they had followed from the

Spire. The other robowolves paced impatiently, awaiting orders. Balthus let out a synthesized howl of frustration and sent a wireless message to them:

COMMAND: DISPERSE > SCATTER PATTERN > SEEK AND DESTROY

The robowolves turned and headed off in different directions in search of their prey. Within seconds they were lost in the blizzard. Unlike normal hunters, they would never tire and never slow because of the cold. It would only be a matter of time before they found their targets.

Red eyes glowing amidst the swirling snow, Balthus prowled onwards.

Robert woke from a forgotten nightmare with a start. Knowing that Sarah and Alex were investigating the floors below, he hadn't meant to sleep, but at some time in the night he'd drifted off. Untangling himself from the soft sheets that had become wrapped around his arms and legs, he looked around the room in confusion for a moment before remembering where he was – the bedroom he'd been assigned in Makarov's tower. Then a sudden realization hit him: Sarah was no longer in the tower.

Sarah, he called out with his mind. *Sarah, where are you?*

There was no answer. Jumping out of bed, he dressed quickly as the computer-generated face of David, his room concierge, appeared on the window.

"Good morning, Robert," the avatar said. Behind him, the dawn had broken but the sun was obscured by clouds rolling in, bringing with them what looked like a heavy snowstorm.

"Morning," Robert said as he walked to the door and passed his hand over the scanner.

"Nikolai Makarov is waiting for you in the garden room on the 153rd floor," David announced as the door slid open. "The others have already been summoned to breakfast. Have a nice day, Robert."

The image on the window faded. A sense of real unease began to spread through Robert as he walked along the corridor towards the central lift. The empty corridors and the expansive view of the gathering clouds through the massive windows seemed suddenly oppressive. Sarah was right, he realized – the tower was a prison. It took her absence for him to understand that.

He met Nestor at the lift. *Are you okay?* the older boy asked.

Sarah's gone, Robert said as they stepped inside and pressed the button for the top floor.

I know, Nestor replied. *I tried to contact her. Alex too. Something must have happened.*

We have to find them, Robert thought desperately, but Nestor held up a warning hand as the lift doors opened onto the grassy domain at the very top of the tower.

Play it cool, Robert. Don't give anything away until we know what's going on.

Trying his best to stay calm, Robert walked with Nestor towards the stone table in the middle of the open space. Breakfast had already been laid out, as much of a cornucopia as the day before. That morning, however, Louise, Wei and Octavio sat in silence and said nothing as the two boys approached. At the head of the table, Makarov sat with a silver knife in his bony fingers, buttering a piece of toast with slow, deliberate attention to detail. He seemed so completely absorbed in the act of spreading the butter to every edge of the bread that Robert wondered if the man even knew they were there. He and Nestor looked at Octavio as they took their seats. The other boy gave an almost imperceptible shake of the head. For a moment the silence continued to hang over the table, broken only by the sound of the simulated breeze through the trees at the edge of the room. Around the glass ceiling snow swarmed and eddied as the blizzard raged outside.

"I see two empty chairs," Makarov said finally, continuing to scrape the knife across the piece of toast. "Can someone explain to me why that is?"

The children looked at one another.

He knows, Louise thought.

Robert jumped from his seat. "What have you done with my sister?"

Nestor stood by his side and placed a hand on his shoulder. *Easy, Robert. This isn't going to get us anywhere.*

Makarov laid the knife down on his plate and looked up for the first time. His eyes were like black pools – bottomless and strange.

"I'm confused," Makarov replied. "I rescue you from the clutches of people who would hurt you. I bring you into my home, feed you and give you everything you could want. Yet you insist on breaking my rules. Prying into my business. I told you not to go below the 90th floor—"

Robert shrugged off Nestor's hand and moved quickly round the table. Makarov lifted a casual hand and flicked a finger in his direction. Hit by an invisible force, Robert flew backwards and landed heavily on the grass several metres from the table.

"Robert!" Louise cried, then looked round at Octavio and Wei. *Enough of this. Let's get him!*

The others made to rise from their seats, but suddenly found themselves rooted to the spot, completely unable to budge.

I can't move! Wei thought desperately. Louise struggled against the invisible force as well. Makarov's psychic power was holding them in place.

Robert got to his feet and ran at the table again, but only got a metre before he also froze in place like a statue. Looking slowly around the paralysed children, Makarov picked up the toast and took a bite from it.

"It seems I've been giving you all too much of a free rein," he announced. "Spare the rod and spoil the child, as my father always used to say. Well, from now on you'll learn that my rules are not to be taken lightly. There will have to be punishments for disobedience."

At Makarov's side, Ilya, the Russian boy from the training zone, teleported into existence. Meanwhile, out of the trees surrounding the edge of the park, the dark shapes of twenty robowolves stalked silently forwards. The robots stood guard a few metres from the table, their red eyes locked on Robert and the others.

Makarov cast an eye over them and nodded approvingly. "The Spire can be a heaven for those who obey my rule. A hell for those who do not." He smiled nastily. "Sarah Williams fled. She has deserted you."

Robert made a choking noise and his vision swam with tears. He wanted to throw himself at Makarov, to kick and tear at the man, but it was as if concrete had been poured over his body. He tried to yell with frustration, but found even that was impossible. Makarov had all of them in the grip of his mind.

"I sense you all trying to fight against me," Makarov told the group, "but as you can see, I'm far too powerful. I was perfecting my mind-control techniques when your grandparents were in nappies. Furthermore, I have an alien with a brain the size of a planet on my side."

Robert looked across at Nestor, who was powerless other than to roll his eyes in desperation. *He's crazy,* Robert thought to him.

No arguments there, Nestor shot back. *What do we do?*

I don't know, Robert replied, suddenly wishing more than anything in the world that his sister was with them. Sarah hadn't given up on them. Makarov was lying – he sensed it.

"You should feel privileged," the Russian continued, clearly enjoying his captive audience. "You are the first to experience the next stage of human evolution. In less than two days, meteorites will rain down on every major city, carrying the virus to all parts of the world. Below, the majority of humanity will live as slaves to my master, the Entity. Meanwhile, we, the immune, will rule as kings in the clouds." He leaned back in his chair with a contented sigh, but then his face darkened.

"Of course, we have the matter of your group disobedience to deal with first," Makarov said, looking up at the swirling snow around the pyramid and then back to the unmoving children around the table. He smiled broadly, revealing brilliantly white teeth. "I'm afraid I'm going to have to make things a little less comfortable for you all around here. Maybe then you'll begin to appreciate how lucky you are to have me."

25

If anything, the blizzard seemed to grow in intensity as Alex and Sarah approached the buildings. They had to hold hands to stop from losing one another in the wall of snow that was being driven towards them. Occasionally Alex would look back, expecting to see the red eyes of one of their pursuers approaching through the pulsating mass of white, but nothing had yet appeared. It was only a matter of time before they were overtaken, however. Visibility was down to just a few metres, so it was impossible to tell how far they had travelled or how far it

was to their destination. For all he knew, they could have
wandered off track in the storm and were heading round
in a circle.

Sarah pulled on his arm and yelled something
inaudible above the howl of the wind. Alex looked round
to where she pointed and made out the shape of a chain-
link fence. They'd made it to the perimeter of the factory.
Spurred on by this knowledge, they doubled their pace.
They reached the fence and followed it along for a minute
before coming to a gate swinging open in the storm.

As they moved through into the factory area, Alex
looked up at a towering sign written in both Russian
and English:

MAKAROV INDUSTRIES COPPER MINING –
WARNING, DANGER AREA

Do you think it's safe? he sent to Sarah, who shrugged.

Safer than being out here. Let's get inside!

He wasn't about to argue. Ahead, the factory buildings
loomed above them like dark giants – hardly welcoming,
but the best offer they were going to get in the storm.
They staggered towards the nearest structure and found
a door. Alex tried the handle, but it was locked. The door
itself felt flimsy and rotten, however. Taking a step back,
he aimed a kick just under the lock and the door flew
open with a crack of metal against wood.

They staggered into a small, windowless room, bare except for numerous items of cold weather gear hanging from hooks on the opposite wall. Sarah pushed the door closed to hold back the storm. They collapsed on the floor, exhausted from the trek across the plain.

"Boots!" Alex cried as he spied a rack of clothing. Pulling himself to his feet, he grabbed a pair of heavy boots with a thermal lining from a hook, tossed them to Sarah and took some for himself. They eagerly shed their sodden trainers and put on the dry footwear. Alex found gloves, scarves and hats for them as well.

"I'm actually starting to feel warm again," he said as he pulled the scarf around his neck.

Sarah clapped her gloves together to get the blood flowing. "Come on. Let's see if we can find someone in this place."

Alex put a hand on her arm as she moved to the internal door. "Take it easy. You saw the sign – Makarov owns this factory."

Sarah acknowledged his point with a nod. "Okay. Let's go slow. If it looks like trouble, we fade out, alright?"

"Alright."

She opened the internal door and they stepped out onto a metal walkway. It overlooked a factory floor that stretched on for hundreds of metres into the distance. Everything was on a massive scale: furnaces the size of houses stood idle, while huge pouring vats hung silently from the ceiling. What light there was came in through grime-covered skylights high above. Alex hit a bank of light switches by the door, but nothing happened – no power. The factory was deserted.

Dead.

"Looks like we're the only people home," he said, picking up a heavy-duty torch from a shelf by the door and turning it on. He swept the wide beam across the silent machinery below.

"Come on," Sarah said, moving to the steps leading down onto the factory floor.

"If there's no electricity, there's no phone either!" Alex replied as he followed her.

Sarah turned on him. "You got something better to do?"

Alex shrugged and waved the torch around the shadows. "No."

Sarah raised an eyebrow. "Are you scared?"

"No way!" Alex called after her as she started off between the rows of smelting furnaces. "I just don't like the idea of wandering around a factory owned by Makarov. It doesn't seem like a sensible place to hide out when we're being chased by a pack of his robots."

Sarah gave no response, so there was nothing to do but follow.

They carried on between the machinery in silence. The stillness of the place was strangely oppressive and Alex began to think he actually preferred it out in the storm. High above their heads, metal chains dangled from the sides of catwalks between the machines. They clattered against one another in the breeze blowing through the factory. Where a giant sliding door stood open on the far wall the snow billowed in, creating a high drift that covered much of the machinery there. All around, in the aisles between the furnaces and work stations, tools and protective equipment such as helmets lay abandoned.

"Looks like this place was cleared out in a hurry," Alex whispered, tapping his boot against a discarded wrench the size of his forearm. "What do you think happened here?"

Sarah looked around. "I'm betting the local meteorite strike—"

She stopped speaking abruptly and grabbed Alex's arm, dragging him to the side of one of the smelters. He opened his mouth to protest, but she placed a finger to her lips.

Quiet! There's something here. Look!

Alex peered round the side of the furnace. In the distance, at the top of the snowdrift, the unmistakable shape of a robowolf stood framed against the swirling blizzard. As its head turned left and right, the searing crimson eyes scanned the factory for any movement below.

Do you think it saw us? Alex thought, turning back to Sarah.

She shook her head, but bent down to pick up a wrench from the floor. *I don't think so, but we should be ready for it.*

Alex nodded and removed an oversized hammer from a hook on the side of the smelter. He stole another look in the direction of the drift. The robowolf had gone.

It disappeared! he told Sarah urgently. *Perhaps it moved on.*

Doubtful, Sarah replied, backing away. She didn't see the movement in the aisle behind her, but Alex did.

"Sarah!" he cried out as the robowolf leaped from the shadows towards her, eyes flashing brilliantly. Alex threw the hammer with all his strength at the charging metal beast. The tool hit it full in the face, sending it off course just enough for Sarah to leap to one side. As the robot passed, she brought the wrench down on the back of its neck. With a howl, the robowolf rolled forward, completely out of control, finally smashing headlong into the side of the furnace. The clang of metal against metal reverberated around the silent factory.

"Run!" Sarah cried as the robot struggled to right itself. She and Alex tore round the side of the smelter and sprinted down the wide aisle that bisected the factory, heading in the direction of the snowdrift.

"We have to get out of here!" Sarah said breathlessly as they ran. Behind them, the sound of the robowolf's feet pounding the concrete floor grew closer as it flew down the aisle after them.

"Then what?" Alex demanded, grabbing one of the discarded tools from the ground as they ran. He spun in time to see the robowolf throw itself at him. He swung the tool and connected with the side of the robot's head, jerking it round. The robowolf staggered to the left, but then slowly turned to face him again. Its eyes glowed an even deeper red – the right pupil flickering on and off as if damaged from the blow. The robot advanced towards him, slowly and deliberately, herding him back towards one of the machines. Concentrating hard, Alex began to fade out, but realized that it would be several seconds before he attained full invisibility.

"Sarah, get out of here!" Alex yelled, but she shook

her head, coming up behind the robowolf with her wrench raised.

"Not leaving you!"

She swung her weapon, but the robowolf anticipated the attack this time, wheeling round and to the side. As the wrench swung uselessly through the air over the robot's head, it struck out with its right foreleg, knocking Sarah down. Alex leaped forward, but the robowolf extended its claws and swiped at him. He let out a cry of pain as the talons ripped into his upper arm, drawing blood. Staggering back, he became fully visible again, unable to keep his concentration because of the pain. As the robowolf advanced, he could have sworn he saw something like a smile pass across its metal jaws. Alex pressed himself against the side of another furnace and tensed, preparing for the next blow...

"Don't move, boy!"

Both Alex and his attacker looked round as one at the sound of a thickly accented Russian voice, deep and commanding. A tall man, dressed in a thick coat with a hood that obscured his face, stepped around the side of the furnace. In his gloved hands he held a sledgehammer raised high above his head. Before the robowolf could evade the blow, the man brought the sledgehammer down squarely on its skull. The robot staggered as the head of the tool smashed through its metal cranium, exposing the wires and circuitry of its brain. The man swung his weapon up and down again with a grunt of effort, hitting the robowolf in the same spot. The skull of the robowolf detached from the body and cartwheeled across the aisle.

Stunned, Alex and Sarah looked from the robowolf's collapsing body to one another and then to the stranger. Their rescuer tossed the sledgehammer into Alex's arms, causing him to stagger under the weight. Without a word, the man produced a large hook from the belt of his coat and stood over the body of the robowolf. He drove the hook through the wolf's steel-plated back leg and used it to start dragging the carcass down the aisle.

"Bring the head," he said gruffly, not looking at either Alex or Sarah. "And pick up any bits from inside. You don't want to leave anything lying around for the other wolves to find. Hurry!"

Alex looked at Sarah, open-mouthed, but she was already on her feet to retrieve the fallen skull of the robowolf. Looking around the floor, she collected several pieces of circuitry and set off up the aisle after their rescuer. Alex brought up the rear, lugging the sledgehammer.

They turned a corner and went down a narrow

walkway walled by racks of tools. The man bent and opened a steel trapdoor set into the floor. Turning, he unceremoniously kicked the body of the robowolf through the gap. It landed a second later with a crash and the man followed down a set of steps. Halfway through the trapdoor, he looked back at Alex and Sarah, who hesitated on the threshold. The man pulled back his coat hood, revealing his face for the first time. He was in his mid-fifties, and although his face was lined from years of exposure to the elements, his eyes were bright and intelligent. The left side of his head was marred by a series of fresh-looking scars that seemed to have been caused by the claws of an animal. His greying hair grew long and fell over his face, obviously to hide the worst of his wounds.

"Well, are you coming or not?" he snapped impatiently. "You can stay here for the rest of the wolf pack to arrive if you like. Just don't lead them to my hideout."

Alex glanced at Sarah, who shrugged. What choice did they have?

They started after the man, taking the stairs down as quickly as they could. As they descended, he pulled on a cord and the metal trapdoor swung closed with a mighty clang, blocking the way back to the factory.

26

Sarah and Alex followed their rescuer down a narrow corridor under the factory floor. Light was provided by a series of bulbs gaffer-taped to the low ceiling. The man had to duck to stop from knocking them down with his head as he passed underneath.

The corridor stretched ahead for about fifty metres, before ending at a short set of steps leading down into an underground room. Sarah judged it was about the size of their entire apartment back in Melbourne, although it felt cramped because of the sheer amount of stuff contained within: workbenches piled high with electronic components, racks of tools, boxes brimming over with old bits of scrap. In the corner she made out a single mattress on the floor and realized that this was where the man lived. Underground, it was significantly warmer than in the factory above, but the place still wasn't exactly luxurious.

"Where are we?" Alex asked as they stepped into the room.

"It used to be a storage area for the factory," the man replied as he dragged the remains of the robowolf across the room and hauled it up onto one of the workbenches, scattering junk in the process. "Now it's just about the most desirable property for a hundred kilometres in any direction."

Shedding his coat, he walked to a bank of car batteries and attached a crocodile clip to one. Immediately, a series of electric heaters positioned around the room hummed into life, casting a ruddy hue across the benches and shelves. Alex walked over and inspected the electrics – everything was battery powered, from the heaters to the lighting.

"Who are you?" Sarah asked as the man returned to the bench and started opening up the belly of the robowolf with a pair of metal cutters.

"Call me Yuri," he replied with a grunt as he prised open the guts of the robot and yanked out a motor. He pointed to the object Sarah cradled in her arms. "Bring me that head."

She walked to the bench and handed Yuri the skull of the robowolf. He held it up, inspecting the exposed brain before reaching inside to remove a circuit board. With a grin, he dropped it on the floor and brought his boot down on the component repeatedly until it was little more than dust.

"Homing chip," he explained, aware that Alex and Sarah were looking at him with concern. "Hard-wired into the brain of every one of those monsters. I just hope we got it before the rest of the pack realize we've taken this one down." He waved his hand around the room. "Take a seat and don't touch anything." He looked at the arm of Alex's coat, which was slick with blood where the robowolf slashed him. "There's a first-aid kit on the shelf over there. Sort yourself out before you leak all over my floor."

With that, Yuri set to work on the motor he'd salvaged with a screwdriver, as if neither of the children existed. He hummed a tune to himself.

Alex moved closer to Sarah. *Do you think he's all there?*

Looks like he's been living alone down here for a while,
Sarah replied dubiously, casting another look around the
room. *Take your coat off and sit.*

She collected the first-aid kit and went over to Alex,
who'd taken a seat in a battered armchair. The wound on
his arm wasn't as bad as it could have been, considering
the razor-sharp talons of the robowolf.

"You were lucky the cut wasn't deeper," Sarah told
him as she applied antiseptic to the four parallel cuts on
his upper arm.

"Lucky, right," Alex replied, gritting his teeth as she
bandaged the wound. In the background, Yuri continued
to work away at the motor, seemingly oblivious to their
presence.

The cuts tended to, Sarah took the first-aid kit back to
the shelf and cast another look around the overcrowded
den that was Yuri's home. The air had a stale smell to it,
but at least the heaters were doing their job. The
temperature quickly became too much after the freezing
air above. Sarah unzipped her coat and threw it down on a
sofa by the door. Yuri looked up sharply at the movement.

"Don't make yourself at home. There's plenty of space
to hide out under the factory. You two need to find your
own room. I can spare you some food and clothes, but
then you'll have to do your own scavenging."

"If you didn't want us down here," Sarah demanded, "why did you help us in the first place?"

Yuri closed the housing of the motor and gave it one last look over. "Because you were bringing the whole wolf pack down on my hideout, clattering around like a pair of fools up there. And because I needed this for Laika."

He turned and gave a whistle towards the open doorway of a darkened anteroom they hadn't noticed before. Something stirred within and there was the sound of metal feet moving on concrete. Thinking of their pursuers, Sarah instinctively backed away. Alex rose from his chair and stood beside her, ready for action.

A robot limped out of the darkness and approached the bench. It was similar in shape and build to the robowolves, although slightly larger and more cumbersome. From the mismatched markings on its body and limbs, it was clear to see it had been constructed from pieces collected from various robots, along with other bits of scrap. Wires were taped to the outside of its frame, which was welded together clumsily in places. Its head was rounder than that of the other robowolves and its oversized eyes glowed green rather than red.

"Don't mind, Laika," Yuri reassured them. "You won't hurt anyone, will you, girl?"

Laika sat back with a *clunk* and raised her forelegs in a movement that approximated a dog begging. An electronic bark escaped her mouth followed by a simulated panting sound that was oddly comical in comparison to the growling sounds of Balthus and the wolf pack.

"It's not a robowolf," Alex said with a laugh, "it's a robomongrel!"

Laika's head twisted in his direction and she let out an abrupt yelp.

"Watch your mouth," Yuri snapped, crouching before the robodog and opening a panel by her front leg. "She's very sensitive."

Alex shrugged. "Sorry."

Yuri removed a component from Laika's leg and proceeded to fit the salvaged motor inside, connecting wires before finally slotting it home. Standing, he patted the robot on the head as if she were a real dog.

"There you go, girl," he said with a newfound softness in his voice. "Getting around should be easier now."

Laika rose and turned in a circle, as if testing out the new motor. Satisfied, she ran excitedly round the table, knocking into furniture and disturbing shelves in her excitement.

"Laika, easy!" Yuri protested as the robodog ran up to Sarah, panting happily. Not sure what else to do, Sarah patted the machine on the head. Laika gave a bark and sat before her.

"She likes you," Yuri said grudgingly. "She has good instincts about people."

"What happened to her leg?" Sarah asked.

Yuri held up the component he'd removed and threw it into a pile of scrap by the door. "Burned out in a fight with a robowolf. They come sniffing around from time to time. We wait for one of them to stray from the pack and take them down. Nobody knows this terrain like Laika and me."

Alex looked at a series of slash marks on the robodog's side. Clearly made by the talons of a robowolf. They approximated the scars on the side of Yuri's face.

"Looks like you've both seen a bit of action," he said. "Did you build her yourself?"

Yuri nodded. "From pieces of the others. First it was just me fighting them out here. Now the robowolves have both of us to fear. Right, Laika?"

Laika gave an approving yelp.

"You used to work for Makarov?" Alex asked Yuri, moving closer to the bench. "Is that how you know this place so well?"

Yuri winced at the mention of Makarov. "Don't say that name around here. All the pain he's caused, I don't want to talk about him."

"But what are you doing here?" Alex pressed. "Where are the others from the factory?"

Yuri sighed and looked down at the bench again. "I was the manager for Makarov's mining operations here in Chukotka. When the meteorite was detected, the plant was evacuated fast. It was just a small fragment and landed many kilometres from here. Barely caused a rumble, but it made a crater in the ice. We thought we were okay, but then people started getting sick."

Alex glanced at Sarah. *The sleepers we saw back at the tower.*

"Makarov's science team came in and transported them to the Spire," Yuri continued bitterly. "For their own good, they said. Now he's keeping them there to use as he wishes."

"He can't do that!" Alex cried. "Why haven't you told someone? The government? The police?"

Yuri grinned humourlessly. "Take a look around this wasteland, kid. Makarov *is* the law *and* the government for three hundred kilometres in every direction. You can walk for a week and still be standing on land owned by him."

"How come you didn't get infected when the meteorite hit?" Sarah asked.

"Because I was in the Spire at the time," Yuri replied, unable to hide the guilt he felt. "Used to live there in luxury along with all of Makarov's other executives. When the meteorite struck, Makarov was already set up for the retrieval operation – spacesuits, breathing masks, sleeper pods. I worked out pretty fast that he knew more than he was letting on.

"When the virus victims were brought into the Spire," Yuri continued, "Makarov started shipping the managers out of Chukotka. Relocating us to operations in other parts of the world."

"He didn't want anyone to know what was going on here," Alex said.

Yuri nodded. "But I wasn't going anywhere. I'm from this part of the world. Those miners are my people. I refused to leave and that's when Makarov set his dogs on me." He brushed a hand through his hair, briefly revealing the scars beneath. "Somehow I made it out of the Spire and crawled to the factory. Makarov assumed I would just die out here in the snow. He was wrong."

Sarah placed her hands on the bench and leaned towards Yuri. "You have to help us. Makarov is holding those miners and their families prisoner, using them as a power source for a meteor beacon. He's in communication with an alien force—"

Yuri held up a hand to silence her. "Please. There's nothing you can tell me about Nikolai Makarov I don't already know. Before I was thrown out of the Spire I had a good snoop around in his restricted level..." His voice fell silent.

"Go on," Alex prompted, but Yuri picked up a tool and continued working on the robot carcass.

"Enough. I've spoken enough about it."

Alex looked at Sarah and shrugged, but she wasn't about to leave it at that. She projected her mind towards Yuri, peeling back defensive layers to reach the things he wasn't telling them about. In the act of suppressing them he had brought them to the surface – his thoughts were an open book to her. She saw the meteorite chamber in Makarov's tower. Yuri had been there. Seen everything.

"What are you doing?" Yuri snapped, backing away from the workbench and clenching his eyes shut. "Get out of my head!"

The man's mind snapped shut like a trap, blocking Sarah out.

"You saw the meteorite fragment," she said harshly. "You know what's going on here. What have you been doing for the last six months?"

Yuri picked up a cutting tool and pointed it at her accusingly. "I've been surviving! And you...you're like Makarov. A mind-controller. Well, you won't get inside my head!"

Alex stepped between them, trying to cool things down. "Okay, okay. We're sorry, Yuri. We're just trying to work out what's going on here." He cast a look at Sarah. *Take it easy. We don't need to be thrown out into the storm just yet.*

Yuri seemed to calm down a little. He threw the tool down in disgust and slumped into one of the chairs. "There's nothing I can do for those miners."

Sarah spoke more softly. "We just want to know what's going on here. Makarov has our friends as well. We need to get help from outside. The world has to find out what's going on here."

"There's no working telephone in the factory," Yuri replied with defeat in his voice. "There used to be a communications set-up at the village, but—"

"Then that's where we're going," Sarah interrupted with determination. "You have to take us. We need a guide—"

Yuri rose from his seat abruptly, anger flashing in his eyes again. "*Have to?* I don't have to do anything other than stay here and protect the last bit of this land that Makarov doesn't control, girl. I'm not going anywhere near that village. There's nothing left there. You'll see."

Beside Alex, Laika lay down on the floor and covered her nose with her forelegs. She emitted a noise that sounded very much like a whimper. Yuri waved a dismissive hand at his dog and turned to the monitors. The storm had passed.

"Good," he said. "Get out and leave Laika and me to what we do best."

Alex shook his head in disgust. "What? Hide underground? Pick fights with Makarov's machines for spare parts?"

Yuri moved swiftly towards Alex, towering over him. His fists clenched and unclenched, but when he spoke his voice was low and even.

"I'll point you to the village, but only so you can see there's nothing left there," he said. "I can spare you some food and more thermal clothing. If you set out now, you'll make it by nightfall. Trust me, you don't want to be caught on the snow plains after dark." He tapped the side of his head with a grimy finger. "Makarov showed me the future. A vision in my mind. Soon the whole world will be like this. Just Makarov and his slaves."

"What about our friends?" Alex demanded.

A sad smile crept across Yuri's face. "Forget them. You can't fight Makarov."

Alex was about to say something else, but Sarah laid a hand on his shoulder. "Leave it, Alex," she said. "He's given up already."

She turned to Yuri. "Give us food and water and show us the way to the village. We've wasted enough time here."

27

Ten minutes later, Yuri led them down another corridor that ended in a steel door. Now supplied with a backpack filled with bottled water and some very tough-looking dried beef, Alex and Sarah followed silently behind while Laika brought up the rear. Throwing a heavy bolt on the door, Yuri heaved it open and sunlight flooded the corridor. As they walked through after him, they were surprised to find themselves standing on the other side of the factory complex, some way outside the perimeter fence. The storm had gone as quickly as it had come and now the sky was brilliant blue.

"That way," Yuri announced, pointing directly ahead across a flat plain of snow that stretched for kilometres into the distance. On the horizon, mountains rose. "The village is beyond those hills. It should take you until sunset to reach it, which is about three p.m. in these parts."

"Thanks for everything," Sarah said harshly and started walking away.

Alex hesitated and turned back to Yuri. "Are you sure you won't come with us?"

Yuri shook his head. "No. The robowolves will catch you before you get there."

"We have to try to contact the outside world. We have to warn them."

"Even if you find the communications gear hasn't been destroyed, there's no one who wants to hear about what's happening here anyway."

"We have to try," Alex replied.

By the door, Laika cocked her head to one side and made a whimpering noise.

"Alex!" Sarah yelled from thirty metres ahead. "Stop wasting time!"

Alex nodded and started after her, but was surprised as Yuri called out for him to wait. The man ran back to the door and produced an item from a hook by the entrance. It was a steel tube about forty centimetres long with a nozzle at one end and a red cylinder at the other.

"It's a portable gas axe," Yuri explained, pulling a trigger at the base of the tool. Immediately a yellow flame leaped from the nozzle. Yuri adjusted the gas flow with a knob and the flame went an intense blue. "If you come up against one of the robowolves use this to blind it. Their visual components are highly sensitive to light."

Yuri killed the flame and handed the tool to Alex, who took it gratefully. He opened his mouth say thanks, but Yuri waved at hand at him impatiently.

"Get going!"

Alex turned and ran to catch up with Sarah, who was already making good progress. Laika let out a bark as he left.

Yuri turned to the door, but was surprised when his dog did not follow.

"Come on, girl," he snapped. "They'll be back. Maybe."

The robodog hesitated before moving after its master.

In the distance, hidden in the shadows of the factory, a robowolf watched as the man pulled the hidden entrance to the basement closed. The wolf knew Balthus, its master, would be pleased they had found the location of the outcast's hideout, but that would have to wait for another day. The children were the priority.

It turned its gaze towards the two tiny figures setting off into the wilderness and sent a command burst to the remaining robowolves scattered around the area:

COMMAND: WOLF PACK > ASSEMBLE > TARGETS ACQUIRED

One by one, the members of the pack pinged back acknowledgement of the message. From kilometres away they began to converge on the signal.

Keeping low to the ground, the wolf began to stalk its prey.

Robert screamed in agony. Five hundred volts of energy surged through the electrified metal floor of the cage, making his body jerk uncontrollably. With effort, he teleported halfway across the room to a cage with flooring illuminated green. He sank to his knees.

"No, no, no," Makarov's sing-song voice echoed from speakers in the ceiling. "You're not paying enough attention to the pattern! I know you don't believe this, Robert, but I'm giving you every chance not to get hurt here. You just have to concentrate."

Robert gritted his teeth and looked round at the window set high in the wall. Makarov stood, silhouetted against the light of the observation room. *Concentrate.* Easier said than done when you'd been teleporting non-stop for an hour. The room in which he was being held was made up of forty caged sections, each with a metal floor that could be electrified at any time. Those cages illuminated green were okay. Some were yellow, which meant they were imminently about to turn red – meaning the floor was electrified. The colours changed every twenty seconds.

Robert knew there was a pattern to it, but just as he thought he was getting it, he'd land in a red cage and he would lose it. He shook his head and tried to clear his head. *Okay,* he thought. *I'm standing on a green square, so the cage three to my left and one forward will be green next turn. Like a knight move on a chessboard.* As the floor under his feet went yellow he teleported into the other cage. The floor was green. He breathed another sigh of relief. He was okay for the next twenty seconds.

"So, what do you think of my little game?" Makarov asked. "It's designed especially for teleporters like yourself."

Robert jerked his head up at the observation window. "I think it stinks." The cage next to him went yellow. That meant the adjacent cells for four blocks were about to turn red, he thought. He teleported five cells to the left and landed in another green.

"Oh, well done," Makarov said patronizingly. "Of course, all this can end right now if you just give me what I want."

Robert teleported into another safe cell and looked up at the window. "No way."

"Come on, Robert," Makarov cajoled. "Your sister never should have been on the lower levels. She knew the consequences of turning against me, but she ran away rather than face them. She left that to you and the others."

Robert wiped his eyes and teleported again – this time into a red cell. The electric shock threw him against the bars of the cage and he barely had time to jump to an adjoining cell before he got caught in the hold of the electricity.

"You're lying," he hissed, kneeling to catch his breath. "She'll be back for us."

Makarov chuckled. "Oh, I don't think so. Nothing survives out there without my permission. Computer, pause the game." Immediately the colours under the cells went out, leaving only grey floor. Makarov moved closer to the window so that his face was visible.

"All I ask is that you acknowledge me as your leader," he told Robert. "Kneel before the Entity and everything will become a lot easier. For you...and for your friends." Makarov pushed a button and the sound of Nestor screaming above a howling wind was piped through the speakers from the adjoining room. After a few seconds, he killed the sound. "Help me persuade them that cooperation with the Entity is the only way forward."

"And what type of cooperation do you want?" Robert asked.

"Bow before my master," Makarov explained. "The Entity regards your type as an anomaly – an unwanted side-effect of the virus it uses to spread its consciousness. If it were up to it, you would all be dead already."

"You're one of us," Robert replied with a shake of his head. "Why are you doing this?"

"When you've lived as long as I have, perhaps you'll understand, boy," Makarov said brutally. "There are only two things worth having in this world: money and power. I already have all the money I could ever need, but there's never enough power. The Entity is going to make me ruler of the world."

"You'll never rule us." Robert turned away from the window and folded his arms by way of ending the conversation.

Makarov sighed in frustration. "Computer, resume."

The *game* began again.

It was just past noon when they saw the robowolf following them. Sarah noticed it first when she stopped to take a sip of water from one of the bottles Yuri had provided. Far in the distance, at least a kilometre away, the wolf was a black speck against the endless white of the plain. It was making little effort to hide itself and appeared not to be moving.

What's it doing? Alex asked with a shake of his head.

I don't know, Sarah replied. *Maybe waiting for backup from the others. Is it Balthus?*

Alex removed the gas axe from his pack and turned it over in his hands nervously. *I can't tell from this distance. Let's keep moving.*

Sarah nodded and they set off at a faster pace. They seemed to be making good ground towards the mountains, but she judged there were still several kilometres to cover. Most disturbing of all was the sun, which was already starting to hang low in the western sky, bringing the threat of night with it. This far north during the winter, the days were short and the nights were long. She glanced over her shoulder as they walked and saw that the wolf was keeping pace with them, neither gaining nor losing ground. It was clearly in no hurry to catch up with them, but it wasn't going anywhere either.

Alex clapped his gloved hands together. "Can you feel it? The temperature is dropping."

"Yes," Sarah agreed. "There's probably only a couple of hours until nightfall. Then it will really drop fast."

Alex glanced to the right and let out a groan. "Another one."

Sarah turned her head. Sure enough, there was the figure of a second wolf, about the same distance away. She looked left and made out the shape of yet another keeping pace with them against the glare of the snow-covered plain. The realization they were being herded on three sides by the dogs dawned upon her. They could not turn right or left or even slow down – the wolves were steering them away from mountains.

"Ever felt like a lamb to the slaughter?" Alex asked, reading her thoughts.

"There's something up ahead," she replied, straining to see. In the middle of the flat plain there was a large indentation in the distance. "Look, it's a crater!"

Alex nodded. "That must be where the meteorite struck."

"And they're herding us right towards it—"

She stopped speaking abruptly as a bolt of pain ripped through her skull. She stumbled forward with a cry as Alex caught her arm to stop her from collapsing.

"Sarah!" he cried. "What is it?"

Shaking her head as the pain subsided, Sarah looked back in the direction from which they'd come. The Spire was still visible in the distance.

"It's my brother," she said, straightening up. "He's in pain."

Alex looked at her with concern. "You can feel that? What's happening to him?"

Sarah clenched her teeth as another wave of agony lashed her mind. It was as if someone had stuck her finger in a light socket.

"Makarov," she said. "He's torturing him."

Sarah closed her eyes and began to visualize a room filled with cages, coloured floors and electricity. Robert was there. She tried to see more, but the vision faded. All she sensed then was the massive psychic power of the Entity, draped around the Spire like a shield. The extreme emotion Robert was suffering had broken through the barrier for just a second.

"Why?" Alex asked.

"Control," she replied. Once again, her brother was in danger – goodness knows what Makarov was doing to the others. Sarah knew one thing: they had to get them out of the Spire at all costs.

Alex began to ask a question, but she waved him into silence. "Right now the main thing is to get to that village. Here's the plan: we allow the robowolves to herd us to that crater. When we get to the edge, we run over the side and fade out. It's probably our only chance to lose them."

"If they don't decide to take us out before then," Alex said pessimistically.

"Well, let's make it before they can do that," Sarah replied and they doubled their pace.

At least it was a good way to keep warm.

Lying flat against the far edge of the meteorite crater, Balthus could watch over the plain as the two children were pushed towards it. Contained in the bowl-like indentation, they would have nowhere to run – a much better plan than risking a chase with them over the plain during the daylight. The girl's power was in its infancy and had no effect on their mechanical minds, but the boy's invisibility was a powerful tool.

Balthus looked round at the two lieutenants lying behind. Although the temperature had dropped almost five degrees in the previous fifteen minutes, they were impervious to the cold, ever watchful for the targets. The wolf-leader looked back at the setting sun and then across at the children growing ever closer.

The kill was almost at hand.

28

The door to the cell slid open and Robert staggered inside. Wei and Louise ran over to help him to one of the metal bunks. The cell in which they'd been placed was cramped and cold. The metal frame beds were fitted with decaying mattresses and sheets that looked as if they hadn't been washed in a long time. The only window was a narrow slit high in the wall. There was a stark difference to the rooms they had been given on their arrival at the Spire.

"Where's Nestor?" Louise asked as they eased Robert

onto his mattress and pulled a sheet over him.

"Still playing Makarov's *games*."

"Why is he doing this to us?" Wei asked, unable to disguise the tremor in his voice.

Robert shook his head. It was a struggle just to keep his eyes open. He couldn't remember a time when he had felt so exhausted.

"I thought it was obvious," Octavio said from the other side of the room, pushing himself into a sitting position on his bunk. "He's trying to break us. Wear us down bit by bit until we can't take any more."

"I'll never give in to him," Louise said vehemently. "I'll never bow down to that alien thing."

Octavio shrugged. "You say that now. But what about after another week of this? Or a month? Or a year? I get the impression Makarov has plenty of time on his hands."

"Why go to all the trouble?" Wei asked. "If he wants to destroy us, he can obviously do that at any time."

"Because he's testing us out," Octavio said. "Seeing how far he has to push us before we'll break. You heard what he said: when those meteorites hit, there'll be more kids like us. The Entity gets the sleepers as its slaves, but Makarov wants to rule what's left. That means learning how to control us."

"I'm glad we're helping with his plans for world domination," Robert said bitterly.

Octavio swung his legs off the bed and leaned forward. "Maybe the best we can do right now is to submit and live to fight another day. At some time in the future there's bound to be a chance to escape or even turn the tables. All he wants us to do is swear some stupid oath of allegiance—"

Octavio stopped speaking as he saw the hard looks of the others.

"One day," Louise said with contempt in her voice. "One day is all it takes to break you."

Before he could respond, the door slid open and Ilya stepped into the room. In the corridor outside, two robowolves stood guard. The Russian boy pointed a finger at Octavio.

"You."

Octavio groaned and pushed himself off his bed. "Not again. It's only been an hour since my last session."

Ilya said nothing as he made way for Octavio to pass.

"Hey," Robert called after him. The older boy paused in the doorway and looked back. "Try to be strong. We've been through worse than this."

"Have we?" Octavio said and walked out of the cell.

As the door slid shut behind him, he started along the corridor to the waiting lift. Ilya entered with him and the lift rose several floors, opening directly into the chamber filled with sleeper caskets. Ilya indicated the way and Octavio crossed the room to where the stairs led up to the meteorite chamber.

"I eavesdropped on your performance in the cell," Makarov said, appearing at the top of the stairs as Octavio ascended. "You're not doing a very good job of winning them over to my cause."

"They won't listen!" Octavio protested.

Makarov narrowed his eyes. "Then what use are you to me?"

Octavio looked down. "They're stubborn and they don't like me very much in the first place. Just give it another day or so and they'll come round." He looked up al Makarov with desperation in his eyes. "I can persuade them, I promise! I have a very low pain threshold – I can't take your trials!"

Makarov's face softened and he placed a bony hand on the boy's shoulder. Again the man had become aged. "I always sensed you would be the first to surrender to me, Octavio," he hissed. "The first to swear my oath of allegiance to the Entity. How frustrating it has been for you to live in the shadow of others. To never take the lead as you should. To take orders from fools like Sarah Williams. No more."

Octavio's eyes widened. "Is she...?" He was unable to say the final word.

"Dead?" Makarov said for him. "Very much so. Or in the process of dying out on the snow. You're doing the right thing, Octavio. The others would push themselves to destruction over her stupid pride. You're saving them from themselves. By collaborating with the Entity we will save millions of lives. There is no way to fight it."

"Robert will never join you."

"You can't save everyone in the world."

Octavio looked past Makarov to the chamber beyond. In the central light beam the meteorite fragment spun languidly on its axis.

"Is that it?" he asked.

Makarov glanced round. "That is the Master. Or his physical manifestation on earth, anyway. The Entity has a million forms on a billion planets."

"Can I see closer?" Octavio asked, moving towards the chamber entrance. Makarov stopped him with a finger in his chest.

"All in good time. First, persuade the others to kneel before me. Then you will be allowed into the presence of the Master." Makarov led the boy down the steps to a table that had been set out with food. "You must be hungry. Eat."

Octavio rushed forwards and grabbed a fork. Makarov smiled as he watched the boy devour the offerings.

"There. See how much nicer it is when you cooperate?"

29

Sarah slipped on the ice and went down heavily on one knee with a cry of pain. Alex grabbed her arm and helped her up.

"Are you okay?"

"I'm fine," she said breathlessly. "Don't slow down. It's getting very dark."

They half-walked, half-ran on towards the lip of the crater as the ground began to slope upwards. The disturbing thing was that the three wolves tracking them had closed in slowly over the previous half-hour, guiding them directly towards the indentation in the ice.

I'm no expert, Alex thought to Sarah, *but this is beginning to look a lot like an ambush.*

Just stick to the plan, she sent back. *The moment we go over the edge, we fade out and try to lose whatever's waiting for us in there.*

Alex nodded and took a final look round. The three wolves that had been their distant companions during their walk across the plain now seemed dangerously close – each less than a hundred metres away – but none of them seemed in any hurry to attack. Balthus was not among them. Clearly the leader of the wolf pack was waiting for them up ahead.

As they began to cross the final few metres towards the edge of the crater, Sarah reached out and took Alex's gloved hand in hers.

It's time, she said. *Start fading out.*

Alex nodded and began to concentrate. He didn't know how easy it would be to focus on both maintaining their invisibility and fleeing from a pack of rabid robowolves, but he was going to give it his best shot. Within a few seconds both he and Sarah were insubstantial in the growing twilight. Behind them there was the sound of metal claws on the ice as one of the wolves bolted forwards abruptly.

Run for it! Sarah cried out in her mind. *Don't stop!*

They both sprinted over the crater edge, somehow managing to keep their footing as they flew over the top and started down the slope on the other side. The crater itself was massive, at least half a kilometre in diameter. It curved down to a dark spot in the centre – a hole in the ice that the red-hot centre of the meteorite had created six months before, punching all the way through to a hidden lake beneath.

Behind Alex and Sarah, the metal paws of the robowolves pounded the snow as they thundered after them.

Look out! Alex warned as they ran. On the side of the crater, three figures stood motionless, waiting – Balthus and two more robowolves. Sarah and Alex skidded to a halt on the treacherously sloping ice.

Now what? Alex asked, aware that the three robots behind them were growing ever closer.

They can't see us, remember? Sarah replied. *Just take it slow. We can sneak past if we're silent.*

They moved across the crater in a wide arc, avoiding a path that would bring them close to Balthus. The three wolves from the plain had stopped in their tracks, looking around as if confused as to where their prey had disappeared.

It's working! Sarah thought excitedly. *We can do this!*

Alex gripped her hand tighter as the head of one of the wolves swung in their direction. Its slitted eyes slowly changed colour, from red to purple. For some reason Alex instantly thought of the dye pack the cops had used on him in the bank. That seemed like a very long time ago now. His stomach sank as the wolf began to advance. Its two companions had turned also and their eyes were flashing purple in the gathering darkness as well.

I have a bad feeling about this, Alex said as he and Sarah backed away. *I think they can see us.*

The nearest robowolf pounced without warning. Alex and Sarah threw themselves in different directions. Sarah became instantly visible as the wolf flew between them. The other two rounded on her, moving in for the kill.

Alex, just get out of here! she thought as she backed away.

He had no intention of running, however, reaching inside his pack and removing the gas axe Yuri had given him. Becoming visible, he struck the ignition and leaped forward, waving the flame in the face of their nearest attacker. The robowolf's head snapped back, purple eyes turning red as it let out an electronic screech like a yelp of pain. Losing its footing on the slope, it hurtled down towards the bottom of the crater. Alex turned the gas control on his weapon, transforming the flame to an intense beam that glowed brilliantly against the gathering darkness.

Stay back, Sarah! he warned as he flashed the beam in the eyes of a second leaping wolf. The robot staggered back, shaking its head as its visual sensors were overloaded.

Sure, she replied, removing a hammer from her pack and bringing it down on the back leg of the third robowolf as it retreated. The wolf slid on the ice as its back leg buckled under the blow.

Sarah and Alex stood side by side as the three battered robowolves regrouped.

How could they see us? Sarah demanded.

I don't know, Alex replied. *Some kind of thermal imaging, I bet. Here come the others!*

Balthus and the other two wolves raced across the crater. They leaped across the dark hole in the ice at the centre, which Sarah now saw was several metres across. The three wolves from the plain waited until the entire pack was assembled. Balthus moved to the front as the others fanned out behind, ready to stop any move Sarah and Alex might try to make in either direction.

Clearly the initial attack was just a preliminary to soften them up – now came the real fight.

This is it, Alex told Sarah, gripping the gas axe and holding the flame out before him. *It was nice knowing you.*

Sarah weighed the hammer in her hand and smiled grimly. *You don't like these odds?*

Not one bit, Alex replied as Balthus grew ever closer. The robot was taking its time over finishing them off and Alex wondered just how much wolf there was in its computer brain. It certainly seemed to take pleasure in the hunt.

As Balthus tensed to pounce, a howl split the air, the noise enhanced by the rough parabola of the crater. For a moment everyone, human and robot alike, froze and looked round as a large, dark shape flew towards them out of the twilight. Then the robowolf farthest to the left flew across the ice as it was struck by a huge figure barrelling out of the darkness.

Laika!

The oversized robodog, made from the scrap pieces of the wolves, swung its foreleg and tore the head off the next robowolf in line. The robot clattered to the ice, sparks cascading from its neck. Sarah and Alex exchanged a look and grinned.

"Let's get them!" Alex cried out loud, feeling a surge of adrenaline as he ran down the slope towards the robowolf on the far right. Angling the gas axe, he turned the flame on its eyes. Blinded, the robot backed away, unable to evade a blow from Sarah's hammer. The clawed end of the tool smashed down on its head, exposing components and the robowolf collapsed – never to rise again.

"That's two down," Sarah said breathlessly as they turned to look back at Laika.

The four remaining members of the wolf pack were circling the big robot dangerously, although Balthus hung back, waiting to see how the fight went. Sarah gave Alex a nod and they ran into the fray as Laika lashed out against her closest assailant.

With a mighty cry, Yuri ran out of the gloom wielding a motor-powered metal cutter with a circular blade on the end. Swiping it across the back legs of one of the robowolves, he brought it down and set about chopping up the machine into several pieces, sending up a great wall of sparks that illuminated the night. Alex, for his part, was becoming proficient with the gas axe, first blinding then using the white hot flame to bore through the metal skin of another robowolf. As the robot staggered, he aimed the gas flame directly between its eyes. The robowolf sank to the ground as its brain was fried.

Further down the crater, Laika was still bravely fighting off Balthus and the last wolf. Balthus leaped upon her back, metal talons digging into her side, as the other wolf swiped at her head. For a moment it looked as if the battle was lost, but Sarah took advantage of the moment to run in and bring the hammer down on the other wolf's back. The robot spun round, claws raised, but Laika grabbed its back legs and swung it over her shoulder – dislodging Balthus in the process. Balthus rolled away, unharmed, but the other robowolf smashed against hard ice in a twisted mass of legs and spilled components. As it struggled to rise, Laika and Sarah jumped in, pulverizing what was left with paws and hammer respectively. In seconds it was nothing more than a pile of trash in the snow.

"Good girl!" Sarah cried as Laika bounded around her. She threw down the hammer and patted the robodog on the head.

"Sarah, watch out!" Alex cried as a dark figure darted across the bottom of the crater in her direction – *Balthus*.

Before she could react, the robowolf leader hit her full force and they flew back towards the hole in the centre of the crater. Sarah heard Alex cry out again…

...then she hit the super-chilled water and fell into darkness deeper than she had ever experienced before. The sheer shock of the cold shut down her muscles instantly, making it impossible to fight the inevitable descent into the abyss – the underground lake beneath the meteorite crater. She was caught in the arms of the robowolf leader, which had become a deadweight, pushing her frozen body to the very bottom of the lake. In the dark, the only light was the red glow of Balthus's eyes. Then the robowolf disentangled itself from her body and swam back up with several powerful kicks of its legs.

Paralysed by the cold, Sarah continued to descend.

The lake seemed bottomless. Her mouth opened and closed uselessly, filling with water. Her eyes stared ahead, although there was nothing to see. Her heart beat one last time and then stopped.

30

Makarov sat at the head of the stone table on the 153rd level of the Spire. He carefully sliced his knife through the piece of bloody fillet steak on the plate before him. He raised the steak on his fork, but paused to look around the table before eating.

"Is anybody hungry?"

Frozen in their seats, Robert and the others were powerless to look away as Makarov worked his way through the food piled on the table. Ilya stood, impassive at Makarov's side, while around the edge of the grassy room a line of robowolves kept a silent vigil – at least forty of them in all.

Makarov bit the meat off the end of the fork and smiled insincerely. "If you'd like to eat, everything is right here for you." He waved the fork around the plates of food. "All you have to do is submit. Kneel before the Entity and surrender your powers to my service. That's all there is to it."

Robert fought to speak against the mind control freezing them in place. "We're not giving up... None of us are."

Makarov looked down and cut another piece of steak. "Perhaps you'll feel differently when you're really starving. This is just our first day." His eyes fell on Robert again. "By the way, your sister is dead."

Robert's vision swam with tears. He wanted to scream out, but was unable to do so.

He's lying, Nestor's voice said in his head. *It's not true.*

But somehow, Robert knew it was.

The voice said one word: *Sarah.*

She floated in blackness, caught amidst tendrils of thought that spread across galaxies.

Sarah.

She opened her eyes and saw a light, shining like a sun in the middle of the abyss. It was at once beautiful and terrifying. Sarah instinctively knew what it was.

The Entity.

Am I dead? she asked, looking around. Apart from the blazing light, there was nothing out there in the blackness.

Yes, the Entity replied. *For now.*

Where am I?

In the place on the very edge of death. I've been wanting to talk to you for so long, Sarah. Ever since we met in the Australian desert.

Sarah waved her arms and spun slowly in the void. There was nothing but her and the light. *You weren't in Australia.*

The Entity laughed. *Oh, but I was. I am everywhere my virus travels. In the rocks of my meteors. In the bodies of the sleepers. In you too...*

You're not a part of me, Sarah replied vehemently.

I am. You know it's true. Every time you read someone's mind or control their actions, you're channelling a little bit of my power. Soon I will be in everything on earth.

Why are you doing this?

Because there has to be more of me. Like all living

things, I have to grow. Besides, everyone is going to be much happier when they're part of my consciousness. You will see. They will contract the virus, fall asleep and when they awake they will no longer feel fear. Or pain. Or doubt.

Sarah tried to swim away through the emptiness – there had to be some way back to life. *People don't want to be slaves,* she said. *They want to be free.*

And has freedom made them happy? I don't see any happiness on your planet, and I've been watching it for a lot longer than you – centuries of your time. The Entity laughed. *Anyway, that is little concern of yours. You are one of the immune. You will have your precious freedom.*

Sarah turned back to the Entity. The alien being shone supernova bright in the centre of an empty universe – streams of light stretched towards her like the tentacles of an octopus.

Freedom? she asked. *Under the rule of Makarov?*

The Entity's light shone a little brighter. *Makarov knows he will never control you. He senses how powerful you will become. That is why he wants you dead.*

But I am dead. Sarah thought of Robert and the others trapped in the Spire. She'd failed them.

Are you? the Entity said. *Say the word and I will send you back.*

Sarah's heart leaped, but she regarded the light with suspicion. *Why would you do that? You know I'm going to come after you. I won't allow you to enslave my friends.*

Because you would be a thousand times more useful to me than Makarov, the Entity replied. *Join with me now and I will destroy him. Free your friends. Level his tower. Wouldn't that be the easiest way to end all this?*

The Entity's words were enticing, hypnotic, but Sarah resisted.

No! Just send me back. I'm not giving in to you.

The Entity chuckled. *I would have been disappointed if you had. One word of warning, however... No being has communion with me and leaves unchanged. Great power is yours, but one day you will use it against your friends. One day you will serve me.*

That's never going to happen! Sarah exclaimed as the tentacles of light withdrew and she spun into a deeper darkness. Echoing in the distance, the voice of the Entity called after her...

Until next time...Sarah...

Suddenly, she had the sensation of falling again and she flailed uselessly with her arms and legs. Pain re-entered the world. And cold. A huge, dark shape descended towards her. Sarah opened her mouth to scream and choked on ice-water...

* * *

Alex paced around the hole at the centre of the crater, staring into the impenetrable water. It had been minutes since Balthus exploded from the dark water and raced across the ice back towards the Spire. Sarah had not reappeared, however.

"She's been down there too long," Yuri said softly, laying a hand on the boy's shoulder. "Nothing can survive in that cold."

Alex kept his eyes fixed on the water. "She's alive. I can feel it."

At that moment Laika burst forth from the hole and leaped onto the ice. Sarah lay slumped, her coat gripped in the robot dog's teeth.

"Sarah!" Alex cried, running over as Laika placed her gently on the ice.

"Good girl, Laika!" Yuri exclaimed, patting his dog on the head. Sarah stirred and pushed herself into a sitting position as the others crowded around in concern.

"It's okay," she said, spluttering water. "I'm okay."

"Incredible," Yuri said as Sarah placed a hand on Laika's flank and pulled herself up. He pulled her soaked coat off her body and draped his own over her shoulders.

Sarah turned to the man and asked weakly, "What caused your change of heart?"

It was hard to see in the growing darkness, but Alex swore for a moment he could make out a reddening of the man's cheeks.

"You can thank her," Yuri replied, indicating Laika, who was nuzzling Sarah's hand with the side of her head. "Wouldn't shut up whining all day. In the end I decided to come for a bit of peace."

"We're glad you did," Alex told him. "Both of you."

Yuri looked with concern at Sarah, who was shaking uncontrollably. "We need to get you back to my hideout. You'll freeze to death out here."

Sarah put her arms in the coat and wrapped it around herself. "No time for that. We carry on to the village."

Yuri was about to argue, but he saw the determination in the girl's eyes. "Okay, okay. It's probably just as close. Come on, Laika. Let's get the sledge."

Laika bounded after her master.

"What happened down there?" Alex asked, helping Sarah back across the crater. "You were gone for minutes. We were sure you were dead."

"I think I was dead for a while." Sarah looked round and saw a strange light over the side of the crater. It took her a moment to realize that it was in fact the Spire – instead now it appeared to be glowing in the night. She could see ribbons of psychic energy emanating from the tower into the sky. The vision was clearer and sharper than anything she had seen before and she remembered the words of the Entity:

No being has communion with me and leaves unchanged.

"What is it?" Alex asked, concerned by the distant look in her eyes as she stared back at the Spire.

"Things are different," she said softly. "I feel different. The Entity told me something down there."

"What?" Alex asked, but Laika reappeared over the edge of the crater before Sarah could answer. She now had a harness fitted over her neck and shoulders which was attached to a metal sledge. Yuri waved from his position at the head of the sledge.

"This is the fastest way to travel out here," Yuri cried as the sledge pulled up and they jumped on. "Laika has the pulling power of ten huskies."

Shivering madly, Sarah pulled a heavy fur over herself as the sledge moved off again – it was surprisingly warm. With another cry from Yuri, the sledge cut across the crater in the direction of the mountains.

31

The village was made up of about thirty single-storey wooden buildings of varying sizes arranged around a large courtyard. In the centre of this area stood a group of squat yellow vehicles with tracks for wheels – transport designed for the icy terrain of Chukotka. The buildings were dark and deserted, with the doors of some still standing open from when they had been abandoned. At the back of the village, a small landing strip had been fashioned on the ice and an antiquated-looking four-seater aircraft stood at one end.

Laika pulled the sledge into the centre of this area and stopped with a command from Yuri.

"This place really is a ghost town," Alex said as he jumped off the sledge and looked around. Wind howled through the gaps between the buildings and the only light was from the moon rising low above the surrounding mountains, giving the place an eerie feel.

Sarah rose from the sledge also, keeping the blanket wrapped around her shoulders. She shivered and Alex looked at her pale skin with concern.

"Are you okay?"

She nodded. "Let's just find the communications gear."

Yuri pointed to the largest building in the village. "The town hall," he said by way of explanation. He looked back at Laika as they set off. "Keep watch, girl."

Laika gave a howl, but stayed put.

The door to the hut Yuri called the *town hall* was unlocked. Yuri reached for the light switch as they entered, but predictably there was no electricity. The Russian reached for a torch from his belt and shone it around the interior, which was a single open area filled with plastic folding chairs, some of them overturned, and a stage at the far end. The place looked as if it had been set up for a meeting, but no one had turned up.

Yuri pointed the torch at a desk in the corner and they started over.

"Looks like Makarov wasn't taking any chances," Yuri groaned as they stopped before the desk.

The communications set-up of the village had been state of the art: a bank of satellite phones, three computers with high-speed internet link-up and webcams, all courtesy of Makarov Industries. Now this equipment was smashed and strewn across the floor. The shattered hard-drives of the computers bore the unmistakable slash-marks of robowolf claws. Clearly Makarov didn't want anyone calling the outside world.

"I told you this would be a wasted trip," Yuri went on. "We should return to my hideout before the dawn comes. Makarov will send more of his hunters."

Sarah took the torch from his hand and shone it around the lonely interior of the meeting hall. She held the beam on a door to the right of the stage marked *Danger* and looked at Yuri questioningly.

"The equipment store," he explained and removed a mini-crowbar from his tool-belt. "Perhaps there's something useful in there."

Sarah and Alex watched as he tore the padlock away with the crowbar. As the door swung open, Sarah angled the torch into the room, illuminating racks of tools, dynamite, C4 explosive and detonators.

"Wow," said Alex. "There must be enough explosives here to level the Spire."

Yuri laughed and shook his head. "Hardly."

Sarah stepped past him and ran a hand over a box of detonators. "Maybe we can't bring down the whole building, but I bet there's enough here to blow that meteorite fragment back to wherever it came from."

Yuri looked at her. "What would that achieve?"

"That's where Makarov gets his power, isn't it?"

"You're right, Sarah," Alex said with a nod. "The meteorite is Makarov's link to the Entity. Destroy the fragment and we destroy that link."

"And his enhanced powers," Sarah added.

Yuri shook his head sceptically. "Even if that's true, how do you plan to get back inside the Spire? Makarov will have an army of robowolves guarding the base."

Sarah thought for a moment. "How about that plane sitting at the back of the village. Can you fly it?"

"The supply plane?" Yuri said. "I can fly, but that machine hasn't been used in months. It probably won't even start."

"You built a robot from spare parts, Yuri," Sarah replied impatiently. "You can get a plane working, I'm sure. Get us in the air and I'll get us in the Spire—"

She stopped talking as a wave of dizziness swept over her and she had to lean on Alex for support.

"Don't feel so good," she said as she fought to stay conscious. The effects of her near-death encounter with the Entity and the extreme cold of the water under the ice were finally winning the battle.

"Yuri, help me!" Alex said and struggled to hold Sarah on her feet. "She's going to pass out..."

That was the last Sarah heard.

Half an hour later, Alex lay back in a bed in one of the empty cabins. The mattress was surprisingly soft and the thick blankets amazingly snug after the cold, damp trek across the plain. In the corner of the room a coal burner flickered, providing heat that would last them through till dawn, Yuri had assured. He looked at the glowing light cast around the wooden walls and felt his eyelids become heavy. He would have surely fallen asleep within seconds, but decided to take one last check on Sarah.

She lay in the bed across the room from him, where they had covered her after she had collapsed from exhaustion, her body covered by a thick set of blankets. All that was visible was her face, which had a softness in sleep that wasn't always apparent when she was awake. Alex guessed she'd been through a lot – during his time with her and the others, he'd pieced together the stories of their first encounter with HIDRA and their life on the run in Australia. He'd had it tough with his Uncle Pete, but it had been a walk in the park compared to Sarah's journey.

"I'm sorry I got you into this," he said as he stood over her, thinking of how he had been the one to bring them to Makarov. *How could I have ever trusted him?* he thought, but already knew the answer. He'd wanted to trust Makarov – because back in Australia he needed someone to trust. One thing was for sure, he was going to make it right – by helping Sarah Williams rescue her brother and the others from the Spire.

"Enjoy your rest," he said. "We've got a war to fight tomorrow."

With that he went to his own bed, got under the covers and was asleep within less than a minute. Across the room, Sarah Williams smiled in her sleep. Although she was outwardly unconscious, her mind was in fact incredibly active...

...reaching out, imagining her thoughts passing through the walls of the cabin and out across the deserted centre of the village. She projects further, back through

the mountain pass, across the plain and over the silent buildings of the copper mine. Finally, the structure of the Spire hoves into view, massive and alien amidst the empty landscape – a finger pointing towards the night sky.

Now Sarah senses the unmistakable influence of the Entity. The alien is projecting an invisible shield around the entire tower, blocking all her attempts to communicate with those inside, and vice versa. Cautiously, she probes the barriers thrown up by the powerful being's mind, aware that if she is not careful the Entity will be alerted to her presence. At last, she finds an area of weakness and pushes into the layers of alien thought, like walking through thick fog with her arms outstretched, expecting at any moment to come up against something solid.

She reaches into the tower and searches upwards, looking for the one mind that she knows is connected enough with her to communicate from such a distance. She finds her brother lying asleep in a room she has never seen before – a hard looking place that reminds her more of a jail cell than the bedrooms they were first given by Makarov. Reaching out to Robert, she makes contact with him...

"Robert."

His eyes snap open, but he isn't awake yet. Robert looks around and is surprised to find himself standing on *a vast, snow-covered plain rather than lying in the bed he collapsed into less than an hour before. A harsh winter sun shines down from the ice-blue sky. Despite the freezing appearance of the surroundings, he feels no cold.*

"Where is this?" he asks, wonderingly.

"A place where our minds can meet," Sarah says, approaching him across the snow. "A constructed reality."

Robert turns and runs to her, throwing his arms around his sister. "Sarah! Makarov said you were dead."

"I was. For a while. Now I'm back."

Robert looks around and marvels at the reality Sarah has created for them in her mind. "It looks so lifelike. Can Makarov see us?"

"I'm shielding us from him," Sarah replies. "He hasn't sensed us yet." She looked at Robert with concern, noting his sunken eyes – he looked dead on his feet. "How are you doing?"

Her brother smiles weakly. "Things have been tough here. Makarov wants us to swear some oath of allegiance to the Entity. He wants us to give up our powers to it. We're not giving in, but it's getting hard."

Sarah touches his shoulders. "Listen. You do what you have to do to survive. Alex and I are coming to get you out of there."

She quickly tells him about her plan to destroy the meteorite fragment.

"The meteor storm is timed to hit midday tomorrow," she continues. "We've got to stop it somehow."

"Destroy the beacon?"

Sarah shakes her head. "That's not enough. Even if the signal is shut down, the meteorites will still be headed for earth. We have to take control of the beacon and use it to deflect the storm."

"Just tell me what you want us to do," Robert says with determination.

Sarah smiles at her brother and strokes a hand through his hair. "I just need you and the others to hold on a little longer for me. Look for the dawn tomorrow – we'll be coming. Do you think you can break out of your cell?"

Robert bites his lip. "Makarov has us guarded by Ilya and about a hundred robowolves."

"All I need you to do is distract his attention while we get close to the Spire."

"What are you going to do?"

"I'm coming after you. I made a promise I'd never leave you, didn't I?"

Robert grins. "You'd better keep it."

"I know things have been hard these last four months, Robert," she goes on. "But as soon as we get out of this it's going to be easier. I know I've made mistakes as a leader—"

"You're a great leader," Robert interrupts. "You saved us from Bright. You knew that Makarov wasn't right from the very beginning. You were right to be suspicious."

"I know. But it's time we started trusting some people again. Like Rachel Andersen."

"You're going to contact HIDRA?" Robert asks with surprise.

"If we can't defeat Makarov they're the only people who know enough about the fall virus to—"

Sarah stops talking as she becomes aware of another, powerful presence in the empty world she has created. Looking round, she sees a pair of eyes in the sky to the east – wide and blazing with hate.

Makarov.

"Get out of here," Sarah orders her brother, shielding her message from the Russian's prying mind. "Tell the others. Tomorrow at dawn we bring Makarov's tower down."

Robert begins to protest, but his sister gives him a look like their mum used to when she wasn't going to take any debate.

"Be careful," he says, planting a kiss on her cheek before fading quickly away. Sarah turns to the horizon, *realizing she doesn't have much longer before the shield blocks her out again. She returns her attention to the Spire itself. For the first time she can sense more than just the minds of Robert and the others – now she can read the electronic thoughts of the robowolves, the commands emanating from the central computer and the beacon signal itself, beaming out deep into space.*

Her power has grown.

She goes deeper into the computer system, pushing through command instructions and programs in search of some way to control the beacon.

"Sarah Williams! How are you not dead?"

Makarov's voice cuts through her mind like a laser, but she ignores it. Already the walls are coming down, shutting her out of the Spire. In the final seconds, she manages to take control of the computer's communication system to send a single, desperate message...

32

Makarov paced back and forth before the illuminated control desk in the meteorite chamber.

"Security has been breached," he hissed. "How did this happen?"

The computer answered emotionlessly, "The girl, Sarah Williams, managed to break through our firewall using her mental powers—"

"I know what she did!" Makarov snapped back. "Is the meteor beacon still operational?"

"She was unable to access the beacon control," the

computer answered. "However, she subverted the communications array for a period of forty-six seconds."

"To what purpose?"

"To transmit an audio message towards a ship in the Bering Sea. The vessel's identification code lists it as the HIDRA Ship *Ulysses*, a Nimitz-class aircraft carrier. The ship is currently three hundred kilometres off the southern coast of Chukotka and on an approach course. It is safe to assume the signal reached them."

Makarov took a deep breath. "Are we in striking distance of their position?"

"Negative. The *Ulysses* is not equipped with long-range missile capability. It does however carry a fleet of thirty hovercopters capable of staging an attack on our location."

"Recommendation?"

"Use the beacon to block communications in a three-hundred kilometre radius. Launch the drone fleet for a pre-emptive strike on the *Ulysses* to knock out their airborne capability."

Makarov smiled. "Good. And send the ship to the bottom of the ocean while you're at it."

"It shall be done, sir."

Makarov watched as the computer activated the fleet of fifty drone-fighters on the 10th floor of the Spire. The drones were pilotless jets especially designed to defend the Spire against an airborne attack. In less than half a minute the launch doors on the 10th floor had opened and the first wave of drones blasted off into the night sky.

Makarov turned at a growl from the door to the control chamber. Balthus nudged Octavio into the chamber and then retreated to the entrance.

"What is it?" Octavio asked. "The others are getting suspicious. I think they know I haven't been suffering the same—"

"Robert Williams has been in contact with his sister," Makarov interrupted angrily. "He continues to plot against me even though it places the lives of your entire group at risk."

"How could he do that?" Octavio replied. "She's dead, isn't she?"

Makarov slammed his palms on the control deck. "Somehow she escaped!"

Octavio backed away, but stopped as Balthus growled dangerously from the doorway.

"I have reached the end of my patience with Robert Williams and his sister," Makarov hissed. In the LCD glow of the command screen, he suddenly looked as ancient as a mummified corpse. "You have until tomorrow to persuade the others to submit to me. Do you understand?"

"I understand," Octavio answered, trying to disguise the fear in his voice. He thought that Major Bright was the meanest person he'd ever met, but he had nothing on Makarov.

"Now, get back to your cell and get the others in line," the Russian snarled, "or at dawn tomorrow I'm going to have them thrown off the top floor of the Spire one at a time. Starting with Robert Williams."

In the flight briefing room of the *Ulysses*, Rachel Andersen stood before thirty hovercopter pilots who were waiting expectantly to find out why they had been called together at two a.m.

"We received a distress signal," she told the group.

Commander Craig hit a control and the audio message that had been sent to them from the Spire began to play out over the speakers.

"This is Sarah Williams to HIDRA," the message began. "Nikolai Makarov is holding my friends hostage. He is also in contact with an alien power that is sending a meteor storm towards earth. Tomorrow at dawn I am going to launch an attack on Makarov's tower to rescue my friends and try to deflect the storm. You must send forces to support us. If the meteor storm hits, the entire world will fall under the control of the Entity." There was a pause. "Rachel, if you're listening – we need your help..."

The message went to static and a murmur went up around the assembled pilots. Rachel silenced them by raising her hand.

"The meteor storm is scheduled to hit us in less than eight hours," she said. "This is our chance to deflect it from earth. Commander."

She stepped aside as Craig addressed the pilots. "We're launching an immediate attack on Makarov's tower. It's located on the Chuckchi Peninsula, almost three hundred kilometres from here."

Behind him a map appeared on the big screen showing the location of the Spire in relation to the HS *Ulysses* in the Bering Sea.

"There's just one complication," he went on. "We've detected a series of aircraft launched from Makarov's position. We can only assume Makarov has found out about the distress signal and has launched a counterstrike against us. We estimate at least fifty jets."

"He's got his own air force?" one of the pilots asked incredulously. "Who is this guy?"

"He's the guy we have to take out to save the world, Lieutenant," Craig snapped back. "That's all you need to know right now."

"What about backup, sir?" one of the pilots asked. "The Russians have a base in Siberia."

Rachel shook her head. "All our communications have been blocked since we received Sarah Williams's message. Makarov has technology in advance of our own."

Again there was a murmur around the room.

"Okay, okay," Rachel Andersen said, leaning over the podium. "Enough talking about it. Your primary objective is to protect the *Ulysses* and take out that airborne force. Secondary objective is Makarov. We need to take control of that beacon or level the tower."

Commander Craig nodded. "Any questions?" There was silence. "Okay, get to your ships!"

Makarov kneeled before the spinning meteorite fragment in the centre of the chamber. The light glowed brighter, indicating connection with the Entity.

"Master. The storm is only hours away. Our time is at hand."

The voice of the alien boomed in reply, "Yet you have

not neutralized the threat against us. Sarah Williams is not in your control."

"She evaded my robowolves on the ice—"

"You attempted to kill her against my orders!" the Entity interrupted harshly. "I was clear she is not to be harmed yet."

Makarov bowed his head a little lower. "I do not understand, master. Why do you need this girl—"

"Do not try to second-guess my intentions," the alien snapped. "You are alive only because of my grace."

"Forgive me, master," Makarov whispered, feeling the power drain from him. He had to place one hand against the floor to stop from pitching forwards. "I beg you, give me the strength to defeat our enemies one last time. Let me prove myself worthy to lead."

"Sarah Williams is coming after you. She will try to take control of the beacon and deflect the storm."

Makarov looked into the beam, eyes wide. "Give me the power to defeat them, master!"

The Entity laughed. "Touch the beam, Makarov. Drink of my deepest powers. But be warned, you might not like the result."

For once, Makarov hesitated as he reached out with his hand. The light around the meteorite was intensely bright – like staring into the sun. Then he looked at the skin on the back of his hand – wrinkled and white, ancient. He plunged his fingers into the beam...

And was engulfed by the pain of thousands of volts of energy passing through him, stronger than anything he had experienced before. Makarov screamed and looked down at his arm. Blue fire leaped towards his shoulder and surrounded his body. He screamed again.

"Master!"

And then it was over. Makarov staggered back from the beam, blinking rapidly. He felt different. Looking around, he caught a glimpse of his reflection in one of the computer screens: wide, staring eyes like reflective discs; elongated arms with ten-centimetre long claws protruding from his fingers; a gaping mouth. He no longer looked human. He looked like something new. Something...

Alien.

"Master, what have you done to me?" he said quietly.

"I have made you stronger," the Entity's voice replied from the light. "Ready to rule our new world. Do you not feel strong, earthling?"

Makarov flexed his clawed fingers and felt the power coursing through them. Every millimetre of his body was now in tune with the alien force.

He grinned.

"I *am* strong, master."

"Then make ready," the Entity replied. "The final battle is at hand."

33

The dawn brought a sky the colour of gunmetal and a watery sun shining across the desolate plain. It also brought a team of forty robowolves, tearing through the snow towards the miners' village. They ran as a pack – a diamond-shaped formation moving with unstoppable ferocity to destroy every last living thing in their path.

Crouched against the side of the mountains behind the village, Yuri watched through a set of ancient binoculars as the last of the robowolves entered the village.

"Do you think that's all of them?" Sarah asked at his side.

"I think it's enough," Yuri replied, looking round at her. The girl showed no signs of her ordeal from the night before. "How are you feeling?"

"Like I could take on the world today," she replied. "Let's do it."

Yuri produced a black box from his side. The box was a trigger and linked to the C4 explosives they'd placed around the village below. Yuri wound the priming handle on the side of the box several times and passed it to Sarah.

"I'll let you do the honours," he said, before glancing round at Alex, who was also crouched on the hillside. "You might want to cover your ears. This is going to be noisy."

Sarah pressed the red button on the top of the box and the explosives Yuri had placed around the village under the cover of darkness exploded. The buildings were ripped apart, burning splinters of wood flying high into the morning air. Simultaneously, C4 charges buried under the central courtyard overturned the earth itself with a deafening *wumpf*. Amidst all of this, the metal bodies of the forty robowolves were cast about, torn limb from limb and then melted in the extreme heat.

Yuri gave a whistle. "Well, there goes the neighbourhood."

Lowering the binoculars, Sarah looked at him. "Now let's go do the same to Makarov's house."

At the Russian's side, Laika gave a low growl, showing her readiness for the fight. Yuri grinned and said, "It will be a pleasure."

"Hey!" Robert yelled, hammering his fist on the door to the cell. "Louise is sick! You have to get her some help!"

After a moment he heard footsteps on the other side. He looked round to the others. *They're coming. You all know what to do.*

The door slid open to reveal Ilya, accompanied as always by a pair of robowolves. Through the windows behind him, the dawn was breaking, hard and clear.

"What is it?" Ilya demanded, looking into the cell.

Robert indicated Louise, who made a good show of clutching her stomach on her bunk. "She's been sick all night and it's getting worse. You have to take her to—"

"Don't listen to him!" Octavio interrupted, jumping up and pushing Robert to one side. He looked at the ceiling and spoke to the concealed microphones hidden there. "It's part of an escape plan, master! A trick!"

Ilya backed away from the doorway and the two robowolves moved in to block any attempt at escape.

"Damn you, Octavio!" Robert hissed, advancing towards the older boy, who jumped back towards the door.

"I'm not going to let you or your sister get us all killed," Octavio protested. "You'll all thank me for this in the end!"

Before Robert could respond, Ilya held his hand up. "Stay back! All of you!" He then turned to Octavio. "The master wants you to come to the 153rd floor."

Breathing a sigh of relief, Octavio moved to the door and squeezed past the robowolves. Inside the cell, Robert and the others looked across at him accusingly.

"Are you sure this is what you want to do, brother?" Nestor asked grimly.

Octavio looked at him over the backs of the robowolves. "You know it is."

"Then do it."

Taking a step away, Octavio raised his hands towards the robots and reached out with his mind. Snatching the robowolves into the air before they could react, he whipped his arms around and they flew towards the window at high speed. The robowolves smashed through the toughened glass and pitched out over the side of the building. The corridor flooded with howling wind. For a second, Ilya watched, open-mouthed at what had just happened. Then he looked round at Octavio.

"You're going to regret that," he said dangerously.

"No he's not," Louise replied, jumping through the doorway and throwing Ilya back against the wall with the power of her mind. The long-haired kid's head took a heavy hit and he slid down to the floor, unconscious. Nestor, Robert and Wei emerged from the cell as doors at either end of the corridor slid open. Robowolves tore towards them from both directions.

"Take care of them!" Nestor yelled above the air that was rushing in through the shattered window.

Wei stepped forward and let loose a stream of fire from his hands that engulfed three of the robowolves. As they ran through the flames, Octavio snatched them up and sent them hurtling through the hole in the side of the building, still burning. Nestor turned his attention to the two attackers approaching from the other direction. He sent a blast of tornado force air down the corridor towards them. As the glass side of the Spire exploded outwards, the robowolves were tossed helplessly into space. Louise ran to the edge and watched as they arced through the air to their destruction far below.

"Cool," she said.

"Good work, Octavio," Nestor said, slapping his brother on the shoulder. "You were born to be a double agent."

"You have to get out of here," Ilya said weakly from his position on the floor. "He'll be sending more robowolves for you. He has an army." They all looked round at the Russian boy. The blankness in his expression was gone now and they sensed that once more the control Makarov exerted over him had been broken. Robert kneeled before him.

"Find the other workers from the Spire," Robert ordered. "Free them from Makarov's control if you can and take them to the sleeper chamber. We'll be there to help after we've taken care of Makarov."

Ilya nodded and pulled himself to his feet. "Thank you," he said as he ran in the direction of the stairs. Robert looked round at the others.

"Makarov is on the 153rd floor. That's where we need to get to."

"Easier said than done," Octavio shouted above the wind. "Makarov isn't just going to let us walk up there."

Nestor nodded. "I know. But we have to reach that beacon. Or tear this tower apart getting there."

As they ran out of the corridor, Robert stole a look across the snowy landscape and thought he made out the shape of buildings on the other side of the distant mountains.

He hoped Sarah arrived soon.

34

Sarah held on for dear life as the tiny supply plane from the village was buffeted around by the harsh winds that swept the empty Chukotkan landscape. She looked round and saw Alex looking a little green in the back seat. Beside her, Yuri controlled the small aircraft expertly, eyes locked on the Spire as it loomed ahead of them.

"No more robowolves," Sarah said, scanning the empty plain below them anxiously. "Do you think we destroyed them all when we blew up the village?"

Yuri said, "Don't underestimate Makarov's resources. Last time I was inside the Spire he was building an army. It looked like he was gearing up to take on the world. I just hope Laika is okay down there." The robodog had been too large to fit inside the small aircraft, so Yuri had sent her towards the Spire on foot – something that she had not been happy about. Seeing the Russian's concern for his pet, Sarah gave him a reassuring pat on the arm.

Ahead, the Spire stood alone amidst the flatness of the ice desert. There was no sign of HIDRA. No hovercopters or jets in the air. Sarah realized that it was up to them – they were the last chance to take out Makarov before the storm hit.

A glass section on the upper levels of the Spire exploded outwards. They watched as fire burst forth from the gap and a body was thrown out of the tower. No one breathed for a second as the dark object fell the length of the Spire, hit the angled glass of the lower levels and spun off.

"It's just a robowolf," Alex said with relief as the body hit the ground.

Sarah nodded. "Looks like Robert and the others are keeping Makarov distracted up there. We need to get inside as quickly as possible."

"Where's this landing strip you were talking about?"

Yuri asked. The Spire was getting so close now it filled the front window of the plane.

"Hold us level around the middle of the tower," Sarah ordered and Yuri pulled left on the joystick, sending the plane round in a wide circle of the Spire.

Sarah closed her eyes and reached out with her mind. This close, the psychic energy used to power the Spire's computer systems shone like a star, incredibly clear to her now that her mind's eye had been opened. She sensed the sleepers in the caskets, the meteorite fragment spinning in its chamber, robowolves in their dozens rushing towards one of the upper levels. *Focus,* Sarah told herself. The amount of information threatened to overwhelm her brain. However, she managed to ride the stream, finding the thing she was looking for: the controls for the landing strip on the 70th floor. She sent an order to simultaneously open the door and extend the strip.

"Something's happening!" Yuri exclaimed and she opened her eyes. As the plane came round for another pass, they made out the large section of wall sliding open on the side of the Spire. Yuri's eyes widened as the landing strip began to extend outwards like a long finger.

"Unbelievable! You're telling me Makarov lands a plane on that?"

"Just take us down fast!" Sarah exclaimed. "Before Makarov overrides the runway control!"

"This plane is not designed to stop in such a short distance!" Yuri protested. "Even if I manage to land on that strip, we'll crash right into the far wall of the tower."

Sarah gave him a hard look. "What choice do we have?"

The Russian thought it over for a second, before giving his head a shake. "Oh well, we've all got to die sometime. Brace yourself for a bumpy landing."

With that, he pulled back on the joystick, sending the plane into a climb away from the building, before bringing it back round in a wide arc. Through the windscreen, Sarah watched the Spire come into line as Yuri pushed forward on the stick, putting them on an angle of descent towards the runway. Then he did something unexpected – he reached down and killed the plane engine. With a sputter, the propeller came to a stop.

"What are you doing?" Sarah said.

"We're going to glide in," Yuri snapped back. "Only chance not to totally demolish this plane."

Sure enough, the plane continued to glide towards the side of the Spire. As they drew closer, the runway began to look alarmingly short. A second later, the wheels of the small plane hit the runway with a jolt. Yuri fought the controls as he pushed the brakes to full. With a screech of rubber, the plane continued to hurtle towards the open side of the building.

"We're going to hit Makarov's jet!" Alex cried as they sped towards the black aircraft sitting before them. Then, without warning, something hit the front of their plane hard – an emergency net that sprang from the floor at the end of the runway. Sarah and Yuri were thrown forwards as their vehicle was brought to an abrupt stop, the force tearing off both wings with a screech of metal. The plane – travelling too fast and too flimsy for the impact against the netting – jackknifed and rolled over twice, completely tangled in the mesh. Finally, it came to a stop in the centre of the circular room, upside down, just metres from the stealth jet.

Untangling herself from her seat belt, Sarah lowered herself onto the ceiling of the plane (which had become the floor) and reached over to help Alex free as well.

"Are you okay?" she asked.

"I think so," Alex replied, before looking round at their pilot. "Nice landing."

"Let's get out of here," Yuri said and pushed open the door of the plane with a grunt, having to force it against the netting. They staggered out and looked back at the remains of the plane: both wings had sheared off and the propeller was a twisted mess.

Three robowolves tore out of the shadows at the side of the stealth jet, jumping at Sarah, gleaming claws extended. As they leaped, she raised her hand.

"No."

The robots twisted in mid-air and crashed to the ground, jerking around as if they were being electrocuted. For a few seconds longer, they continued to thrash madly, before coming to a rest, the red light of their eyes slowly dimming to black.

"How did you do that?" Alex marvelled.

"I'm not sure," Sarah said, looking around the room. The walls seemed to glow with an energy only she could see. The Spire was hers to control now, as were the electronic brains of the robowolves. She walked to the control panel and passed a hand over it. "Computer, where are my friends?"

"Currently on the 141st floor," the electronic voice replied. The jungle level, Sarah recalled.

"Call the lift, please."

"Nikolai Makarov has ordered a lock down of all—"

Sarah snapped, "Call the lift."

"Yes, Sarah," the computer answered, a dull, submissive tone coming to its voice. "Is there anything else?"

"Where is Makarov?"

"On the 153rd floor."

"Give him a message from me," Sarah said. "Tell him I'm in charge now."

"Yes, Sarah."

"And tell him I'm coming for him."

"Yes, Sarah."

The lift doors pinged open and Sarah turned to Yuri. "Come on."

Alex gave her a look. "You're not messing around, are you?"

"I'm just getting started," she replied with a grin as Yuri came up with the bag of explosives slung over his shoulder. "I'm going to take care of Makarov then get control of the meteor beacon. You two are in charge of releasing the sleepers and taking care of the meteorite fragment."

Behind her, the lift doors opened and she stepped inside.

"Good luck," Alex said as the doors closed on her and the lift began to ascend. He looked round at Yuri. "Let's take the stairs. The meteorite chamber is just a few floors below us."

35

The airborne battle against Makarov's drone fighters had raged around the HS *Ulysses*. The drones were light, flimsy aircraft equipped with basic weaponry, but they were fast moving and highly agile. The more sturdy hovercopters were having a hard time against the larger force. Although they had engaged the drones closer to the Chukotkan coastline, they had been driven back towards the *Ulysses*. The hovercopter lead pilot barked a warning to the bridge as another drone broke through their protective formation and hurtled towards the deck, kamikaze-style. It exploded in a ball of flame, metres from the flight tower of the *Ulysses*.

As the explosion rocked the lower levels of the ship, Rachel Andersen joined Commander Craig in a room adjacent to the observation cell holding Major Bright. Through a two-way mirror it was possible to see the giant man handcuffed to a metal chair in the centre of the empty room. He looked directly at the mirrored glass on his side, eyes blazing with anger, as if trying to make out who was in the chamber beyond. Rachel walked to the glass, gave their prisoner the once-over and sighed.

"This had better be good, Commander," she said. "I don't have time to waste on this madman and neither do you."

"I want to put Major Bright into the fight against Makarov, Colonel," Commander Craig replied. "Those drones are keeping our hovercopters too busy to get anywhere near the Russian coast, let alone the Spire. We can't provide backup for Sarah and the others. But Bright can."

Rachel shook her head. "Are you serious? The minute we let Bright off his leash, he'll turn on us. You know he can't be trusted."

"Except there's a more dangerous enemy out there now. An enemy that doesn't care about the major's plans to take over the world – it's too busy with its own. Present Bright with the choice between rotting in that cell and the chance to get involved in the fight, sir. He's a soldier. He'll take it."

Despite the craziness of the scheme, Rachel played along. "And how do you propose getting him to the Spire?"

"He can teleport large distances, right, Colonel?"

"Only when he has serum," Rachel corrected. "He used the last of his supply in Melbourne."

Commander Craig gave an embarrassed cough. "I always assumed some samples of the super-serum might have fallen into your possession…"

Rachel gave him a hard look and he stopped talking.

"I'm sorry, Colonel, I've overstepped the mark," he began, but stopped talking as Rachel removed two vials from her jacket. "Is that what I think it is?"

"Two samples of the serum survived the destruction of Colonel Moss's experiment." She turned them over in her hand. "I should have destroyed them myself, but just couldn't bring myself to do it. They were so hard come by. And at such cost."

Craig smiled slightly. "And do you always carry them around in your pocket, sir?"

Rachel looked back at the glass, her expression

unreadable. "Okay, so I had the same idea as you, Commander. Bright could mean the difference between winning and losing this one. But once he's in the Spire, how do we know he isn't going to swap sides on us?"

"He might be crazy, but he's still human," Craig replied. "That's got to be enough incentive for him to side with us rather than some alien monster."

"And once the battle is over?"

"No two ways about it, he'll try to escape at the very least. That's why I want to go along for the ride." He patted the pistol on his hip. "Make sure he behaves himself. Even if he doesn't, he'll act as another problem for Makarov to worry about – give Sarah and the others the chance to get the upper hand."

"Don't make the mistake of underestimating him, Commander," Rachel said. "Or have you forgotten what happened in the desert?"

"Oh, I haven't forgotten, sir," Craig said darkly. "I won't let him off the hook a second time, I promise."

"I don't like sending my men on a suicide mission."

"Unless they volunteer for one."

Rachel studied the Commander and saw he was deadly serious. An explosion shook the ship as another of the kamikaze drones made it through the hovercopters.

"Don't make me regret this, Commander." With that, she walked to the door into the cell and threw it open.

Major Bright looked up and grinned. "Well, well, it's Colonel Dr. Andersen. I was beginning to think you'd forgotten about me. Even your interrogator seems to have lost interest. I haven't seen him in days."

"We've had better things to do than worry about you, believe me," Rachel replied as she entered, closely followed by Commander Craig. "I've got a proposal."

Rachel held up the two vials of serum, along with a syringe-gun from her pocket. Bright's eyes widened at the sight and he fidgeted in his chair, pulling against the restrain on his left wrist irritatedly.

"What do you want from me?" he said.

Rachel noticed the beads of sweat that appeared on his forehead and realized that he would do anything she asked in return for another shot of the super-serum. Was it really so addictive? she wondered. Or was it just the power that he craved?

Bright leaned forward and licked his lips impatiently. "Well?"

"I want you to do what you do best," Rachel said, and laid the syringe-gun on the table before him. "Cause some havoc."

* * *

Alex led Yuri into the circular chamber containing the rows of sleeper modules.

"The meteorite chamber is up those stairs," he said, but Yuri was already on his way, opening the bag containing the explosives as he went.

Alex made to follow him, but stopped as he saw Ilya appear from beside one of the sleeper caskets. The Russian kid held up a hand.

"It's okay," he said. "I'm free of Makarov's control. His attention is too distracted to notice."

Alex nodded and approached the casket Ilya was standing beside. The boy indicated the bearded man inside the module. "It's my father. I came here to wake him."

Ilya reached for the *door open* control on the casket, but Alex placed a hand on his arm.

"No!" he said. "Not until we've deflected the meteor storm. If we unhook the sleepers, the beacon will shut down."

A pained look passed over Ilya's face, but Alex said to him reassuringly, "Just a little longer."

A sound from the corner of the sleeper chamber made Alex look round, and he saw a group of the tower workers huddled together.

"I freed them from Makarov's control," Ilya explained. "With my mind. Did I do good?"

"Yes," Alex said. "Tell them as soon as Sarah and the others take control of the beacon, we'll wake the sleepers and get out of here."

Ilya went off to reassure the women, speaking to them urgently in Russian. Alex just hoped it would be as easy as he had made out.

A tornado raged through the tall trees of the rainforest on the 141st floor. Nestor walked along the jungle floor, arms stretched out before him, blasting robowolves in his path. Beside him, Wei ignited the trees, sending up a wall of fire that began to spread though the rainforest, fanned by the howling tornado.

Robert looked around at the others as they fought back robowolves attacking on all sides. They'd become cornered as they fought their way up the stairwell and forced onto the 141st floor. Now the ground was littered with smashed components from the machines, but still they came – a seemingly endless supply from the depths of Makarov's lair.

"We don't have time for this!" he yelled to the others. "We have to get off this level!"

Octavio sent a robowolf sailing through the air into the distance with a push of his hand. "Yeah, but how?"

"They're blocking our way back to the stairs!" Louise added as an attacker imploded before her. Robert looked round and saw the red eyes of robowolves moving in the trees near the stairwell entrance. Despite the dampness of the atmosphere, the fire Wei had started was spreading fast, sending up a choking black smoke.

Over here!

They all looked round at the familiar voice in their heads. Sarah approached through the trees.

"Watch out!" Nestor cried as a robowolf jumped at her, teeth and claws bared. Sarah showed little concern, however, giving it the barest look before the machine crashed at her feet, motionless.

"Sarah!" Robert cried and ran towards her, throwing his arms around her as the others joined them.

"How did you trash that wolf?" Octavio asked, looking down at the motionless body of the robot.

"Magic," she replied with a wink. "Makarov's on the top floor. Let's take him out."

"But the computer has the lifts locked down," Nestor protested as she grabbed Robert's hand and began leading the group through the smoke.

"Not for me!" she yelled over her shoulder. Sure enough, the lift doors were standing open for them as they crossed the final few metres.

"I knew you'd come back!" Robert said, looking up at his sister, tears forming in his eyes. She put her arms around him and gave him a hug.

After the chaos of the battle, everyone breathed a sigh of relief as the doors closed on them and the lift car began to ascend. A few seconds later, the doors opened onto the 153rd floor. The grassy area was deserted, silent. For a moment they all looked at the scene, trying to take in the unexpected emptiness.

"I thought Makarov was supposed to be up here," Louise whispered.

Sarah nodded. "Let's be careful."

They stepped out of the lift as a group, Sarah leading the way. As the doors closed behind them, they walked across the grass towards the stone table in the centre. Outside the pyramidal glass ceiling the Chukotkan sky was a brilliant blue. Inside, a strange silence had fallen, relieved only by the synthetic breeze blowing through the leaves of the trees.

It was almost peaceful.

"Where is he?" Nestor asked in frustration.

The silence was broken by a slow handclap from the

trees, then a familiar figure appeared, albeit strangely deformed from the man they knew. Makarov looked bigger, physically stronger than before, but at the same time his body was hunched, as if every muscle in his body was twisted in knots. He regarded them with hungry, staring eyes, like those of a predator, as he approached.

"Well done," he said, giving a final clap as he stopped on the other side of the stone table. "I'm really surprised you made it this far. You certainly put up a good fight. Of course, you've only faced a small proportion of my army so far."

He snapped his fingers and Balthus teleported into existence by his side. Followed by another robowolf. And another. And another.

Sarah and the others looked round wildly as Makarov's robots snapped into existence all around. Within a few seconds, there was a hundred or more. Every pair of robowolf eyes was locked on them with murderous intent. Beside Sarah, Robert and the others slowly sank to their knees on the grass. She was about to order them to fight when she found herself doing the same – unable to control the actions of her own body under the greater power of Makarov's mind. She met his eyes and he sneered at her in triumph.

"So," he spat, "this is how the world ends…"

36

The windswept mountain overlooked the plain of ice upon which the Spire stood. With a squawk of protest, a group of gulls rose into the air as two figures materialized out of nowhere. Commander Craig looked round, disoriented from the effects of the teleport. He held his gun on Bright.

"This isn't Makarov's tower," he said.

"Look over there, flyboy," Major Bright replied sharply, indicating the skyscraper rising in the distance. "Teleporting isn't an accurate science. You're lucky we made it this close."

It had taken three jumps to get to their present location: the first from the interrogation room on the *Ulysses* to the coast of Chukotka, then another into the centre of the peninsula, and the third to their present location. Craig squinted at the building. He estimated it was about twenty kilometres away.

"Teleport us there," he ordered.

"I need another shot of serum."

"No way," Commander Craig replied, looking at Bright with suspicion.

"The teleports have drained my power. If I don't get another shot, we're walking."

Reluctantly, Craig reached inside his jacket and removed the syringe-gun with the final vial. Bright rolled up his sleeve and presented his arm with a grin.

"You'd make a great nurse, Commander Craig."

"How fitting that it should end here, Sarah," Makarov pronounced, waving a hand around the park on the 153rd floor, "where we first met."

Now, with Sarah's team subdued and the robowolves at attention, a strange silence had fallen over the glass pyramid once more. Sarah looked at Makarov's transformed frame with shock and disgust. As he limped before them, he looked like something from a horror movie.

"What did the Entity do to you?" she asked, every word an effort to get out.

Makarov waved a hand. "Just a few upgrades to my psychic ability. One cannot achieve mental perfection without paying a physical cost."

"It's made you into a monster," Robert said at her side.

"I wouldn't expect a child to understand," Makarov spat at him, before turning his attention back to Sarah. "But you. I see you have been in the presence of the master. You have sensed its power. Been transformed in some way by it."

"That thing is pure evil," she said. "It's not too late to break free of its control. Help us turn back the meteors—"

"Silence!" Makarov snapped, swiping a clawed hand in her direction. He regained his composure with some effort. "We should not spoil this moment with argument. After all, we are in the perfect place to view the meteor storm that will herald a new beginning for the human race." He looked up at the sky above the pyramid roof. "Here we can watch the fire raining down on the globe. You are all privileged. You will be here to witness the next stage of our evolution…"

A booming voice from the trees cut through Makarov's words. *"Please!* If I'd thought he was going to torture us all with an election speech, I'd have gotten here sooner."

Makarov's eyes widened as he turned and saw Major Bright standing before the treeline. At his side, Commander Craig rolled into a shooter's stance, his rifle raised.

"I wouldn't do that," Bright said as the commander pulled the trigger...

Makarov raised his hand. The bullet changed direction in the air and flew backwards, ripping through Craig's shoulder. With a cry, the commander hit the ground.

"Thanks," Bright said, looking from his wounded companion to Makarov. "I've been wanting to do that since I met him."

Makarov pointed a finger at the ground. "Kneel before me."

Bright laughed and shook his head, approaching slowly across the grass. "I don't think so. On my way over here, I was actually debating whether we should team up. But now I meet you, I can't see myself partnering up with something only half-human." He slammed a fist into his other palm. "So, I'm gonna smack you all the way back to Siberia."

With effort, Sarah turned her head and caught

Nestor's eye. He nodded at her – Makarov's hold over them was slipping. With Bright as a distraction, there was just too much going on at once.

Everybody get ready, she sent to the others. *We're taking down Makarov with Bright.*

Like the plan, Nestor replied. *But who's going to take down Bright?*

We'll cross that bridge when we come to it.

"Balthus, kill!" Makarov screamed.

The large robowolf flew from the horde of waiting robots, teeth and claws aimed at the major's neck. With incredible speed, Bright caught the robowolf by the head, twisted it round and placed a hand on either side of its jaws. Giving a cry of effort he wrenched his arms apart, tearing Balthus's skull in two. There was an arc of electricity. The robowolf collapsed with a final howl, spilling components on the grass.

"Balthus!" Makarov whispered.

"Sorry about your dog," Bright replied. "Guess I'm more of a cat-lover."

Now! Sarah cried out with her mind.

Around her, she sensed the others break free at once – too much for even Makarov to control. He backed away, looking at them wildly as they rose from their kneeling positions.

Major Bright looked round and gave her a wink. "Surprised to see me?"

"Nothing surprises me any more," she said, keeping her eyes on the Russian.

Makarov threw his head back. "Robowolves! Destroy them all!"

Bright laced his fingers together and cracked his knuckles noisily. "Here we go."

A robowolf launched itself through the air at him. Drawing back his fist, Bright smashed it clean across the level, grabbed another as it attacked and proceeded to swing it around his head like a club.

Sarah and Nestor backed away as the scores of robots circled them, red eyes glowing furiously. One of them advanced towards her and she reached out with her mind, just as she had before. Making contact with its electronic brain, she subverted its programming with ease. It turned and swiped its claws across the side of another robowolf, spilling its electronic guts, and then leaped to Sarah's defence. Wei, meanwhile, threw up a wall of fire behind them that fried a group of wolves charging their rear.

Nice work! Nestor said as he directed a blast of air at a group of racing wolves, lifting them clean off the ground and into the air. The robots slammed into the side of the pyramid and carried on through. Massive shards of glass from the shattered section rained down, impaling several of their attackers in the process. Sarah saw this and had an idea.

Louise! Octavio! she said urgently. *Think you can bring down the whole ceiling?*

The Colombian kid looked round the gigantic glass pyramid and then back to her. *We can give it go.*

Then do it! she commanded. *Let's take down as many of them as we can at once.*

Nestor cast the robowolves running at them back with a blast of air. Octavio and Louise stood side by side and raised their hands. A mighty cracking sound filled the area.

"Take cover!" Sarah screamed as every pane in the pyramid roof shattered at once. A second later the air above them was filled with millions of shards of razor-sharp, toughened glass. She threw herself under the stone table, along with Nestor and Wei as the missiles hit the ground. Robert teleported into existence behind them, one arm wrapped around the injured Commander Craig. Looking out from their cover, Sarah watched as robowolves were torn apart in their tens – impaled, crushed and sliced by the knife-like shards. The sound was deafening.

As the cacophony finally ended, Nestor asked, *What about Octavio and Louise?*

They pulled themselves out from under the table, but they needn't have worried. Both Octavio and Louise stood unscathed amidst the devastation, having shielded themselves from the storm. The ground was now a sea of glittering shards, many of them impaled deep in the ground. All around lay the broken bodies of the robowolf army. With the glass gone, the wind howled relentlessly across the surface of the level. To one side, Major Bright brushed a glass fragment off his shoulder and nodded approvingly at the destruction.

"Not bad," he said. "Couldn't have done it better myself."

Makarov stumbled back towards the lift. One of the shards had escaped his shield somehow, for there was a line of blood across his left cheek from where it had been slashed open. He looked drained of power, pale and death-like. The remaining few robowolves leaped across the bodies of their fallen comrades to protect their master.

"Don't let them follow!" he ordered hoarsely as he broke for the lift.

"He's going for the meteorite chamber!" Nestor exclaimed. "We have to stop him getting back to the Entity!"

But Louise was already there, blocking Makarov's escape. He looked round wildly as Wei fried the last of the robowolves with a ball of flame. Their melted bodies pooled across the grass and solidified into an unrecognizable mass.

"Stand aside or die!" Makarov hissed at Louise as Octavio went to her side. The two kids looked at one another and then back at Makarov.

"Die," they said together, and threw out their hands. Makarov was hurled backwards towards the open side of the Spire. At the very edge, he fought against the invisible energy, managing to pull himself back.

"Nestor, finish him off!" Octavio yelled.

His brother stepped forward and directed a hurricane force blast of air at Makarov. With a final, ghastly howl, the Russian flew off the side of the Spire and disappeared.

"Yeah!" Louise cried as she raced to the edge with Nestor and Octavio. The side of the Spire stretched down, but Makarov's body was gone – swept away on the wind.

"Can we get out of here now?" Wei asked at her shoulder.

She looked round at him. "I thought you liked it here."

The Chinese boy rolled his eyes.

"We have to take care of the meteor storm first," Sarah said and they looked round at her. "The beacon control must be on the same level as the meteorite fragment, right?"

Octavio nodded. "Next to the sleeper chamber. I've been there."

"Okay," Sarah said. "Let's take care of the Entity once and for all. This isn't over until he's defeated. Right?" She looked across at Major Bright, who smiled at her knowingly.

"Right," he replied.

Sarah turned to Robert, who was crouching beside Commander Craig. "Is he alright?" she asked.

Craig pushed himself into a sitting position with a wince of pain, keeping pressure on his wounded shoulder with a hand.

"I'll live," he said.

"Think you can fly a jet out of here?" Sarah asked.

"Sure," Craig replied, eyeing Major Bright warily, "but—"

"No buts," Sarah said firmly. "We're in charge here. Robert, teleport the commander down to the 70th floor. Power up the stealth jet."

Robert nodded and grabbed Commander Craig's arm.

They teleported away a second later. Sarah looked round at the others as the lift doors slid open in readiness for them.

"Let's finish this."

37

They ran between the rows of sleeper modules towards the chamber containing the meteorite fragment. Alex appeared at the top of the steps as Sarah and the others ascended.

"Makarov?" he asked.

Sarah nodded her head at Louise, who said, "He took a trip off the side of the building."

Alex grinned, but then became serious again. "Me and Yuri have been busy. Come and see."

He led the way into the smaller chamber, where Yuri

was placing the last of the explosives around the surface of the meteorite fragment. The beam shone at half-strength, indicating that the Entity was not in contact. Sarah hoped it stayed that way.

"My god," Bright said reverentially as he cast his eyes over the object floating in the beam of light, "it's true. A fragment of the Tunguska meteorite. Amazing." He walked towards the beam, entranced.

Sarah looked at Alex, who was watching the major with caution.

I don't trust him, Alex sent to her covertly, shielding his thoughts from Bright.

One bad guy at a time, Sarah answered. *We take care of the Entity first, then worry about what we're going to do with Bright. He might be crazy, but I don't think the major wants to see the world destroyed before he can own it. Has Yuri finished rigging the meteorite?*

Alex gave the Russian a nod and pulled the detonator from his pocket – a squat black trigger that fitted inside his palm. *Armed and ready.*

"First we need to deflect the storm," Sarah said. "We'll use the beacon."

"Perhaps one of these computers controls it," Wei suggested, looking round the technology-covered walls. Sarah considered this for a moment, but then shook her head. Her eyes fell on the meteorite and she suddenly had no doubt.

"The fragment *is* the beacon," Sarah told the group. "We can use it to control the storm."

"You can turn the meteors around?" Nestor asked.

"I don't know," Sarah replied. "It's going to take a lot of strength and I'm going to need some help."

She placed her hand in Nestor's and walked towards the beam. He got the idea and beckoned to Louise, who took his other hand. The group came forward and linked hands, forming a circle around the light beam. Even Yuri joined the group. Wei extended his arm to Major Bright to close the circle.

"You're joking, right?" the towering man said, before taking the kid's hand. "What are we going to do next? Sing a song?"

"Everyone concentrate," Sarah ordered. "Close your eyes."

Around the circle, all eyes shut, including Bright's. Sarah made contact with their minds and channelled their energy back through her own. She felt her own power increase in turn. Taking a deep breath, she removed her hand from Nestor's and placed it against the surface of the rock...

The meteorite was unexpectedly cool to the touch at

first, but then a warmth began to grow. Sarah couldn't resist opening her eyes. The light beam shone brighter now. The smooth, mirrored surface of the rock began to vibrate under her hand. First it rippled and then began to rise in a series of peaks and dips – like spikes on the back of a porcupine. The spikes undulated and danced. It was as if the solid matter had become liquid and insubstantial. She sensed the power in the rock and the massive amount of psychic energy being used to guide the meteors towards their earthly targets. Sarah closed her eyes again...

...and is there, floating in space amidst the speeding meteors. She looks around and sees the extent of the storm – fifty objects in total. Ahead, the earth appears like a giant blue and white marble. It seems dangerously close.

She also senses the presence of her friends – joined with her mentally as well as physically. Their thoughts come through in an excited jumble as they experience the vision of the storm.

"Concentrate," she orders. "We have to take control. Focus all of your attention on me. On my voice."

One by one, she feels them settle and channel their thoughts towards her once more.

"Good," she encourages. "Very good."

Now she directs her mental powers to the beacon itself, the complex web of signals – one for each of the meteors, each with a different approach vector. Alter those signals just a little and the objects will go off course. Alter them a lot and the storm can be sent on an implosion course. She begins to manipulate the beacon, drawing the strands together, making them converge at a point in space...

"Sarah."

The voice is familiar from her meeting under the ice – the Entity. Suddenly, the alien mind is right alongside her.

"What are you trying to do? You know this is only delaying the inevitable."

Ignoring the voice, she concentrates on the beacon. She feels the others losing their focus in the presence of the alien.

"Sarah, what is it?" Nestor asks. "It's—"

"Concentrate on me!" she snaps. "Don't listen to its lies and don't let it weaken us!"

"The earth will be mine eventually," the Entity continues, its words rippling through her mind and the minds of the others like searching, grasping tentacles. "You know it is true. If you stop me today, you will just make your eventual defeat all the more terrible."

Sarah keeps attention on diverting the course of the meteors. Slowly, one by one, their paths begin to converge. Two of them on the edge collide with such force they split apart, sending a cloud of dust and debris out across space. It is working...

"I can't allow you to do this, Sarah..."

Searing pain rips through her mind, passing on to the others. It is everywhere, engulfing everything. Beyond her own agony, Sarah senses her friends screaming in similar torment under the Entity's psychic attack. It's like someone taking an electric drill to their frontal lobes.

"Don't make me tear your minds and bodies apart," the Entity hisses. "Leave my beacon alone. Nothing can withstand me."

"Make it stop!" Wei cries out...

Nestor's hand begins to slip from Sarah's grasp...

The circle starts to break...

Fighting the pain, Sarah directs her strength into keeping them together. Even though they try to pull away physically, she will not allow it. She holds them in the circle just as surely as Makarov had paralysed their bodies earlier.

"Just a little more," she assures them.

"You're letting it kill us!" Octavio screams.

Unexpectedly, it is Major Bright's voice that comes

through next. "You're not dead yet, boy! Finish it, Sarah!"

The Entity howls with rage and the pain and pressure on their brains increases... For a moment it seems their heads will be crushed in the grip of the vice-like alien mind...

Focusing again, Sarah throws everything she has into the beacon. Now the meteors are speeding towards a single point. A collision occurs between the lead meteor and three others directly behind it. They create a cloud of flying rock that explodes across the void...

A fourth rock flies in and is ripped apart...

The cloud grows as one after another of the meteors zooms in and is pulverized by the massive forces.

The storm is destroying itself.

"Sarah," the Entity whispers, its voice becoming fainter as its missiles are destroyed. At last the psychic assault diminishes and the pain in their brains begins to fade.

"You're beaten," she replies with grim satisfaction.

The Entity laughs. "Nothing happens without my consent. This is not over between you and me..."

Its voice fades.

The last of the meteors flies into the cloud and disappears. Sarah looks at the dust forming a silvery streak across space and...

...opened her eyes, as did the other members of the group. They stared at one another with amazement. Around the room she could see from the drained expressions on the faces of the others that they had experienced the agony of her battle with the monstrous alien force. For a moment there was only stunned silence, then Louise broke the spell.

"You did it, Sarah!" she exclaimed.

"*We* did it," Sarah corrected, rubbing the bridge of her nose to alleviate the residual ache from her fight with the Entity. Alex touched her arm with concern, but she smiled at him to show she was okay. He looked just as exhausted as she felt. But it wasn't over yet. From somewhere within the Spire there came a rumble. This was followed by a vibration that went through the walls and floor, as if something had shaken the building to its very foundations. The Spire, the technology, the beacon and even the architecture of the building was intimately linked to Makarov and the Entity. Now, with one of them dead and the other defeated, the building's stability was severely compromised.

"We don't need the beacon any more," she told Nestor. "Take the others and free the miners and their families. Yuri, take them to the bottom of the Spire."

The Russian placed a hand on her shoulder. "Thank

you for giving me the chance to put things right here."

Sarah smiled. "Give Laika a hug from me. Now get going."

"What about you?" Nestor asked as he started to move.

Sarah nodded to the fragment. "I have to finish things off here. Commander Craig is piloting the stealth jet out of here, so as soon as the miners and other workers are safe, get to the landing strip three floors above."

Without another word, Nestor left Sarah, Alex and Major Bright in the meteorite chamber. He led the others quickly down the steps and into the larger area below, moving to the nearest sleeper casket and pressing the button to open the lid. As it swung up, he removed the skullcap from the head of the bearded man inside. Almost immediately, the sleeper's eyes flickered open and he sat bolt upright, speaking quickly in Russian. Yuri ran to the miner's side and started reassuring him. Nestor turned to Louise, Wei and Octavio as another rumble went through the Spire.

"Wake them all up!"

The building shuddered again and somewhere a window exploded in a shower of glass. A fourth, even deeper rumble went through the building. The floor shook hard enough to send the caskets skittering across the floor.

Octavio looked at the ceiling and guessed what was happening. "I get the feeling Makarov's tower isn't so stable without the Entity holding it together."

"Then let's make this fast," Nestor said and they started moving around the caskets, waking the sleepers one by one.

Inside the meteorite chamber, Sarah turned her attention to the Spire's central computer.

"Something interesting?" Major Bright asked, moving next to her. She gave him a quick, wary glance – the man who had tried to imprison or kill them so many times. A wry smile passed across his lips, as if he read her thoughts.

"War makes strange bedfellows, doesn't it?"

Sarah ignored him and was pleased when he wandered away, examining the walls of the chamber. She didn't want him standing over her shoulder while she tapped the secrets of Makarov's computer. Alex appeared at her side.

Can we just blow up this place now? He cast a look at Bright. *The sooner we get out of here, the better.*

Not yet, Sarah replied as she moved to the main computer terminal. *There must be something on here about the fall virus. Makarov manipulated it to harness the psychic power of the sleepers. Perhaps there's the information we need for an antidote.*

She passed her hand over the terminal and the screens lit up.

"Hello, Sarah," the computer said. "How can I help you?"

"I want you to upload all the information from your memory about the fall virus onto the central computer of the stealth jet," she ordered.

"That constitutes over a million terabytes of data," the computer replied impassively. "The transfer will take several minutes. My systems are not working at optimum level. May I ask..." The computer's voice became slurred and deep at this point. "Where is Nikolai Makarov? I do not...detect his signature...in the Spire."

"What's wrong with it?" Alex asked.

"The sleepers are being disconnected. We're removing its power source."

Another rumble went through the Spire. The computer spoke with agonizing slowness, "This building...is unsound..."

"Just transfer the data," Sarah ordered.

"Yes...Sarah..."

Over the next minute the computer set to work while Sarah paced impatiently before the terminal. Finally, Nestor's voice sounded in her head. *We've opened all of the caskets. Yuri is taking the miners and their families down the stairs to ground level.*

Good, Sarah replied. *Get the others to the stealth jet. Alex and I will be along in a minute.*

Just make sure you are.

As Nestor signed off and she sensed them leave the chamber outside, a voice Sarah hoped never to hear again sounded from the direction of the meteorite fragment. The Entity.

Sarah. Join with me.

"I sense..." the computer continued in the same laboured drawl, as if every word was an effort. "The structural integrity...of the Spire...has been compromised. A fatal collapse will occur...within the next eight... minutes."

"Don't worry about that," Sarah said as the alien voice spoke again.

Sarah. This is your time. It's not too late!

She looked round at Alex, but he showed no sign of having heard anything. Bright, however, had moved so close to the light beam he was almost standing inside it.

As he reached up with his hand to touch the still-spinning rock, Sarah cried out.

"Major, no! It's not safe!"

The Entity's voice sounded in her head for a third time. *Sarah, are you really going to let Bright usurp your place beside me? How disappointing.*

Oblivious to the communication from the Entity, Bright looked round at her. "Not safe?" he said. "Not safe for you, maybe." He turned back to the meteorite and looked at it with awe in his eyes. "I thought that I had found real power when I was first injected with the serum. How wrong I was. Now I can sense true power. When it fought us for control of the beacon...it was like being in the presence of a god."

With that, he laid his palm on the surface of the meteorite fragment and the extraterrestrial artefact ceased to spin. Instantly, Bright's body went rigid, as if held in the grip of an electric current. His head slowly turned to face Sarah. When his lips moved, it was the Entity who spoke:

"Sarah. This is your last chance. Join me or see your friends destroyed at the hands of the major."

Sarah walked into the centre of the chamber. "Let him go. It's over! The meteors are destroyed. Makarov is dead. There's nothing left here for you now."

Like a puppet under the control of the Entity, Bright cocked his head on one side and his features contorted into a frown. *"But I am immortal. Defeat me today and I will be back tomorrow. Or next year. Or next century. I will always be here."*

"And there'll always be someone like me to fight you," Sarah said defiantly. "Leave earth alone."

"Such spirit. I would have made you a queen. Ruler of the world." Bright reached out towards her with his free hand. *"To join me is to live for ever."*

Alex watched in horror as a strange, vacant look passed over Sarah's face. She took a step towards the meteorite fragment, as if under the spell of the Entity's hypnotic words.

Sarah...

With a cry, Alex threw himself between her and the beam, holding the trigger aloft.

"Let go of the rock, Bright!" he cried out. "I'm ending this right now! I'll press the trigger!"

Bright pointed his hand at Alex and blue electricity shot from his fingers, blasting the boy back against the wall. With a cry of pain, Alex landed on the floor, smoke rising from his body where the electricity had touched. Bright hit him again, sending more electricity surging through his body for several seconds. The bomb trigger flew from his hand and rolled across the floor towards Sarah's feet...

Still in a trance, she reached down and picked it up. She turned it over in her hands as if trying to remember what it was. Finally, she placed her thumb over the red button.

"*Sarah, no!*" the Entity screamed from Major Bright's mouth. "*You will not do it. You will—*"

Her eyes became focused again. She looked at Bright and the meteorite fragment under his hand.

"Don't ever tell me what to do," Sarah said. "Either of you."

She pressed the trigger.

The C4 pack strapped to the back of the meteorite was small, but as it exploded it had the effect of breaking the fragment into a thousand pieces that flew outwards in every direction. Sarah was thrown backwards by the force of the blast, shielding her face as razor-sharp shards of rock flew all around. The noise was deafening, followed by a cacophony of shattering glass and plastic caused by rock shrapnel embedding itself in the computer screens that covered the walls.

As the noise subsided, Sarah lowered her hands from her face. Her forearms were criss-crossed with tiny shrapnel cuts, but nothing serious. The floor was littered with pieces of meteorite, ranging from the size of her finger to a quarter metre in length. The beam in the centre of the room had extinguished and where the meteorite fragment once hung in suspension, there was now only empty space. There was no sign of Major Bright either. Carefully getting to her feet, Sarah took a few steps towards the centre of the room. Then she saw the major...

...sitting with his back propped against the far end of the chamber where he'd been thrown by the explosion. The position in which he'd landed was oddly casual, as if he'd merely sat down for a rest. Major Bright's eyes shattered the illusion, however – they were blank and staring, locked on the floor between his splayed legs. A slender meteorite shard almost as long as Sarah's forearm was embedded in the major's chest – straight through the ribcage and into his black heart. Blood pooled across the floor from his corpse.

Sarah looked away from the horrific scene and took a deep breath. She quickly put aside her shock, however, as a vibration went through the entire building. Moving over to where Alex was lying, she checked his body to make sure that none of the flying shards had seriously injured him and then eased him into a sitting position.

"Bright?" he asked weakly as his eyes flickered open. "The Entity?"

"Both taken care of," Sarah replied. "With one bomb. Your bomb."

"Does this mean you trust me now?"

"I'm thinking about it," she said wryly. The Spire shook again. She looped her arm under Alex's and helped him to his feet. "We need to get out of here. This entire building is going to collapse."

They moved to the main computer terminal, which had suffered the worst of the explosion – the screens were completely shattered and smoke was rising all around. As they stood before it, the computer began its final message.

"Complete...structural...collapse...in...four... minutes..."

"Do you think it's finished uploading the virus data?" Alex asked, still leaning against Sarah for support.

"I don't know," she replied. "Let's get to the jet. We'll do it the quick way."

Robert! she called out with her mind. *We need a teleport!*

There was no response.

Robert!

Again nothing. Sarah exchanged a worried look with Alex. "Something's blocking my communication with him."

Alex felt it too. The building vibrated again and they started to the jet the long way – down the steps from the meteorite chamber and across the room with the sleeper modules, all of which were now empty. The jet was three floors above – Sarah estimated they could make it if they were fast, but Alex was still weak from the battering he'd taken. The lift was just ahead of them...

The doors slid open and a massive figure stepped out. It was broken and bloodied, but still alive and looking at them with pure malice in its thoroughly insane eyes.

Nikolai Makarov.

"Going somewhere?" he hissed.

38

Sarah and Alex backed away as Makarov advanced towards them.

"It will take more than a dive off a building to kill me," he said.

Sarah shook her head in disbelief. "How could you..."

Makarov held up his hands – the formerly long nails on his fingers were ripped to the bone. "I've got a good grip," he said. His shattered, twisted body shuffled along, completely transformed from the man Sarah had met just a few days before. Here was the price of greed and uncontrolled ambition. The price of allegiance with the Entity. Makarov must have read her expression, because he stopped in his tracks.

"You dare to pity me!" he said. "The greatest power in the universe flows through my veins!"

Sarah drew herself up and faced her attacker. "You know, Makarov, I've met your Entity and I've worked something out. You think it's a great power, Bright thinks it's a god, but I know what it really is. It's a parasite. A parasite that spreads across the universe infecting every life form that it comes across."

A ghastly grin spread across Makarov's maw, revealing jagged, broken teeth. "You can't fight the inevitable. You'll join us or die."

Now it was Sarah's turn to smile. "Oh, didn't you realize? We destroyed the meteor storm. And I just blew up your meteorite fragment. So no more link to the Entity for you."

Makarov's eyes flickered as he processed the information, then they widened with anger. He threw himself at her and Alex, teeth gnashing in a blind fury. They dodged to one side and he smashed into a sleeper casket. Makarov spun, blood pouring from his forehead. Sarah cursed inwardly: every second they were delayed brought them closer to the destruction of the building. They had to get moving.

With a howl, Makarov grabbed one of the overturned caskets and heaved it in her and Alex's direction. They avoided the missile by ducking to the floor. The casket smashed against the wall, showering them with plastic and components. Sarah grabbed Alex's arm and pulled him back.

The voice of the computer rang out through the chamber: "Warning, complete...structural...collapse... in...three...minutes..."

"We don't have time for this," Alex said as Makarov circled for another attack.

Sarah felt suddenly more exhausted than she ever had in her life: the meteor storm, the Entity, Bright, and now Makarov to fight once more. Taking a deep breath, she steeled herself for one final battle.

"Let's all go to hell together," the Russian hissed, sensing her prepare.

Sarah backed away with Alex, but stopped as she sensed someone appear behind her. Looking round, she saw her brother.

"Need a lift?"

Robert threw his arms around her and Alex. The corridor faded away...

...and they teleported into the windswept chamber containing the stealth jet. The engines were powered up and humming, but the wreckage of the light aircraft they'd flown into the Spire was still lying in a crumpled mess in the centre of the runway.

Sarah grasped her brother's hand. "Well done!"

"I had a funny feeling you needed help," he said.

"Just over two minutes until the building comes down," Alex reminded them, checking his watch. They stumbled towards the waiting jet.

Nestor appeared from the back. "Commander Craig is out for the count," he said urgently. "He collapsed while he was trying to prep the jet. He isn't going to be able to pilot."

"Don't worry about it," Sarah said. Leaving Nestor and Robert to help Alex on board, she ran up the steps at the back of the jet. "Octavio, Louise – get out there and clear that mess off the runway."

As they ran past, she moved over to where Wei was crouched over the unconscious body of Commander Craig.

"There's no way he can fly us out of here," Wei said.

"He doesn't have to," Sarah replied, kneeling down and placing her palm on Craig's cheek. In that instant she was connected with the commander's unconscious mind – a myriad of unconnected thoughts and images. Wei watched with fascination as she took a breath and removed her hand.

"What did you do?" he asked.

She gave him a wink. "I just took a flying lesson."

With that, she ran through to the cockpit and took the pilot's seat. The jet was powered up and ready to go. As she looked over the array of readouts and switches they all made perfect sense – courtesy of the knowledge she'd harvested from Commander Craig's mind. Nestor appeared in the doorway.

"Take the co-pilot's seat," Sarah ordered. "I might need you to help out."

"You can fly a plane now?"

"Benefits of my enhanced powers," she explained. "Looks like we've got something to thank the Entity for."

Through the front window of the plane, she watched as Louise and Octavio raised their hands at the wreck of the other plane and pushed it off the side of the building. *Good work, you two,* she sent to them. *Now get in the jet. We're out of here.*

As they ran across the runway, she fired the boosters and grabbed the joystick. In the back of the plane, she heard the door slam shut as Octavio and Louise got on board. The runway stretched ahead.

"I hope you know what you're doing," Nestor said from the co-pilot's seat.

"So do I. Otherwise, this is going to be a really short flight."

Sarah pressed forward on the stick and the jet started to roll forwards. Then, without warning, it skidded to a halt. She looked round the controls wildly, trying to work out what she had missed.

"Makarov!" Nestor cried, pointing forward.

Sarah looked up and saw the Russian standing before the runway. His arms were outstretched as he held the jet in a telekinetic field. His final grasp at control. Their eyes met.

Let us go, Makarov, Sarah told him. *It's over.*

His answer spat hatred. *Never.*

From the depths of the building there was a tremor that signalled the terminal stages of the Spire's collapse. The tremor continued to grow in strength as the building began to implode. Through the window of the plane, Sarah saw realization dawn upon Makarov that his Spire was about to destroy itself. His eyes widened in desperation. She pushed the engine throttle to full and the jet broke free of Makarov's control, hurtling towards the open wall of the chamber so fast that he was unable to avoid it. Sarah fancied she heard his scream as the undercarriage of the jet ran over him, but knew that had to be her imagination, the sound of the engines was so loud. Then the jet hit the narrow runway, carrying on inexorably towards the point of no return – open air just fifty metres ahead – even as the Spire began to list to one side.

The jet made the end of the runway and seemed to drop, but Sarah pulled back on the joystick with all her might. Beside her Nestor gave a cry as the nose of the plane pushed upwards. The jet angled round as it climbed. Sarah took a second to glance out of the side window and grinned with satisfaction at what she saw.

The Spire was falling.

Yuri led the group of dazed men, women and children across the snow plain as a great rumble split the air. A few of the miners stopped to look back, but he waved them on frantically.

"Keep moving, you fools!" he cried, pushing one of the men on. However, he couldn't help but look back himself...

The lowest levels of the Spire seemed as if they were literally being swallowed up by the ice, sending up a great cloud of dust as the soil beneath the permafrost was disturbed. He cast his gaze up the length of the building as every piece of glass shattered simultaneously, filling the air with millions of shards that glittered in the morning sun.

As he watched, fascinated by the terrible destruction, Yuri saw a dark, bat-like object fall from the centre of the building. He followed its path down to earth, vaguely realizing that he was watching the demise of Nikolai Makarov. What remained of the man hit the crumpling lower levels of the building and was swallowed up in the deluge of glass and steel.

Finally, a mighty whine filled the air, a sound of metal shearing against metal. The central structure of the Spire broke in several places like a fractured bone and the tower toppled towards the north. It hit the ice with a ground-shaking boom. A cloud of snow and dust was thrown hundreds of metres into the air, momentarily obscuring the crash site.

As the Spire came to rest, Yuri looked round at the group of miners and their families and laughed.

"It's over."

Someone cried out, pointing out towards the ice as a dark figure very much like a robowolf came barrelling towards them. But Yuri held up his hands to show it was okay…

Laika bounded up, almost knocking him off his feet.

"Okay, okay!" he laughed, patting her head. "I'm glad to see you too!"

Laika looked round the group, searching for Sarah and Alex, but Yuri shook his head. He pointed to the white exhaust trail cast across the blue sky by the stealth jet as it climbed.

"It's okay, girl," he said. "They made it."

39

Commander Craig's eyes flickered open and he looked around the cabin. He saw Robert crouching beside him and frowned. "Who's flying this plane?" he asked, trying to sit up.

"Don't strain yourself," Octavio replied. "Sarah has the stick."

"What the—" Craig began, but gasped with pain as he tried to move.

"Do as you're told and lie down," Louise ordered and pushed him back on the sofa. Craig started to protest more, but then fell into unconsciousness again.

"Is he going to be okay?" Robert asked, looking down at the commander with concern.

"He's lost a lot of blood," Octavio said. "We need to get him some medical attention soon."

"I'll tell my sister," Robert said and moved through the cabin. On the other sofa Wei was watching over Alex, who had dropped into an exhausted sleep. Robert carried on through the open door to the cockpit. Sarah sat in the pilot's seat, looking completely at ease. She checked one of the instrument panels and then turned her attention back to the blue skies ahead. Beside her, Nestor had the co-pilot's chair.

"So, what's the plan?" Robert asked.

Nestor said, "We've got a plane and a full tank of fuel. We can go anywhere we want, right?"

"And we've also got injured people back there," Robert reminded him. They both looked to Sarah.

"We're going to HIDRA," she said bluntly. "They're the only people who can help Commander Craig." She looked round at her brother. "Besides, it's time to stop running, don't you think?"

Robert nodded.

"Okay," Nestor said, "and just how do we find HIDRA?"

Sarah pushed forward on the joystick, sending the jet into a gentle descent. "They're sending a hovercopter to escort us to their mobile base in the Bering Sea. Switch the communicator to channel 64. They're about to broadcast a message. I've sensed it."

Nestor exchanged a glance with Robert as he adjusted the comm controls. "You're getting scary, you know."

Sarah looked round at him with concern. "Am I?"

"I'm joking," he said. "I think—"

He stopped short as the voice of a HIDRA communications officer crackled in his headphones. "Southbound jet, this is HIDRA Mobile Pacific. Please identify yourself and prepare to receive approach coordinates for a landing on our vessel."

"Tell them Commander Craig needs medical help," Robert said. "And about Yuri and the miners. They need picking up."

Nestor explained their situation and relayed a series of longitude and latitude numbers to Sarah, who programmed them into the on-board computer like she'd been flying for years.

"We're on our way," she said as she angled the jet towards the waiting HS *Ulysses*.

* * *

The stealth jet was larger than the normal aircraft designed for landing on the carrier, but the pilot executed the operation perfectly – easing off just before hitting the deck, then applying the brakes gently enough to bring it to a halt just metres from the end of the runway.

"Textbook landing," the landing crew controller yelled as he ran to meet the now stationary plane with his men. "Commander Craig must be piloting."

"Uh, I don't think that's the commander, sir," his second-in-command said, indicating the teenage girl in the pilot's seat.

The controller shook his head, but then waved his arms. "Well? What are you all waiting for? Let's get them out of there!"

The next few minutes were a flurry of activity on the deck as the crew secured the jet on the swaying aircraft carrier. Medics ran in and removed Commander Craig and Alex on stretchers. Finally, Sarah and the others emerged from the back of the jet and walked uncertainly onto the deck of the *Ulysses*. Cold sea air blew across the deck, bringing with it a mist of salt-tinged water.

"Wow," Nestor said, looking around the ship. "This is big."

"Yeah," Sarah agreed, "HIDRA don't do things by halves." Her eyes fell on the still-smoking wreckage of one of Makarov's drone fighters at the other end of the deck. "So, they got involved with the fight as well."

At her side, Robert nodded. "Looks like it. But where is everyone?"

Apart from about twenty or so members of the ground crew fussing around the jet, the deck was completely deserted.

"What were you expecting?" Octavio said. "A hero's welcome? The HIDRA command are probably congratulating themselves on saving the world. And we'll probably get locked up for flying a jet without a proper licence."

Sarah laughed despite herself. "I'll tell them it's in the post."

The squat shape of Lt. Kaminski appeared from the control tower halfway down the ship and beckoned them over. Leading the group, Sarah crossed the deck to meet him. As they came together in the middle, the lieutenant held up a hand.

"That's far enough," he said abruptly.

With a hydraulic hiss, the entire section of runway upon which they were standing shuddered and began to descend into the ship. Everyone apart from Kaminski looked around in surprise as they dropped away from the upper deck. A few seconds later the platform came to a halt – all around was darkness in the belly of the HS *Ulysses.*

Louise's hand slipped into Sarah's. *I'm not giving up without a fight.*

Let me light things up in here, Wei added, appearing at her other side.

Take it easy, Sarah ordered them both, trying to sound more confident than she felt. *Let's not jump to any—*

All the lights in the hold flicked on at once, momentarily blinding. Then Sarah made out the shapes of people standing around – some in overalls, some in combat fatigues, some in the black and gold uniform of the HIDRA command – at least two hundred of them. The entire crew of the *Ulysses* was assembled. All eyes were turned in their direction.

Then the cheering began.

The clapping and whooping of a couple of hundred people was deafening. Sarah and the others looked round in bewilderment at the sea of faces and finally to each other, smiles spreading.

"There's your hero's welcome, Octavio!" Nestor yelled at his brother.

Octavio shouted something in reply, but it was lost in the din as the crowd piled in, slapping their shoulders, hugging them, shaking their hands.

At first Sarah tried to keep track of the others as they became lost in the tide of well-wishers. Finally, she gave up, going with the flow of congratulations and thank yous. Then, a familiar face appeared through the crowd.

"You saved us," Rachel Andersen whispered in Sarah's ear as she threw her arms around her. "You saved us all."

Sarah pulled away and saw there were tears in the woman's eyes, which she wiped away quickly. "Colonels aren't supposed to cry," she said with a smile. "What about Major Bright?"

Sarah shrugged. "He didn't make it."

"Too bad," Rachel said. "I was getting used to having him around."

They both laughed as the crowd jostled them. Rachel's face became more serious and she leaned close to Sarah again.

"I've ordered the stealth jet to be refuelled and prepped for departure. It's yours to take wherever you want. I won't try to stop you."

As Robert found his way through the crowd, Sarah put her arm around him and looked at Rachel.

"We thought we might stick around for a while," she said. "If you've got space for us, that is."

Rachel grinned back at her. "I thought you'd never ask."

Epilogue

The night sky over the Pacific Ocean was alive with colour: blues, purples, greens, oranges – an amazing symphony of light falling in great streams from east to west. Sarah Williams sat on the edge of the deserted flight deck, legs dangling over the side of the ship, and watched the show. So engrossed was she in the ever-changing patterns of light, she didn't even sense Alex approaching until he was standing beside her at the edge.

"It's beautiful," he said, also looking up at the night sky.

"Dr. Fincher says it's the result of particles from the meteor storm skimming the upper atmosphere," Sarah replied, eyes fixed on the sky. "Completely harmless. Just space junk getting burned off in various colours."

"How poetic," Alex said. "You know, you probably shouldn't be sitting like that on the edge. The ship is liable to sudden lurches. You should move back."

Sarah looked round at him. "Why, are you afraid?"

"No, it's just—" He stopped himself and grinned. "Perhaps I'll join you."

Sarah looked back at the sky as he took a seat beside her. For a moment they sat in silence.

"Where are the others?" she asked finally.

"Watching the news," Alex replied. "Things are getting back to normal around the world. But it actually looks like the meteors had a good effect: as soon as news about the storm got out, just about every conflict on the face of the earth declared a ceasefire. The destruction of the world put things in perspective, I guess."

"I wonder how long that will last. What about Makarov?"

"It's being covered up," Alex replied. "The destruction of the Spire is being put down to an action by radical anti-capitalists. It seems the other six Spires also collapsed without the Entity's power to hold them up. That's getting blamed on—"

"Radical anti-capitalists as well?" Sarah finished for him.

"How did you guess? NASA is reporting that the meteor storm was destroyed by a freak surge of solar radiation. They're calling it an act of God. So much for being heroes."

Sarah smiled into the night.

"Back in Chukotka," Alex said hesitantly, "you said that the Entity spoke to you when you went under the ice."

"So?"

"So, I was wondering if you'd heard from it since we defeated Makarov. Is it still out there?"

For a moment he thought Sarah wasn't going to reply, but at length she spoke. "I can sense it. Waiting."

"But we blew up the meteorite fragment, right?" Alex said.

Sarah shook her head. "That was just a small part of its power. I saw it. The Entity is massive, ancient. Its influence spreads across galaxies. I should have died under the ice, but somehow it brought me back."

"You said it told you something," he said. "Want to let me in on it?"

"It said—" Sarah's voice cracked unexpectedly, but she continued. "It said I'd betray you all one day."

Alex placed a hand on her shoulder awkwardly. "I wouldn't believe a word that thing said."

Sarah nodded and looked away. If there were tears in her eyes, she wouldn't let him see them.

"I was thinking," Alex said, deciding to change the subject, "we should probably give ourselves names or something."

Sarah looked at him out of the corner of her eye. "What are you talking about?"

"Well, we're a team, right? And we've all got special powers, so maybe we should each have a special name that reflects that power. Like in comic books."

"Such as what? Invisi-boy?"

Alex groaned. "No! Something cool. Like *Stealth*."

"Stealth!" Sarah exclaimed, unable to control her laughter.

"And you could be something like...*Perception*. Because you have the power of mind control..."

Sarah held up a hand. "I think maybe you should just stop while you're ahead. Not that you're ahead."

"I'm serious!" Alex protested. "Listen, I was talking to some of the others and they think we should even get suits."

"Oh, get real!"

Their voices carried on into the night. Meanwhile, the

HS *Ulysses* ploughed through the dark waters of the Pacific as high overhead the last of the meteor storm burned out across the sky.

The light show also shone over the plain in Chukotka where Makarov's Spire had been demolished.

Ground zero was a giant crater, filled with twisted metal and a billion tiny shards of glass – all that remained of the Spire. In the morning a HIDRA science team would arrive to start sifting the rubble for anything that remained of the Entity's technology. For now, the perimeter of the three-kilometre-wide site was patrolled by only a small force of very cold, very tired HIDRA commandos.

They didn't notice as the figure of a man pulled himself from under the wrecked foundations of the Spire and walked towards the edge of the crater. He carried on towards the west, seemingly oblivious to the cold, although his clothes were in tatters. After a while he stopped and looked up at the lights flashing across the sky.

Major Bright, a voice spoke to him on the wind.

Yes, he replied. *Am I dead?*

No. You're very much alive. You are a part of me now.

Major Bright looked down and ran a hand over his chest. The last thing he remembered before he emerged from the rubble was the wound in his heart that the shard of meteorite had caused. Somehow the wound had healed.

And I am a part of you.

Pressing his hand against his ribcage, Bright felt the meteorite shard throb inside his chest. The Entity was inside him. It had saved him. He felt its power coursing through his veins, making him stronger than ever before.

I have so many plans for you, Major. You're finally going to achieve your full potential.

Major Bright grinned and told the Entity, *You know, I think this is the beginning of a beautiful friendship.*

He started walking towards the west.

Read on for a sneak preview of the superhumans' ultimate battle to beat the Entity...

ENEMY INVASION

ENEMY INVASION

Prologue
Wilkes Land, Antarctica

The helicopters came just after dawn, two of them flying low along the coast from the direction of the Shackleton Ice Shelf. Dr. Jan Petersen spotted them as he was prepping the snowcat for his weekly trip to the Casey Research Station, twenty kilometres west. Squinting against the brilliant blue of the Antarctic sky, he watched the helicopters make a circle of the three buildings that made up the Wolfe Station and then touch down on the snow.

Helen Brooks walked out of the communications

shack to see the unexpected visitors. Winter was coming and the Wolfe Station was preparing to close until spring, so they were the only two researchers left on site. Normally the station, an offshoot of Casey, would have closed weeks before.

But the discovery out on the ice had changed all that...

"Who are they?" Brooks said.

Jan shook his head. "Beats me. There's no flag or markings on the machines."

Men wearing the heavy-duty thermal coats, gloves and boots necessary for the harsh Antarctic environment began to pile out of the helicopters. Jan started towards them as the chopper rotors slowed. Three of the men ran to meet him, bent low so their heads wouldn't be taken off by the still-spinning blades. As they straightened up, Jan noted they were all tall, but the man in the middle was a giant, well over two metres. Despite the sub-zero cold, this man pulled back the hood of his coat. Jan was immediately struck by his piercing blue eyes and the scar running down the left side of his face. The crew cut and lack of a beard indicated that the man hadn't spent much time in Antarctica, where facial hair was a must if you wanted to stay warm.

"Hi," Jan said, glancing over the two men flanking the

blue-eyed one. They looked back at him expressionlessly, eyes hidden by mirrored goggles. He noted the automatic rifles slung over their shoulders.

Blue-eyes gave him a smart salute and said, "Dr. Petersen?"

"Yes."

"My name's Major Bright," he said with the unplaceable accent of a man who had lived all over the world. "We're here to take over this operation."

"Take over?" Helen spluttered, always fast to anger. "Why?"

Bright gave her a look like the question was stupid. "Why do you think?"

She began to say something else, but Jan held up a hand for her to be calm. "On whose authority are you doing this, Major?" he asked.

"HIDRA's. I'm sure you've heard of the Hyper Infectious Disease—"

"I've heard of your organization," Jan interrupted. "You have no authority here. This is a research station run by the Australian government—"

"Not any more. We have reason to believe there's a contamination risk from the object you discovered."

"You're talking about the fall virus? There's absolutely no reason to believe—"

"It's a done deal, doctor," Bright cut him dead. "You're under my authority now. Both of you."

"We'll see what the guys at Casey Station have to say about that," Helen said, bristling. "I'm getting them on the radio."

She started stomping back towards the communications shack before anyone could argue. Bright nodded to his men, both of whom followed. Jan looked after them, taken aback at how quickly things were moving. Major Bright took his arm and began to lead him towards the helicopter.

"Don't worry about your partner, doctor. My men will make sure everything is taken care of. Right now I need you to guide us to the discovery site." Jan tried to protest, but Major Bright's hand was firm on his arm. "I won't take no for an answer."

Before the doctor knew what was happening, he'd been bundled into the back of the nearest chopper. Two burly men sat on either side of him, as if worried he might try to jump out. Major Bright took a seat opposite and produced a tablet PC as the helicopter rose swiftly into the air.

"Mark the location of the crater," Bright shouted above the noise of the rotors.

He handed Jan the tablet, which showed a map of

Wilkes Land. Seeing he had little choice, Jan tapped the screen in the area thirty kilometres south of Wolfe Station where the object had been discovered two weeks before. A flashing marker appeared.

"Very good," Bright said, passing the tablet through to the pilot. "Now, who else knows about the object?"

Jan shrugged. "Well, apart from Helen and I, just a few people at the Casey Station. We kept it as confidential as possible."

"What about other research stations in the area?"

"There's the Russians at Vostok and the French at Concordia Station. But they have no reason to be looking for anything in that sector."

Bright smiled thinly. "We'll see."

"Where did you guys come in from?" Jan asked. "Is your ship close by? Are there HIDRA scientists on board?"

Major Bright gave no response and merely stared at Jan expressionlessly until he looked away. They sat in silence for the rest of the ten-minute trip, Jan feeling more and more uncomfortable sandwiched between the big men. None of the members of Major Bright's group looked or acted like scientists. They were soldiers. HIDRA or not, it was clear the military was moving in to claim the amazing find they'd made on the ice. And all he could do was grin and bear it.

Finally, the crater in the ice appeared through the windows on the right. "That's it," Jan said, although it was pretty obvious they'd reached their destination – the crater was almost two hundred metres across. The helicopter descended and landed near the edge. The soldiers pushed Jan out after Major Bright and they walked down the snowy incline to the rim of the giant bowl.

"Amazing," Major Bright said as they looked across the indentation.

Jan nodded in agreement. A meteorite strike on a continent the size of Antarctica was common enough, although the size of the crater was unusual (as was the fact that no one seemed to have picked it up, but given the amount of meteorite activity in the last six months, that was forgivable). No, the truly interesting thing about this crater was under the ice itself. It was as if the meteorite had hit the permafrost and burrowed deep inside. In the centre of the crater the ice had turned the deepest black and it was possible to see a spherical object, like a giant lump of coal far under the surface. From this object spread dark, slender veins, as if the matter at the centre was bleeding material out through the frozen Antarctic ground. It looked like a spider preserved in ice.

The second helicopter landed on the other side of the crater and Jan saw that there was some kind of camp over there. Bright scanned the opposite rim with a pair of binoculars, then handed them to Jan for a look.

"The Russians!" Jan said. "I might have known the Vostok boys would come sniffing around." He shook his head. "Those sneaky…"

The unmistakable sound of gunfire echoed across the crater. Jan brought the binoculars back to his face. A scientist he recognized was running along the edge of the crater. One of the soldiers aimed a rifle at his back and fired a burst of rounds. The man's body jerked and went down. Bright's men were shooting the members of the Russian scientific party. Gunning them down in cold blood.

"What is this?'" Jan demanded, hardly believing what he was seeing.

Bright smiled coldly. "Just protecting our find, Dr. Petersen."

Jan lowered the binoculars and backed along the edge of the crater. "You're not from HIDRA."

"Duh. You think?"

Jan's legs felt too weak to run. "Helen is calling the Casey Station – you can't get away with this."

"No one from Casey is going to answer that call,

doctor," Bright said, producing an automatic pistol from the folds of his coat.

Jan stammered, "Wh-why?"

"Because we've already been there."

Major Bright shot Jan three times in the chest. The scientist staggered back over the edge of the crater and slid down the curved side, leaving a smear of crimson blood on the ice, all the way to the bottom.

A soldier appeared at Major Bright's side. "The Russian team has been neutralized, sir," he reported. "As has the woman at Wolfe."

"Very good."

"Orders, sir?"

Major Bright looked across the crater and surveyed the dark, spider-like infection running through the ice. His gaze focused on the hard, black mass in the centre.

"Dig it up," he ordered.

To find out what happens next, read

Coming soon

ISBN 9781409526711

A meteorite has struck earth without warning,
unleashing a deadly alien virus. Thousands fall victim…
but not Sarah and Robert. Instead they develop strange
side effects – psychic abilities. And that makes them a target
for HIDRA, a rogue international agency determined to turn
them into lab rats, just like the other kids they've already
captured – kids who can control fire, create storms and
tear steel with their minds. If they work together, these kids
might just stand a chance against HIDRA…

ISBN: 9781409508571

**For more thrilling reads log on to
www.fiction.usborne.com**